I love novels like this, fictional narratives, set-in real-world circumstances. Hunter has many years of intimate experience in Africa, and I was able to get a good sense of his in Malawi. He brings the settings of his story alive with explicitly descriptive detail. His complex, yet easily related to narrator is authentic, knowledgeable, and believable. The plot is whimsical. As a devotee of books like this, I highly recommend this one. Thumbs up, Hunter.

—Amal Sedky Winter, *Escape to Aswan*

When Tom Craig, a hard-boiled reporter arrives in Malawi to investigate a series of bizarre murders, he looks up his old flame, Joss. But when he meets the once breezy, sensual Joss, he smells a rat. The novel, "Joss" is a page-turner, set in an African country, off-the-beaten-track. Hunter's novel has an authentic feel of a writer who knows the continent very well. I couldn't put it down.

—Gretchen McCullough, *Confessions of a Knight Errant*

JOSS

The Ambassador's Wife

by
Frederic Hunter

Cune

Joss, The Ambassador's Wife
© 2023 Frederic Hunter All rights reserved.
Cune Press, Seattle 2023

Paperback ISBN 978-1-951082-52-9
EPUB   ISBN 978-1-61457-460-6

https://lccn.loc.gov/2022950761

Hunter, Frederic, author. Joss the Ambassador's Wife / Frederic Hunter. 2nd. Seattle : Cune Press, 2023.

   pages cm
   ISBN: 9781951082529 (paperback)
   ISBN: 9781614574606 (epub)

Bridge Between the Cultures (a series from Cune Press)

The Passionate Spies	John Harte
Music Has No Boundaries	Rafiq Gangat
Arab Boy Delivered	Paul Aziz Zarou
Kivu	Frederic Hunter
Empower a Refugee	Patricia Martin Holt
Afghanistan and Beyond	Linda Sartor
Congo Prophet	Frederic Hunter
Stories My Father Told Me	Helen Zughaib, Elia Zughaib
Apartheid Is a Crime	Mats Svensson
Girl Fighters	Carolyn Han
White Carnations	Musa Rahum Abbas

Cune Cune Press: www.cunepress.com

For my son Paul

For my son Pat

Chapter One

MALAWI IS GREEN AND UNSPEAKABLY BEAUTIFUL. Its small mountains rise unexpectedly off the plains. Its sunsets grab the breath right out of your lungs. Its length stretches more than five hundred miles in the deep trough of Africa's Rift Valley, but at no point is it more than one hundred miles wide. The country nestles against a long, narrow body of water, the southernmost of the Rift Valley lakes, achingly lovely, known in colonial times as Lake Nyasa, but more commonly now as Lake Malawi. On maps the country and the lake look like longtime lovers snuggling spoons in an embrace that never ends.

If that image seems tender, what is happening right now in Malawi is not: a string of twenty-plus murders. They will intrigue readers of mine in California who do not even know that Malawi exists. Foreign correspondents like to believe that they do serious journalism. But they know that a good murder story garners more readers than reports of diplomatic negotiations or summit meetings. And this murder story is a good one because the murders are committed by a leopard. Yes, a leopard. Or perhaps a leopard-man. That ambiguity makes the story worth a visit, especially since, afterwards, I am headed north to Kenya to do the wildlife situationers that my editors ask for every year or so.

A story that will fascinate readers is not my only reason for going to Malawi. Another reason is a woman: Jocelyn—known to me as Joss—the wife of the American ambassador.

On the flight up to Blantyre, Malawi's commercial hub, I spend almost the entire trip thinking about Joss. I take out photos I've slipped into an envelope in my typewriter case. There is one, taken two years before, of the two of us standing before a bookstall on the Left Bank of the Seine. It was a turbulent time in Paris—students were rioting—and not only there. America appeared to be tearing itself apart. Opposition to the Vietnam War had caused Lyndon Johnson to declare that he would not run for re-election. Assassins had killed both Martin Luther King and Bobby Kennedy. But that was not our business. We were two people who wanted to shut out the world and be together. Joss succeeded in concocting some reason for a trip away from her family and we spent a week together, moving inside a cocoon of passionate self- absorption. That trip caused me trouble with my editors at the Big Guy—I have always thought of my paper as the Big Guy in California—because they did not want me on vacation just then and I went anyway. Looking at the photos—there were others of us when we were first together in East Africa—I have no regrets, even if we ended that week in Paris agreeing never to meet again.

I've also brought the latest of the family photos that Joss and Max send out at Christmas. Joss has scissored Max out of the pictures and so I see only her and Pepper, their daughter. These photos arrive folded into a note that never says more than "Miss you—Merry Christmas!" And if Joss seems never to change, Pepper, who looks to be a great, bright, grinning kid, gets a little bigger each year.

Putting the photos away, I wonder how I go about contacting Joss once I arrive in Blantyre. I muse about simply calling the ambassador's residence. In my ruminatings, Joss answers the phone. The minute I hear her voice, I break into smiles. "Joss," I say, "is that you?"

In my mind's eye I see her shiny dark hair falling across the earpiece of the phone and her lips at the mouthpiece. She says, "Tommy! You in town?"

"When can I see you?"

"Darling, when we last said goodbye, you claimed you'd never—"

"A man can change his mind. I have to see you." "I heard you were living with someone in Joburg. Not burning the candle at both ends, are you?"

"I hear you're living with an ambassador. Pretty pleased with yourself, huh?"

"You at the Mount Soche?" she asks. "I could probably slip away for an afternoon."

So we set up something for tomorrow afternoon—which means a couple of hours of the best lovemaking I've ever had—and I think about how beautiful every part of her is. But she rings off; someone is coming who may overhear us. Part of the pleasure of this game we play is that it has to be clandestine, furtive, our passion a secret we share.

Once this fantasy passes, I know our meeting can be nothing so simple. Joss is now the newly arrived American ambassador's wife. Everywhere she goes in Blantyre, her identity will be known. No slipping into a hotel for an afternoon of love. I wonder if this predicament amuses Maxwell Hazen. Joss, so it is said, has had many lovers. As has Max. They make each other aware of these indiscretions. Private misbehavior seems to provide them a way to keep in touch. Joss has told me that she and Max argue ferociously about these affairs. The unique aspect of our involvement, Joss assures me, is that our off-and-on affair is a secret we've kept to ourselves. Joss swears she has let Max know nothing about it. That means we have a singular attachment, a special love. Despite my journalist's skepticism, I hope this is true. But in a place like Blantyre, the American ambassador and his wife have a kind of celebrity status. I wonder how they're bearing the scrutiny. It will be a matter of crucial importance to Max, now that he has achieved an ambassadorship, that their reputations not be tarnished. So Joss cannot come to the hotel to see me. I'll have to find some way to gain access to the residence.

By great good luck I have a pal in Malawi to help me with tips and contacts. The first thing I do, once I've rented a Land Cruiser at the airport and checked into the Mount Soche Hotel, is to seek out a run-down section of Blantyre. Here the Land Cruiser jounces over potholes. Urchins and bystanders watch the vehicle pass, the urchins wondering if they will ever ride in so fine a chariot. I park on a commercial street full of shops run by East Asians, where buildings, some wood, some stucco, badly need paint. There are decaying office blocks with dark hallways and the stairwells smelling always of piss and rooms with dirty windows sparsely furnished where little work is done. I lock the vehicle and check all the doors. I greet the urchins, some who hang back, others who approach me for handouts, and give two of the biggest of them coins and instructions to keep my property safe. Then I head toward a storefront over which hangs a sign: BLANTYRE STAR Your Eye on Malawi - Subscribe Today.

The dimly lit newsroom contains half a dozen desks. Most are piled with newspapers. There are two phones and three ancient typewriters. Two men work at layout sheets. They wave in greeting as I enter. I make my way to the dark back of the room where an African sits at a stool pulled up to a desk in a slouch I know well. He hunts-and-pecks at a standard-model typewriter. I sneak up and cork him on the shoulder. "All lies!" I tell him.

He turns to look at me, then brings a hand up to protect his eyes. "Oh, the whiteness! The whiteness! It hurts my eyes to look at you, my friend." He stands to cork me with the hand not shielding his eyes and we clasp our right hands, grab each other's thumbs and give one another friendly shove.

This man is Bakili with whom I worked for a time on Nairobi's Daily Nation—and for African wages. In those days Bakili hoped to parlay his presence in Nairobi into some kind of overseas training in America, Britain, or even Germany. We often ate dinner together—there was a curry place called the Three Bells where the food was good and cheap—and Bakili would try out on me his stratagems for going overseas. As a young man with a job and some money, Bakili was a magnet for girls. He introduced me to those who were daring enough to be seen with an American paleface.

We would go on excursions in a beat-up Volkswagen bug I rented from a place called Odd Jobs in Muindi Mbingu Street. We took girls out to watch animals at the Nairobi Game Park and up to Lake Nakuru to see the flamingoes, to visit Karen Blixen's house at Ngong, to watch the planes take off and land at Embakasi. One weekend we rented a small house in Mombasa and took two nurses-in-training down to the Indian Ocean coast. Since neither girl wanted to be stuck all weekend with the white guy, in the middle of the night they switched beds. Bakili and I had three joyful nights going to bed holding onto one nurse and waking up holding onto the other.

Alas! all of Bakili's overseas plans failed.

Eventually his father called him home, wanting him present at Malawi's independence celebrations. In addition, he announced it was time for Bakili to marry and perpetuate the clan. Furthermore, his father said, he had found just the woman for him. So Bakili left Nairobi. He married the woman his father had chosen. She lives up-country—there is a lot of up-country in Malawi—tending his farm and raising their two children while he holds down a money-economy job in Blantyre.

Bakili gazes at me and shakes his head. "You hear there's a leopard-man on the loose," he accuses, "and you run up here to write that we are savages."

"But you are savages!" I tell him. "To show you what a generous albino I am, I'll buy you dinner."

"To pick my brain!"

"That takes ten seconds."

I take him out for a quick beer and ask his assessment of the stories I may pursue. Bakili reports on President Hastings Kamuzu Banda's plottings to become president for life and hints that the leopard-man killings are a reaction to his putting a stranglehold on access to the presidency. "This," he says, "is not the way the so-called democratic forms we inherited from the Brits are supposed to work."

When I urge him to tell me more, he laughs. "Would I deprive you of the opportunity to ply your trade, to chat up bigwigs in interviews? Not a chance of it." He does, however, give me the name of an African anthropologist who teaches at the country's best secondary school. Despite the risk in talking to me, this man may be able to provide an anthropological perspective on the leopard-man killings.

When I ask about possible American government aid to the President's project to move the national capital from the south to Lilongwe in the Central Province, Bakili, who is no admirer of Banda, claims a national capital at Lilongwe is simply the latest scheme to put money into the old man's pockets. He checks to see if anyone overhears our conversation. Even when no one seems to, he lowers his voice when he says the word "Kamuzu."

I ask if the new American ambassador is pushing the development scheme. Bakili's info—from what sources I have no idea—is that the American dollars are designed to wean Malawi from the orbit of South Africa's apartheid regime while keeping it firmly anti- communist. "My hunch," he says, "is that American capital is positioning itself to take over the South African mines if there's a race war down there."

Then he grins at me. "Feed me dinner some other night," he says. "There's a party tonight at my place. Want a girl while you're here?"

"I might if your taste in women were bett—"

"My taste in women," he interrupts, "is superb."

When I shake my head at this, he says, "I have a town wife now as well as the one up-country. You'll see my taste in women."

"Insatiable!" I exclaim. "That's what your taste in women is." We laugh together and he tells me he has to get back. Believe it or not, he's on deadline. He writes down the name of the anthropologist and his address on a sheet in the notebook he always carries, tears it out and gives it to me.

I ask him, "How's the new American ambassador?"

"Manipulates the"—he lowers his voice—"dictator like a puppet." He adds in a normal tone, "He doesn't talk to folks like me."

"And his wife," I ask. "What's she like?

"They keep her under wraps. The kid, too. They think we'll contaminate them." He grins and shoves me in the chest. "I am ready to party! See you tonight! Bring a bottle."

—m—

If anyone might know that I've had a relationship with the new American ambassador's wife, it would be Bakili. Because I met Joss on the terrace of Nairobi's Norfolk Hotel, a place where we used to drink at night after work. But she walked into my life after Bakili returned to Malawi.

The Norfolk is a famous hostlery from the colonial days, just across the road from what is now the University of Nairobi. Wild tales hold that colonials used to ride their horses onto the bar terrace and even into the dining room. But when I was at the Daily Nation, the clientele was generally young professionals, maybe some students and professors and the predictable clusters of tourists. That particular night in 1962, eight years ago, we were drinking and munching the hamburgers that were necessary to lure tourists. We were a mixed group of riff-raff: some African students, playing at doing homework, two of us from the Nation and a couple of Brits, born in Kenya, one bearded, the clean-shaven one with an African girlfriend. Out of nowhere a slim young woman in a tee shirt and shorts, backpack and hiking boots, entered the terrace from the road. She stood looking around. Her black hair was cut short then and she wore no make-up, not even lipstick. She glanced around the terrace, swung the pack off her back and, grabbing it, walked over to us. "Mind if I join you?" she asked. "You're the only crowd out here who looks as disreputable as I do."

"What do you say, chaps?" asked the bearded Brit. "Do we really look as disreputable as all that?" But he quickly stood—as did I and the other Kenya-born Brit—because of course we wanted this plainly beautiful woman to glorify our table. We opened up space and reached for chairs. Since I was closest to her, I took the backpack, grabbed her wrist and ushered her into a chair beside me.

"Glad to have you join us," I told her. "I'm Tom."

She said, "You're an American. I can hear it in your voice."

"I am," I said. "But I've been here long enough to feel Kenyan."

She put her hand on my arm and smiled and leaned forward to kiss my cheek. The others applauded. "Kiss us all, lassie!" cried the bearded Brit.

"She only kisses fellow-countrymen," I shouted as we sat down. I signaled a waiter and ordered a beer and a burger for her.

She leaned close to me. "I've been in West Africa, speaking French," she told me. "I haven't heard American English in I-don't-know-how-long." She reached out her hand and we shook. "I'm Jocelyn," she said. "Joss."

I assumed she was a student. Possibly an anthropology grad student as I had been not long before. I felt a kinship with her. We stayed with the others for a couple of hours, talking and drinking. When the circle broke up, it was after midnight. As we left the terrace, the pack on her back again, she asked me, "Do you know a cheap place where I could stay? I can't afford the tab here."

I was surprised. "You have no place to stay?" I asked.

She shook her head and grinned. And I grinned back at her.

In those days my lodgings were a single room at the back of an Asian store in Bazaar Street. I entered from the rear. The room had a washbasin in one corner and a small refrigerator in another. My clothes hung on nails and hangers beneath a shelf where I'd stacked underwear and books. The double bed was unmade and, as I brought Joss into the room and looked at it, I wondered how long it had been since I'd washed the sheets.

I'd gotten a straight-back chair—a towel was hanging over it to dry—and a cheap but sturdy wooden table I used as a desk. On it were a lamp and piles of reference books and newspapers next to my two most valuable possessions: my Olivetti portable typewriter and Grundig short-wave radio. Stacks of books stood like mini-Stonehenges on the floor throughout the room. The door was ajar to a small compartment attached to the room. It was almost large enough—but not quite— to house the toilet and the telephone-shower that were in it. There was a drain in the floor and I sometimes showered standing on the toilet. I always left the door open, hoping to dry the place out.

"Will I knock over books if I set this down?" Joss asked.

I took the backpack from her and set it on the chair. "Now you know what the room of a freelance journalist looks like."

"I've always wondered," she said.

"You're welcome to stay."

She looked at me gratefully. It was a kind of magical moment that went on and on without really taking any time at all. Then she kissed me, very fully. "Do you mind if I take a shower?" she asked.

"I may even have a second towel," I said, pulling a dry towel from the shelf next to the underwear. Giving it to her, I took hold of her hand. I wanted to kiss her again. "I won't be long," she promised.

While she showered, I turned off the overhead light and got into bed, wondering what would happen. The lamp on the table was the only illumination. When she left the shower, she came into the room to dry off. I pretended to be asleep—she must have known I wasn't—and narrowly opened my eyes to watch her polish her body. After a moment I sat up. "You're incredibly beautiful," I said. I watched her buff herself dry. She smiled at me, without a trace of self-consciousness. Then she folded the towel over the chair, turned off the lamp and came to bed. We kissed again and she asked, "Why are you wearing shorts?"

—m—

We were together for more than a month, making love with the frequency of honeymooners. I could not quite believe what was happening to me: that a woman of intelligence and loveliness would walk out of the night in a tie-dyed tee shirt, shorts and hiking boots and expand my existence, enhance my emotions, in a way I had never dreamed possible.

At the end of our time together we went camping on the Serengeti plains. That was like being Adam and Eve at the beginning of the world. Adam and Eve lived in the moment. They did not worry about the past or future and neither did we. I knew, of course, that Joss had a life – probably a grad student's life – before she appeared on the Norfolk Hotel terrace that night. But I did not ask her about it. We lived with an immediacy that did not worry about tomorrow. I went to work during the days. I picked up free-lance stories when they floated by. At night I was with Joss. We did Nairobi and we made love. On the weekends we went camping.

Sometimes I would watch her. I would think she might be – or had been - three or four different women. I wondered if I would recognize any of them if I bumped into them on the road up ahead. Would I meet her at a party somewhere in the future and wonder who she was? If I came on to her and we connected again, would we realize we'd been lovers?

When we camped, we slept on plains so abundant with wildlife that we had no fear of being attacked by predators. Who would want to eat us when a juicy little Thompson's gazelle was so easy to catch? We slept, wound about each other, in the same sleeping bag. We woke at dawn to watch zebras and gnus, gazelles and waterbuck, topi and kudu, Cape buffalo, lions and elephants come to a water hole to drink. When they had drunk their fill, we would wriggle out of our bag and bathe in the cool morning air, as naked and as unconscious of our nakedness, as the animals themselves.

Eventually I got a request from a paper for which I served as a stringer. It asked me to provide dispatches from southern Africa. This was an opportunity I longed for. It might lead to a staff position and end my hand-to- mouth existence as a stringer. One night while we were camping on an enormous plain dotted with kopjes, rock hillocks, I told Joss about it. Our campfire was the only man-made illumination for hundreds of square miles.

Having eaten, we sat close to one another, our backs against a log, sipping wine, watching the stars. I said, "One of my papers wants some coverage from South Africa. I have to go down there for a while next week."

"What is it?" she asked. "An audition?

"Maybe." I held my breath, then plunged ahead. "Want to come along?" She looked at me as if I were joking. "Why not?" I said.

For what seemed forever she did not speak. Finally she said, "You should know: I'm married."

The words stunned me. I did not move. I sipped my wine and finally said, "Come anyway. I'm not prejudiced against married women."

In the silence that followed I could not believe what we were discussing. She was married? I had been making love daily to another man's wife? I had been feeling my emotions expanding, growing toward a possible commitment… And she was married! Finally, I looked over at her. Joss said nothing, staring sadly into her glass of wine.

Finally, I asked, "Does he know you're here?" Joss shook her head.

"Does he know you—?"

"He plays around all the time," she said. "He knows I hate it. That's why he does it." Then she added, "And I do it to him because he hates it."

I nodded. But I had never heard of such a relationship.

"It's strange," she said. "We love each other too much to divorce. And hate each other too much to be happy."

I felt like railing at her, giving her hellfire-and-damnation. But in Kenya such things were not done by the people I knew. In Nairobi no one ever took a high moral tone with a friend.

"We think a baby will make a difference," Joss said. "So that's the plan."

I smiled at this and looked at her a long moment.

I put my arm about her and kissed her sweetly as if kissing her goodbye. In the morning we drove back to Nairobi and I got her a room at the Norfolk.

—⋙—

After leaving Bakili, I drive into the center of town and stop at the American Cultural Center to see the Public Affairs Officer, the Embassy's public face. He's Bill Sykes, a fellow Californian by origin, maybe forty-five, tall, with the ready smile of a man who wants to be liked. He invites me into his office and pours two cups of coffee from a burbling coffee maker. It sits on a bookshelf below one of several large National Parks posters with the logo "See America!" written across them. Scanning the posters, I realize that, beating around Africa for ten years, I've seen more of it than I have of my own country. Sykes hands me a cup of coffee. "Ever been to Malawi before?" he asks, gesturing to a chair and settling in behind his desk. "Can't be much here to interest a newsman."

"I'll do a situationer," I tell him, "and they'll bury it next to ads for panty hose."

"Can I make that sweeter?" Sykes asks. He opens his bottom desk drawer and pulls from it a bottle of whiskey. He sweetens both coffees. "The Assistant Secretary of State for Africa's arriving in about ten days."

"Lilongwe project?" I ask.

He nods. "Anything for you in that?"

I shrug, reluctant to tell him that while the Assistant Secretary's visit is an-all-hands-to-battle- stations deal for him, it's a yawner for my readers. I pass it off and Sykes shrugs. He replaces the bottle and relaxes into his desk chair, his feet on a drawer. "Any chance of my seeing the Ambassador today?" I ask.

"He's tied up this afternoon," Sykes tells me. I wonder if it's true or if every interview has to be negotiated. Probably I should have set up the appointment from Joburg, but I didn't want Joss to hear from her husband I was arriving.

Sykes asks, "Wandering Africa the way you do, you ever run into Hazen?"

"Once in Morocco. Rabat. You're sure he couldn't fit me in today?"

"A doctor's seeing his daughter," Sykes explains. "He wants to be there."

"What's wrong with his daughter?"

"Acute depression."

I think: What? The kid I met a bit over two years ago in Morocco seemed well adjusted. In any case, children tend to adjust easily.

Sykes adds, "I guess the flight down here from Europe really got to her. She had to fly down unaccompanied. She's been under a doctor's care ever since. Malawi can do that to you."

"The kid flew down here alone?"

"Hazen hated to have that happen. But there was no other choice." Sykes continues, "The Hazens have really had a rough go. Mrs. Hazen was in an auto accident in Europe. She's had extensive reconstructive surgery."

Joss!

I am stunned. An image of her face swims into my mind. Such a beauty! I wonder how reconstructive surgery has altered her face. Then out of nowhere my mind sees the image of a car wreck I came upon in southern France some years ago: a small sports car mangled beside a road lined with poplars. I see the body I saw then: a young man lying beside the car, face cut, bloody. Oh, Joss!

Then I hear Sykes saying, "We all admire the way Hazen attends to her. But it's put the kid in a tailspin." I ask about the care she's getting. "An African doctor's treating her," says Sykes.

"Mrs. Hazen's under the care of an African doctor?"

"No, the child. He's a guy who trained in the States." My expression telegraphs what I'm thinking. Sykes shrugs as if he agrees. "Hazen says we oughtn't to be out here if we scorn the people we serve," Sykes explains. "Well, maybe. But if she were my kid, I'd get her the hell of out here." Then he adds, "But I'm not bucking to be Secretary of State. That's off the record, of course."

Sykes walks me to the Land Cruiser and I ask what my chances are of seeing the President. "Let us handle that for you," he says. That's a surprise. Usually I set that sort of thing up directly with the President's office. Why would I go through Hazen? That way I'm beholden to him. Sykes explains, "Hazen can probably get you in. You won't see the President otherwise."

Well, well, I think. I wonder if I believe that. "Old Kamuzu admires the fact that Hazen really knows Africa," Sykes says. "He understands that they're good for each other. If Malawi progresses so will Hazen. And vice versa. So the President trusts him."

"And to see the President," I ask, "I have to see Hazen first? Is that the game?"

"Hazen's walking on eggs," Sykes says. "He wants to do good—as well as make good. This Lilongwe involvement is just being finalized. First American money in ages. President doesn't want any bad press."

I have the feeling that Sykes is offering me a deal that I don't think I like. He and I take each other's measure.

"If we got you in to see Kamuzu," says Sykes, "would you do a piece on U.S. money helping Malawi? Africa moving forward? That sort of thing?"

I shrug. There's no use telling him I don't work that way—because I may have to. "The leopard-man murders will get a lot more play in my paper," I tell him.

"How about laying off that? It just reinforces stereotypes about Africa."

"You know, you won't get positive foreign press out of here as long as a leopard-man keeps killing government ministers."

Sykes nods ruefully. "Then maybe no coverage is the best kind," he says. "Malawi needs that Lilongwe project." Then he promises to set up something with

Hazen and says he'll call the hotel.

He watches me drive off. I turn the corner and pull off the road. I lean against the steering wheel and put my head in my hands. I ask, Joss, Joss! My beauty! What in God's name has happened to you?

Chapter Two

B ACK AT THE HOTEL WHERE I'VE GOT ACCESS TO a phone, I get to work contacting sources suggested by Bakili. I set up appointments for the next day with Blantyre Mayor John Kamwendo and Ian Galbraith, a British colonial holdover in the Justice Ministry. I'll talk to Kamwendo about the impact of the murders on Blantyre's morale and steps being taken to apprehend the killer. I'll ask Galbraith the same questions and also query him about the expanded use of traditional courts in settling this matter.

I also talk with Dannie van der Merwe, a South African seconded by his government to run the Malawi Information Services. Not enticed by the game Sykes and Hazen have on offer, I ask him to set up an appointment with President Banda. He suggests I bring a list of questions I intend to ask. I try Dr Chitambo, the anthropologist. He can see me this afternoon and gives me directions to the school. Securing this interview will mean that I've used the day for more than getting things set up. Good.

Before leaving the hotel, I open my envelope of photos and extract the air letter that came to my one-room office in Johannesburg three or four months ago. No return address. Postmarked Paris. I recognized the handwriting immediately. I had not really heard from Joss in almost two years. I let the letter sit for two days. I knew I should burn it.

The text was vintage Joss: one paragraph, no periods, only dashes.

"Max has received an ambassadorship at last—Malawi—We arrive there in a few weeks—I am here putting poor Pepper into a summer camp cum psychiatric boot camp—Max insists that she needs tests—Department has agreed to foot the bill—We have argued about this-as about everything and as usual I lose—Max is quite pleased with himself—Has people calling him Ambassador-Designate—It's the culmination of 20 years of ass-kissing—About time his tongue got a rest—If duty brings you to Blantyre your girls will be undyingly grateful and delighted to warmly welcome you!"

—⁂—

The note was unsigned. Joss never signs a communication to a man. I was pleased for Hazen. I'd met him only once, but he struck me as a hard-working Foreign Service officer, well-informed about Africa, where he's served much of his career, and worthy of promotion to the yearned-for ambassadorship.

I read it over, yet again, and look up the number of the ambassador's residence, secured from Hazen's predecessor. I dial. The phone rings repeatedly. I'm about to hang up when a woman's voice answers. "Mrs. Hazen, please," I say.

"This is she," comes the reply. I frown. This is the thin, uncertain sound of an older woman. It's not Joss's melodious voice.

"Joss?" I ask. "Is that you?"

"Who is this, please?" replies this old woman's voice.

"This is Mrs. Hazen?" I ask again.

"Yes," comes the answer. "I'm the Ambassador's mother. Jocelyn's not available right now. Can I take a message?"

I wonder: Will this call put Joss in an awkward position? Her mother-in-law must know she's had men on the side. But certainly she has not expected them to be calling in Malawi. "I'm a school friend, phoning from the United States," I say. "I just heard she'd been in an accident and I hope she's all right. How is she coming along?"

"She's doing very well," says Mama Hazen. "Can I tell her you called?"

I give her the name of my first college roommate and ask after Pepper. "I met her once," I explain.

"She really hasn't taken to Malawi," says the woman. "It's such a change from West Africa. She's got a bug or something, but she'll be fine."

I thank the mother-in-law and ring off, saying I will write Joss a letter. Fortunately, the woman did not sound suspicious of me as another of Joss's men; she simply sounded befuddled. Perhaps Mama Hazen, like her grand-daughter, has not really taken to Malawi. She may actually think I've called from the States.

—∿∿—

As I shake his hand, Dr Chitambo beams with delight. Tall, with close-cropped, tight-coiled hair and a long face that ends in a mustache and beard, he wears the educated professional's badge of suit and tie, as well as pointed European shoes that have failed to win a purchaser there. He's pleased that an American journalist has sought out his expertise and is happy to allow me to record our conversation on the tape recorder that dangles on a strap from my shoulder. He understands that I've come seeking insights into the leopard-man murders. He leads me into the school's small museum.

There he points out masks and ritual regalia, musical instruments, drinking pots and a hundred other items, most covered with dust and labeled with tags from which the ink is fading. He leads me to a back corner. There a naked light bulb shines down on a man- sized dummy modeling a remarkable garment of black cloth painted yellow and white to resemble the pelt of a leopard. It includes a long tunic and trousers. The headpiece is a papier-mâché mask of a leopard's face with openings for eyes and mouth attached to black cloth, painted again, that covers the back of the wearer's head and neck. The tunic's sleeves end in black work gloves, sewn to the garment. They feature knife-sharp claws fastened to the fingers. Dr Chitambo takes a glove and turns the palm upward so that I can see the blood stains that cover it. I take out my notepad and do a feeble sketch of the model.

"I confess I don't know the history of this item," the anthropologist tells me. "It was collected long before I arrived here." He speaks with a British accent shorn of the musicality of his native language. "There were apparently incidents like these we're having early in the colonial period."

I ask, "Who wore this garment? Are there records?"

"That's a dilemma," claims Chitambo. "Legend has it that he was a man convicted of killing twenty people in an effort to overthrow the colonial government. The colonial regime was repressive, of course." He smiles and lifts the arms of the tunic, careful not to touch the claws. "The skin is outsized, you see. No leopard is this large."

I ask if the present leopard murders are the work of Banda's political rivals. Dr Chitambo is reluctant to comment. He seems uncertain that politics actually drove the murders in the colonial era. He hints that, instead, the missionaries who started the school fabricated the leopard-man suit as a way of combating an African superstition. They showed students the leopard suit, he contends, in order to convince them that men did not actually transform themselves into leopards, but merely dressed up in leopard suits. I persist with the question about what's happening now, even make an elaborate show of turning off the tape recorder and assuring the anthropologist that I will not quote him on this matter by name.

"Please, don't," he says finally. "I have a family."

Then he whispers. "The government is no longer colonial, but it's still repressive. There's disorder in our national life: huge disparities of wealth, opportunity, access to jobs. Need I go on?"

I gesture that I understand.

"People want change," he continues. "But the President and his cronies block all dissent. If development money comes into the country, they pocket it. So a leopard-man gets loose in the streets. It kills the President's cronies. Some believe it is witchcraft, but most people understand what it is."

"Is it only cronies of the President who've been killed?"

Chitambo shrugs. He's reluctant to be drawn into a discussion of politics.

"I take it people on the other side of the rivalry have also been victims," I say, testing him. He shrugs. "Have they all been killed by leopard-men?"

He whispers, "I suspect there are sorcerers on both sides of the rivalry."

"Am I correct," I ask, "in thinking that some people actually believe that a man can transform himself into a leopard?"

The anthropologist regards me with patience. He's an old hand at trying to explain Africa to white men like me who see the world quite differently, men who have allowed rationality to cut themselves off from a world that Africans know exists. "For you there is no spirit world," he declares. "Am I right? All that exists can be measured, categorized, placed under a microscope."

Now I shrug. I gesture for permission to turn the tape recorder back on. He nods his permission.

"And so for you," he continues, "a spirit's transformation from a human to an animal form: that's an impossibility. Am I right?"

I nod that this is correct. He bestows on me a patient smile.

"But resurrection," he says, "virgin birth, raising the dead: these are also self-evident impossibilities. Am I right again?"

Once again I agree that he is correct. My culture has its irrationalities, just as his does. Many people in my culture hold to an irrational faith that these matters are or were actualities. He gestures me to turn off the recorder once more and I oblige him.

"You assume that I fear the government," he says, "and I do. But not alone because it quashes dissent." He leans closer and lowers his voice. "I also know that at night the President turns himself into a vulture. He can fly anywhere. Even into my house. He can harm me. He can eat my children."

I nod solemnly and start to note down the quote in my notepad. Dr Chitambo places his hand lightly on mine as it attempts to make a note. When I glance up, he is once again smiling patiently. He raises a finger and waves it back and forth. I stop writing and thank him for the interview.

—〰—

Bakili's party reminds me of my beginning days as a journalist in Nairobi. His wooden house in an area not far from the office of the Blantyre Star has wide porches and an overhanging roof. Above the noise of the Land Cruiser's engine I hear the music and laughter of the party a block before I find the house. I see revelers moving about inside, some chatting as they hold dark, tall bottles of beer, others nibbling snacks, still others flinging their arms and shaking their hips to the music of a three-piece band made up of musicians who live in the neighborhood. Guests also gyrate and talk on the porch, men trying to line up women to take home, women trying to connect with men who will proposition them. Men who have given up on this game—or have not yet begun to pursue it—talk together or drum their hands on the balustrade and shake rattles made of bottle caps.

Entering the house, I'm greeted by a stunning young woman, acting as a hostess, who is a walking song of praise for the mixing of the races. She seems to know who I am, introduces herself as Beryl, Bakili's wife, and welcomes me to the house. When Bakili appears, I draw him aside to extol his taste in women. Grinning with self-congratulation, he informs me that Beryl likes white men, but is spoken for. "Her father was a District Commissioner," he whispers. "So she's forgiving of white men's faults."

"Where did you find her?" I ask, admiring her across the room.

He grins. "Under a toadstool."

As he introduces me around, African city girls soon come up to say hello. All are alluring and alluringly available. They present themselves as friends of Beryl, but it is more likely that they are students at the secretarial school she owns and manages. Some want to examine an American journalist to see what he looks like and has to say for himself. Others have heard that I'm on an American expense account and that alone sparks their interest. Still others are attracted to the fact that I am staying at the Mount Soche; some of these women have never entered the hotel. They would enjoy spending a night there just to see what the rooms look like. Later they would share this information with jealous friends. I find these temptresses attractive. Their eyes especially. Their gaze is full of mystery. And yet the brown pupils also flash and sparkle, the liveliness shimmering against those eyes' white backgrounds.

They wear bold colors—yellows, oranges, mauves—set off well by the dark chocolate of their skin. That skin possesses a lustrous smoothness that women with white skin do not have. Their white teeth explode out of their smiles. Their hair—always an African woman's beauty challenge—is woven by some of them into threads of intricate sculpture. The music is energetic, the motions of the dancers sexy, sinuous, flowing like liquid. Soon I'm snacking, quaffing beers and moving to the rhythms, all the while flirting with every girl who says hello.

By 1:00 a.m. I have been dancing for several hours. I'm a little drunk and I've shed my shirt and safari boots. I'm barefoot and naked to the waist. I've been with the same girl for over an hour. She's probably no older than nineteen. We've sat together on the balustrade of the porch for many minutes wondering if a sorcerer who has transformed himself into a leopard is walking through this quarter. When I pointed in jest at something moving up the street, the girl cuddled against me, pushing her breasts against my chest. She's told me very sweetly, very seriously, that the leopard-man murders terrify her, that she wants me to protect her.

She wishes she had witchcraft to transform herself into a tiny mouse. As such a small creature she could hide safely, she says, in my pocket until the murders are solved. I've found that idea so charming that I've jotted it down in my notebook. In fact, I am thinking of beginning my piece on the murders with her story.

She's enticed by the idea of having her name in an American newspaper. Pleased with ourselves, we've exchanged boozy kisses and now we are gyrating in close proximity on the dance floor, not holding one another, but thighs rubbing groins, our legs intertwined as our arms flail. Sometimes we dance back-to-back, rubbing our asses together. Bakili watches me, a leering grin on his face. "Take her! She wants you!" he calls.

The girl grins. "The bedroom's free for the moment."

I am tempted. This is very much the sort of good time we had in Nairobi. There, taking a girl to the bedroom was one of the reasons for a party. For some time, this girl has excited my groin, something she undoubtedly knows. She is young enough to feel a genuine, if only transitory, attraction to me, young enough not to be jaded by the aftermath of parties like these. And I feel attracted to her.

The band takes a break. Suddenly a car horn shrills repeatedly somewhere in the neighborhood. The silver sound of chatter and laughter falls silent. The merrymakers look from one to another as if a warning has sounded, as if someone's life has come to an end. I realize that these Africans live differently with death than do Americans. We keep it out of our homes, on the other side of our gates, away from our neighborhoods. These Africans know that it inhabits their neighborhoods. An ominous stillness wraps itself about the house. The girl with whom I've been dancing throws her arms about me as if now is the time for me to hide her in my pocket.

I kiss the girl's forehead, pull her arms off me and jive over to my shirt and boots. Once I've donned them, the girl and I search out Bakili. "Time to call it a night," I tell him. He cocks his head as if to ask: Really? "I'm here to work, believe it or not, and if I stay here a minute longer..." Bakili smiles, assuming I'm taking the girl to the hotel. He and Beryl and I shake hands and I stumble out of the house to the Land Cruiser. The girl follows me. I tell her I have to work. She asks for a ride. As we circle the block, she makes clear her willingness to spend the night. When I decline, I feel certain she will tell her friends that white guys don't know how to show they're men.

When we pull up before the house, guests have spilled onto the porch and the unpaved road. They are staring down the street at something I cannot see. The girl hears the undercurrent of murmurs that spread through her friends. She huddles beside me again, frightened. Bakili hurries up to the Land Cruiser. "There's been another murder," he says. "You better follow me."

Chapter Three

S BAKILI GOES FOR HIS VOLKSWAGEN BUG, PARKED BESIDE the house, party guests open the doors of the Land Cruiser and pile inside. Soon the vehicle is warm with humanity and ripe with the smell of sweating bodies. When we arrive, three blocks away, at the scene of the murder, neighborhood people stand in the unpaved street in nightclothes, sleeping cloths and shorts. They gape at the body of a well-fleshed man. He seems to have fled his night sport in haste for his suit coat lies beside him in the dust. His shirt is unbuttoned. His suit trousers are fastened at the waist, but the fly is not zipped. His face and chest have been raked by claws; blood oozes from the wounds. His throat is a bloody mess. The flesh has been ripped away, exposing the windpipe.

My fellow party guests leave the Land Cruiser and move out silently to peer at the body as if to identify it, then move to other onlookers to question them. Bakili starts toward a group of men standing beside a black Mercedes. I follow him. In the midst of this group a man in a chauffeur's uniform gesticulates wildly to men who have the look of detectives. Bakili and I take out our notepads. The Mercedes is parked on a cleared patch of ground that stretches before a two-story wooden structure removed from the squalor of its surroundings like a lady with pretensions of grandeur. Beside the Mercedes are two police vans. It requires no extraordinary perception to understand that the establishment, ostensibly a bar serving a clientele drawn from other parts of the city, is actually a brothel.

Bakili and I move through the onlookers. They open a path when they see that I am a white man. We make our way to the group around the chauffeur. Bakili nods to the detectives. When one of them looks up as if to challenge me, I show him my press pass. He relents.

Understanding what's being said does not require fluency in Chichewa, the local language. The eyes of the chauffeur, the dead man's driver, still bulge out from the fright he experienced. He pantomimes a feline creature moving along the street while he dozed in the Mercedes. He claims it pounced on the hood of the car. He gestures to a balcony on the brothel's second floor, thrusts his arms forward and opens his hands wide, the fingers outstretched, to indicate the leopard's claws. He jumps forward to suggest the cat's leap from the balcony.

When the police go into the establishment, Bakili and I compare notes. My surmises prove correct. The leopard—or leopard-man—sprang onto the victim, the Deputy Minister of the Interior Affairs Ministry, as he fled the brothel, alerted by the chauffeur's blasting the car horn.

The police pull a young woman from the brothel.

Her hair's peroxided and coiffed in an enormous Afro so that she seems to have a shaking, golden aureole about her head. She's crying and tears have savaged her makeup. She no longer seems the sexy sophisticate she aspired to being, but rather a frightened child who wonders what bad luck will befall her for giving the bigwig value for his money. She wears pink slippers with a fringe of faux ostrich feathers and holds a thin dressing gown over her nakedness. She corroborates the story of the chauffeur, using some of the same gestures. As the police lead her away, I wonder what sort of treatment she will receive at their hands.

Bakili moves beside me to whisper, "I better go write something that won't get me tossed into jail with the sweetie." He starts away, then turns back. "Want to see how your ambassador plays puppet master to our President?" He suggests that I drive out to Hazen's house and instructs me how to find it. "These leopard murders terrify the President," he says. "Hazen talks him through them, even in the middle of the night." Bakili and I shake hands. He hurries away. Most of his guests follow behind him. The girl I danced with looks at me. When I shake my head, she moves off with Bakili.

I move into the darkness at the edge of the crowd and watch the neighborhood people from a vantage point where I hope they won't notice me. It's clear from the hushed tones and gestures that the onlookers are talking about the "cat" and its attacks on its victims. They seem worried lest it attack them. Soon they'll suspect that any element out of the ordinary will threaten their safety, including a white man watching them from the darkness. I take off.

—m—

I find the American ambassador's residence without difficulty. It's a gated property, situated at a T junction, with a stucco wall surrounding it. Shards of broken glass have been fixed along the top of the wall to discourage thieves from climbing over it. An asphalt road passes in front of the house; a murram access road joins it just across from the driveway. I park on this murram road well back from the T junction, turn off my headlights and watch the house. It's large, with hallways of rooms spreading out from both sides of a central parlor. As I recall from an earlier visit, a terrace leads off the parlor and overlooks a spacious lawn and a swimming pool. I sit waiting, for what I'm not sure.

If it's true, as Bakili contends, that the President will telephone Hazen, seeking his advice about what to do in the face of yet another murder, I suppose I should admire Hazen. I should be proud that an American diplomat has gained the President's trust so quickly.

I can understand why Kamuzu Banda has his worries. Despite its beauty, Malawi is a curious country, little known and rarely visited. Landlocked and donor-dependent, it's doomed to perpetual poverty. It came to nationhood in 1964 with a set of insoluble problems. Its citizens in the north, for example, have little in common with their brother Malawians in the south, where Blantyre was sited in the late 1800s by Scots missionaries who sought to replace the principal occupation, slave-raiding, with commerce. In a perfect world, a newly independent black-run African state would turn its back on the apartheid regime in nearby South Africa. But Malawi has no such luxury.

Possessing no industry and few natural resources, it must content itself with being a labor reservoir for South African gold mines. Indeed, it's grateful to send its young men there for work and rites of passage into manhood. At this time, in 1970, that fact makes it anathema to other newly independent African states.

The intransigence of the imperious Dr Hastings Kamuzu Banda sours its reputation even further.

As I watch the house, I wonder which of the bedrooms is occupied by Joss. She is the most beautiful woman I have ever known. Modern life offers up every day countless images of women who are—or who are purported to be—beautiful, sensual, sexual. So a man sees beautiful women—or at least images of them—all the time. Less often he sees them in the flesh. And he's privileged to know a beautiful woman—to be her intimate companion—almost never. I have had that privilege. Jocelyn has high cheekbones and a lovely mouth, full of perfect teeth, with a well-formed indentation stretching between the peak of her lips and the beginning of her well-modeled nose. She wears her lustrous black hair in a variety of styles: sometimes long and parted naturally along the crown of her head, sometimes in bangs and a bob of the sort made famous by the silent screen star Louise Brooks, sometimes in a shiny ponytail. Her eyes hold a thousand expressions. They flash. They mist over with emotion. They invite intimacy in the early morning. They glaze over with boredom. Twinkle with merriment when she's amused. Narrow with accusation when she's miffed. Assume an imperiousness when she raises a critical or questioning eyebrow. Go absent when she wishes to be elsewhere. She has a smile that any man would strategize to bring to her face. And her beauty seems perfectly natural. It does not occur to one that she spends inordinate time nurturing her beauty. But, of course, she does.

If Jocelyn is consummately beautiful, she is also consummately perverse, the most difficult, the most damnably vexing woman I have ever met. But she gets away with it. She has allure. She has sex appeal. If she looks at a man, he feels a stirring in his groin. Whatever It is, she has it.

Vexing though she may be, I begged her to leave her husband and marry me. As, I'm sure, other lovers of hers have done. She refused. Because of the child, she said. But she could have brought the child with her. Because she would want to be faithful to me, she said, and did not trust herself. Men came after her and she was weak. Because, she argued, seizing an afternoon of love-making in Rabat or a week of it in Paris, with our mutual passion at flood crest, was better than living each day together. But I suspect she refused me because the real pleasure of her existence is to make her husband's time on earth a hell. And so I determined to get on with my life and never to see her again.

But as is customary with Joss, the matter was not quite so simple. After I received the letter about her coming to Malawi, she began to tiptoe once again through my dreams. I did not want to call out her name while Maggie, my companion in Johannesburg, was in my bed. Sometimes I would force myself awake, get up and walk through the quiet house. Once or twice, Maggie appeared to ask if I was all right. I began to feel that it was dishonest to let this situation continue. Either I should tell Maggie about the letter and my relationship with Joss or I should take a trip to Malawi, see Joss again and determine whether or not the attraction was over. I sensed that discussing this situation with Maggie would be the wrong move. I did not want to invite her to leave my house; I did not want to invite her to leave my bed. Because the truth is I like her very much. I feared that once I confessed to her that I was still thinking about Joss, she might assume that leaving was the only course that preserved her self-respect.

Watching the house I see that under a tree that shades its entrance a night guard sits. Now and then he stokes a small fire flickering in a metal pan. I gaze at the structure, thinking about Joss, about the Hazens' daughter Pepper, even about the ambassador's mother, all of them sleeping somewhere inside. I wonder what changes Joss's accident and reconstructive surgery have wrought in her marriage to Hazen. Are the two of them getting on now? Does she ever recall lovers? I fantasize about leaping over the stucco wall, slipping into the house, and moving through the corridors, seeking my Joss.

Suddenly, someone leaves the house by a side door. A woman. She wears a white dressing gown of a light material that trails behind her as she moves. My heart leaps. It's Joss. She knows I'm waiting for her.

Then I realize that my fantasies are deluding me. I'm dreaming, only half awake.

Strangely, the momentary dream brings to mind an experience I'd had in Morocco, in Rabat. I'd interviewed the embassy's political officer, an Africa hand I'd never met before, and he'd invited me home for lunch. He wanted to pick my brain as much as I desired to pick his.

I followed him in my rental car out to his home in the suburbs. It was a neighborhood of houses surrounded by high walls that protected the homes from the clatter of street life. Inside, the place was dark with high ceilings to keep the home cool in the heat. It was decorated in Maghrebi style: few carpets on the tile floors and large brass trays on the walls. The furnishings were US government issue, bland couches and chairs given interest by local weavings made into cushions. My host gave the family whistle, shed his suit coat and tie, and took the light sport coat I wore as a way to carry my reporter's notebook. A servant appeared wearing a white tunic and trousers, complete with red sash and fez, and took the coats. With the servant came a bright child, five, maybe six, full of smiles at the sight of her father. He paid her little attention. She said hello, but did not rush to him for a fatherly hug. He went to the drinks cart to make us gin tonics. While her father prepared the drinks, I introduced myself to the girl, explaining that I was a journalist. She told me she went to school. A servant Mamadou walked her to and from the schoolyard.

I asked, "What's your favorite subject: Arabic? Math?" She could not have been studying much math because she seemed just to have started school.

"Oh, I hate maths!" she burst out. Then she caught herself and answered as she had apparently been trained to do. "I mean… I don't much care for maths. Daddy helps me sometimes. Then it's okay."

I winked at her and confessed, "I never 'cared much' for math either." She grinned at me and I felt I'd made a friend.

The host asked, "Is Mommy joining us?"

The child answered, "I think so." Then she hollered, "MOMMY!"

The host handed me my drink and frowned at his daughter. "Don't yell, Pep. Ladies don't yell.

The woman of the house entered, grinning at the child, greeting her, "Hello, sweetie! How was school?" She stooped for a hug. She wore a djellaba with a stretch of local fabric around her head. When she rose from the hug, we half-smiled at one another. I was wondering if I could continue to pick her husband's brain over lunch en famille. I considered the woman part of the furniture, a dutiful Foreign Service wife, accustomed to feeding strays for lunch, who wore Moroccan dress around the house as a way of absorbing local culture.

A strange sudden silence fell across the room. I felt it, ignored it. I assumed it sprang from some tension that was none of my affair.

The woman went to the drinks cart. She told her husband, "I'll have bourbon today." He seemed surprised and maybe a little disapproving.

He glanced at her carefully. "Everything all right?" he asked as if thinking some domestic calamity had complicated her morning.

"Of course," she said. "Will you introduce me?"

"Hello," I said with a smile. I gazed at her, but my attention was on her right hand, to see if she would offer it to shake.

The man said, "Tom Craig, the journalist." As I looked at the woman, I felt oddly that we'd met. Then just as he said her name - "This is my wife Jocelyn" – I got it.

"Welcome to Morocco?" she said. "You just passing through?"

An icy wave flashed across my body. My scalp prickled as if my hair were standing on end. My Joss! I had not seen her since our passionate month together in East Africa years before. "Journalists keep moving," I mumbled.

She turned back to Hazen – for, of course, her husband was Hazen – while he prepared her drink. I sipped my gin tonic and inspected her. She'd put on a few pounds. Wrinkles showed in her neck. But still a magnificent woman.

She glanced at me. The old attraction immediately pulsated between us. I felt sexual energy reverberating in the room. I saw that it also affected Joss. I felt nervous. I was tingling. I stopped thinking about picking Hazen's brain over lunch.

When I'd known Joss in Nairobi, she had used the surname Bennett. When she confessed to me that she was married, she refused to give me her husband's name or occupation. I had assumed he ran a business somewhere. So I had no way of knowing that the political officer I'd been interviewing was the husband with whom Joss had such a troubled relationship. But they'd accomplished the child Joss had said they were planning to have. I supposed things were tolerable between them. The child was certainly bright and sweet.

Joss said, "Visitors in this place feed our souls, Mr. Craig. Where are you based?"

"Johannesburg."

"You're a long way from home."

We exchanged banalities. I sensed that Joss had handled this situation with other lovers. She knew how to dissemble and I relaxed. We were exemplary. In fact, the child helped us out.

She asked me, "Would you like to see my kittens?"

"I would love to!" I told her. I was delighted to have a moment away from that magnetic attraction I felt for Joss.

"They were just born," the child said. "They're blind." She led me out across a patio to a large box containing a mother tabby and her litter of wiggling kittens, their eyes still firmly shut. "One died, but three are left," she said.

"Oh, I'm sorry."

"That's what happens sometimes," the child replied matter-of-factly. She gave me one of the kittens and took one herself. She petted it tenderly. "They're so cute. I wish they weren't blind." She looked at me. "Don't you?"

"Why don't you pray for their eyes to be opened?" I suggested. "That might help." I was playing a little joke on Joss. She hadn't been to a church in years and suddenly her daughter would be believing in miracles.

The child gazed at me as if I were an oracle of wisdom. "Really?" she inquired. "I just ask God?"

I nodded. Pepper handed me her kitten, put her hands together and shut her eyes. Her lips began to move. I watched her. I loved her guilelessness and was grateful that kittens' eyes always open after a few days.

At lunch I sat across from Joss. After Hazen pontificated about Morocco, we made small talk, chatting mainly about places they'd been stationed. Joss and I made casual remarks about our lives over the past half dozen years, statements that passed as light conversation, but were, in fact, set forth in order for us each to fill in for the other the vanished years. It was not hard to piece together that she and Hazen had been married for more than a decade and that Hazen was ambitious for an ambassadorship. I explained that journalism in Africa kept me moving so much that I'd never had time to get married. Shamelessly I mentioned that I had met a woman who'd walked out of the darkness one night in Kenya, but had been with her too short a time before our paths went in opposite directions. I suggested that I hadn't quite gotten over her.

While we were eating dessert, Hazen got a call. He was needed back at the embassy. Joss fetched our coats and Hazen and I returned to our vehicles. I had repented of my wooing at lunch and knew what would happen if I stayed. In case Hazen had sensed the unusual energy in the air, I wanted to be sure he saw me leaving. I did not want suspicions that I had lingered to exacerbate any troubles in the marriage. I told Hazen that I had to get on the road. I was heading on to an appointment later that afternoon in Casablanca, I said.

He explained the road I should take to connect with the highway and we shook hands. Our cars headed off in opposite directions.

I hadn't gone far when I felt in my coat pocket and realized that my reporter's notebook was no longer there. I knew immediately what had happened. Even so, I pulled off onto the shoulder and searched the car. No notebook. It contained notes of interviews, the names and addresses of people I needed to contact, as well as snatches of reportage. I could not leave it behind. In lifting it, Jocelyn understood that fact. As I returned to the neighborhood, Pepper appeared from behind the wall surrounding the house. With her was a Muslim servant in djellaba and knitted cap. I stayed in the car until they disappeared around a corner. I parked the car well down the street and went back. My heart was beating wildly.

Joss was waiting at the door of the house. Hearing my footsteps she opened it. "I wasn't sure I could get through lunch," she said. I kissed her fiercely.

"What about the cook?" I asked.

"I sent him to the market."

We dashed to the bedroom shedding clothes. We pulled back the bedspread and made eager love.

After a time we rested, wrapped about each other. I was staring at the ceiling. "You didn't recognize me, did you?" she said.

How could I have recognized her? When we'd been together, she'd been so slim, always in shorts and safari boots, a shirt and sunglasses. She'd been deeply tanned. Sometimes she had seemed several different women to me. But none of them was a Rabat housewife in djellaba and a Moroccan scarf. "Of course, I recognized you. I was being discreet."

"You've had so many women since me that—"

"I recognized you instantly. I like your kid."

"The best thing that ever happened to me." A slight pause. Then: "Thank you."

"For what?"

Another pause. "The compliment, of course." We returned to our labors. While an air-conditioner hummed, I examined her body for old times' sake, covering it with kisses. On her right rump I discovered a small tattoo in the shape of the African continent. I put it entirely in my mouth and gave it a tender bite. She remarked, "There's more of me than there used to be back there."

"Prime real estate!" I pinched the tattoo. "This wasn't here the last time I visited this site."

"Max was furious I got it," she said gaily. "Pepper loves it!"

I lay beside her, fondling Africa. We kissed. We agreed to meet the following month in Paris. Our bodies slid together again.

As I was dressing, I said, "Why not divorce him? Get free of him."

"No divorce. I like living overseas." Joss was in her djellaba again, remaking the bed. "Except," she added, "when his lover visits. She's my cousin."

"Your cousin?"

She nodded. "She was here last week." She stood to her full height, her hands on her hips, the injured wife who's just had an adulterer in her bed. "I told Max: She's not coming in this house! She's not seeing my kid. My dear husband! Fucking my cousin in my house."

"Well," I reminded her, "you've been fucking me in his. "

"You're not a cousin!"

"Are there rules in families?"

"She hates me, that bitch. Says I stole Max from her when he was on home leave. We did sort of run off. But I didn't steal him. He begged me to marry him."

"Leave him! Isn't that better for Pepper?"

"I'm not going to be a single mother," she declared. "Working all day, parenting all night. Hoping he sends me child support this month. Worrying how that lovely child will turn out. I'll ruin his career first!" She raised a fist and lifted the middle finger to her absent husband. "Foreign Service careers are not hard to ruin," she went on, "especially if a man's as ambitious as Max. He knows I'll do it." Joss smiled, pleased with the problems she could cause him.

I had just made love to her. The smell of her body was still on mine; the taste of her still in my mouth. As she grinned at the revenge she could wreak on Hazen, I watched her, amazed, repelled. I took my notebook—it was on the nightstand beside us as we made love—and got back onto the road to Casablanca. I felt more physically alive than I had in months. I also felt a little put off by her—and ashamed of myself because I knew that, even though her perversity distressed me, I would still meet her in Paris as we'd planned.

A noise—I'm not sure what—startles me. I come out of my reverie. I'm only half awake, parked outside the American ambassador's house in Malawi.

I see the night guard prancing before the entrance of the house. Perhaps he made the noise that startled me. With an almost military stiffness, he braces himself to a soldierly stance, holding a panga, a machete. He salutes, touching the tip of the panga to his forehead as a man—Hazen? It must be—hurries from the house to a black Cadillac parked beyond the tree. An American ambassador must drive American. So Bakili is correct. Hazen makes night calls. But so what?

With my windows rolled down, I hear the Cadillac's engine ignite. The night guard trots down to the gate and opens it. The Caddy slides down the driveway, turns right toward town and disappears. I listen to the whisper of its motor diminish beyond earshot and wonder if I should follow the car. But surely at this time of night the ambassador would quickly realize he was being followed. Would that serve my purpose? If I follow him, what will I learn? I watch the night guard close the gate. Does he lock it again? He returns to his fire and crouches in such a way that I can no longer see him. Perhaps he's stretching out for a snooze.

What now, I wonder. It's 2:30 in the morning. A government minister lies dead outside a brothel not far from the city center and that fact so disturbs the president of this tiny slice of a country that he telephones the American ambassador in need of his solace. Joss is inside that house, ever more the prisoner of the fate she's chosen for herself, and that fact so disturbs me that I cannot think about the leopard-man murder. I can think only about Joss. The woman is perverse, spiteful, a bitch. But I know I have to see her.

Sitting in the darkness I wonder about the stucco wall. Could I scale it? Could I find an unlocked door or open window and steal inside the house? Could I find the room Joss occupies? And enter it? And slide into her bed? I fantasize for a moment that this happens. I look down at her sleeping figure, her serene and beautiful face, as I did in Nairobi when I came home late from sending stories from the Reuters office. In my fantasy I slip out of my clothes. Naked, I feel a chill. I glide between the covers toward her warmth. I move beside her, slide my arms about her. She recognizes my touch. She turns toward me, wraps her arms about me.

"Hello," she whispers. "I wondered when you'd come." We kiss. Our bodies join as easily as they always have.

What adolescent fantasy! I should have grown beyond such dreams. Especially since Joss is now in recovery from an accident. Still, I must see her, even if she's damaged. I keep wondering about the wall, getting inside it. Does it completely encircle the property? What about the shards? Do they project from the entire wall? I try to recall if the guard locked the gate.

I sit in the darkness a long while. Eventually I strike a deal with myself. If the gate is locked, I will not try to scale the wall; I will return to the hotel. If the gate is open, I will slip inside. If the night guard confronts me, I will ask if this is the home of the South African ambassador. When he tells me it's not, I'll leave. If the night guard does not detect my entrance, I'll move toward the house and try the doors.

As I tiptoe across the lawn, I hear the night guard's snores. As I circle around the near wing of the house, I see light spilling from a window. I move slowly toward it, then push beside a large bougainvillea that grows next to the window.

Peering through the vines, I can see that the room is a kitchen. A woman stands in a black nightgown, her back toward me, her graceful back. Her hair has a dark sheen and her stance, so erect as she drinks, sets my head to spinning. I feel a tingling along my spine. She's drinking a glass of water—there's a carafe of it on the counter beside her—and the moment has the simplicity of a Vermeer painting. My black-haired Joss is just a woman, standing now, unconscious of her mystery and the desire it wakens in me, in her kitchen in the middle of the night, alone with her thoughts.

My own thoughts rove back to a moment the morning after our first night together. A chill on my skin awakened me. My bed had been warm all night with her beside me, but suddenly I was cold. She was gone. Rising to an elbow, the smell of Earl Grey tea filling the air, I looked over and beheld her standing in just the same way, positioned against the drawn window shade, drinking tea, her nakedness, covered by the shirt I'd worn the night before, hardly distinguishable in the dawn light. "Are you really here?" I asked. "Or is this a dream?"

After a moment she turned, perfectly at ease. She smiled at me and said, "I like tea in the morning. Do you?"

"Yes, I do."

"Don't get up," she said.

She shed the shirt and brought two cups of tea. We drank our tea together in bed. Finally she put both cups on the floor. "Hello," she said. She gave me an amorous smile.

"I'll get some protection," I told her.

"You don't need to protect yourself from me," she said. "I'm already taken care of. In the States they've developed a pill. A woman takes a pill to protect herself these days." She smiled at me. "We can do this whenever we want. Without preparations."

What a marvelous idea! "This must be a dream," I told her.

Standing now beside the bougainvillea I remember the laughter of that morning and her warmth and our laziness together. I was late to work. I smile at the memory and reach through the vines to tap on the glass. As soon as she turns around, I will step into the light and show myself. And what will be will be. Soon I'll know if there's still magic in this relationship.

As my fingers extend toward the glass, a woman enters the kitchen. I pull back. This new woman must be Hazen's mother. She's much older, her gray hair askew, squinting against the overhead light that accentuates the wrinkles in her face. She speaks to Joss, then she spots something on the floor. She steps back, chagrined, stamps her foot repeatedly. Is it a cockroach she's chasing? Failing to pulverize it, she raises her hands and shakes her head, overcome by bugs.

As she watches this old woman's dance, the demeanor of my beauty changes before my eyes. The womanliness Joss exuded standing alone with her thoughts drops away. She seems to deflate; her posture shifts to fatigue, to sexlessness. In an instant all the juice in her dries up. She reaches to a place I cannot see and brings back to her body a pair of crutches. She adjusts these under her arms and moves herself out of the kitchen. I watch her depart, feeling that the real Joss, the Joss I watched alone with her thoughts, still exists. I wonder: How do I make contact with her? And I wonder, too, if contact is really the course to pursue. I cannot enter the house tonight, not with her mother-in-law wandering about.

Alone now in the kitchen, the older woman screws the cap back onto the carafe of water. She returns it to the refrigerator, spots the bug again, stamps her foot several times more, gives up the fight and takes from the refrigerator a container of milk in the shape of a tetrahedron. She gets scissors from a drawer, snips open the container, and pours milk into a glass. She knocks at a swinging door I have not noticed and suddenly through it a child appears. Pepper. Wan and very thin, she moves as if she's walking on eggs, as if she has waited to enter until her mother left the kitchen. She tiptoes to a chair, scrambles across it onto the top of the kitchen table. She sits cross-legged, all bones and angles, her nightie looking like a sack full of sticks. She smells the milk before drinking it, a Foreign Service kid with experience of bad milk. She takes a swallow and leaves a mustache of white liquid on her upper lip. She and her grandmother talk. She giggles. Her laughter seems to turn on a light inside her. I saw that light go on two years ago when she showed me her kittens.

Suddenly Pepper spots the bug. The sight of it energizes her. She slides from the chair, rises to attack, stamping her foot. She demolishes the bug and grins in triumph. The older woman smiles; she pats the child approvingly. Pepper leans down, then rises holding a smashed cockroach between her forefinger and thumb. She shows it proudly to her grandmother. The woman recoils, horrified. Pepper pantomimes putting the cockroach into her mouth. The older woman gasps, grabs her arm. Pepper shows her the cockroach—she hasn't eaten it—and breaks up laughing.

I myself laugh aloud. And quickly silence myself lest the night guard hear.

The grandmother marches Pepper to the sink. There the child disposes of the bug and obediently washes her hands. Pepper takes her glass again. She seems suddenly dead tired. I'm distressed at how thin she looks. When she lifts her glass of milk, she holds it with both hands. She gazes toward the window. I watch her, unable to decide if she is sickly or just gawky and thin because she's growing. Now she leans forward. She peers out the window. Has she seen me? I retreat into the darkness behind the bougainvillea and push my way back onto the lawn.

As I return to the Land Cruiser, I realize that Pepper has her mother's sense of humor. I think of Joss. We were lovers. Were we ever friends? If I see her, will she tell me what it feels like now to be her? Could we talk together as people whose love for each other transcends passion to include friendship?

Driving back to the hotel, groggy with sleep, I think of Joss moving across that kitchen. That vessel of mystery and desire on crutches! How can it be? I watch the road I'm moving over as we move over the courses of our lives. Perhaps it is not a good idea to contact her. Maybe I already know what I came to find out.

Chapter Four

SUNLIGHT SLAPS MY FACE AT ABOUT 7:00 O'CLOCK and wakes me. When I am unable to fall asleep again, I pull myself from bed, don exercise clothes and go out for a run. Down the hill from the hotel lies an African market. Market women are just beginning to set up their stalls for the day's palaverings and friendly hagglings over price. They watch as I move past, calling to one another to notice the crazy white man. Some of them cry out to me, offering their wares. I circle back and jog in place as I examine their produce. I indicate my admiration of their headscarves, of the elaborate ways they're tied. They jabber to me in dialects I cannot understand. Bounding off, I hear them giggling at my antics.

As I approach the center of Blantyre, I hear shouts and suddenly I'm at the fringes of a crowd of angry protesters, jamming the entrance of the central police station. Most of them are peasants in worn clothing. They carry hoes, shovels, and pangas, and raise them, shouting demands. Although most of these people possess no items that can be wasted, a few carry placards, crudely lettered. They are in Chichewa, but I can guess what they say: "Find the Leopard-Man!" "Safety, Security, Work!" "Justice Now!"

Uniformed police with truncheons appear from inside the station to reinforce the stone-faced officers being jostled by the crowd. In order to take up defensive positions, they push back the protesters yelling at them, threatening to use their truncheons. The crowd takes offense. Refuse and rocks start flying. The unarmed police retreat into the station. The others use their truncheons. Several of them are felled by rocks. Police rush out the station doors. They raise rifles and fire warning shots. They roll out hissing canisters of tear gas. The crowd flees, screaming, elbows flying, trampling one another. I whiff the acrid smell of the gas and move along with the crowd to avoid being trampled.

As I trot away to escape the gas, heading in a direction opposite from where I came, a white man strides up beside me and takes my arm. It's Sykes, the embassy Public Affairs Officer. "My car's down this way," he says. I run beside him. We reach a Chevy sedan and jump inside where the air is not yet affected by the gas. "So you heard the news, huh?" he asks. "Leopard-man took another one. You doing a story?"

When I nod, he says, "Hazen will shit." Which strikes me as a curious reaction by both him and Hazen. What do they expect a journalist to do? We're the guys who write about events like this. Our editors may not find the events compelling, but we still report them.

"Can I see him today?"

"Not if you're covering this."

"The leopard-man gonna take a bite out of Hazen's ass? Is that his worst nightmare?"

"His fondest dream," says Sykes. "Figures there's a promotion in it." We smile and he adds—unnecessarily—"That's off the record, of course."

The excitement dies down. The crowd disperses. Sykes says, "If you really want to talk to Hazen, come to the Midweek Smash." In answer to my frown, Sykes explains, "The Hazens hold a 'Smash' for the entire staff every Wednesday afternoon. Good for morale at a post like this. And not a bad place to pick people's brains."

"I just appear?"

"Anytime after 2:00. Bring your bathing suit."

By the time I head for the residence for the Midweek Smash, I've seen the Mayor, the British holdover in the Justice Ministry, and the South African who heads up Malawi's Information Services. Both expats have requested that I not use their names; that makes it difficult to source the stories. Furthermore, it's impossible to suggest in reportage that the body language of unnamed sources confirms that the leopard- man violence has political roots. Mayor Kamwendo has acknowledged that the murders are depressing the city's morale; they're also jangling the nerves of city employees who keep a roster of the victims and fear that some of their number will become targets. A Banda loyalist and professional optimist, at least to a foreign journalist, Kamwendo expressed confidence in the police and was certain that there is only one culprit, a crazed sorcerer, probably not even a Malawian. He's assured me that this person will soon be found and brought to justice.

The Justice Ministry Brit has taken a similar line. He's told me he supports the expanded use of traditional courts, arguing that there's no way the leopard-man can be tried in a court which denies the possibility of a man transforming himself into a leopard. Asked about a political dimension, he smiled with tell-tale wryness and insisted that he stays out of politics.

The South African van der Merwe has parroted the same line, but with facial expressions that confirm the murders are political. He's confided to me his opinion that Banda should expose himself more often to foreign journalists. "The President's a realist," he's told me. "He rules a tiny country that possesses only one resource: laborers. He's convinced that Malawi must engage South Africa in order to get his people jobs rather than to vilify it and keep them poor and unemployed. I keep telling him that if he would give people like you a chance to explore realities with him, they'd see he's a man of vision." Van der Merwe's suggested the possibility of an interview with strict boundaries, with certain subject areas embargoed.

Although journalists customarily conduct their interviews, not let the subject conduct them, I've indicated interest in this possibility, maybe even a willingness to play by these rules. Securing the face-to- face meeting is at this point the primary objective. So I've given van der Merwe my questions for Banda. He's promised to push Banda about an interview and to press him to provide responses to my questions. If the good doctor does not see me, I may still be able to work whatever answers I get into quotes. I'll be able to file something that the Big Guy can use immediately or amplify with further information later on. That's the editors' call.

Enroute to the residence, I'm keyed up about seeing Joss again. If I felt differently last night, that notion fled with the daylight. The sight of her standing alone in the kitchen, even with her back toward me, has made me hope that the accident hasn't ruined her beauty, after all. In that brief moment before her mother-in-law entered, her mystery and seductiveness seemed unchanged. So maybe the reconstructive surgery has been a success. Regardless of the outcome, I'll be interested to see if the old animal attraction still exists between us.

Why do a man and a woman suddenly feel that strange sexual magnetism? It can't simply be the contour of their faces, the symmetry of their lips, the set of cheekbones. Some researchers hypothesize that it's pheromones. We exude these and others respond to them. Will that still be the case with Joss and me? I've dressed with careful casualness, two-thirds of me excited once again at the prospect of being in Joss's presence, the other third wondering what has come over me that I'm acting like a horny high school kid, especially when I've got a relaxed, intelligent and attractive companion in Joburg.

As I drive over to the residence, passing African women moving along the roadsides with their immaculate posture, their backs straight as they carry bundles on their heads and babies on their backs, my fantasies get the best of me. I imagine that as I leave the Land Cruiser parked outside the house I watched last night, Maxwell Hazen appears dressed in tailored slacks and a leisure shirt with a cravat at the throat. And although it's not a garment you can hang in a closet, he's also wearing, cloaked in modesty, that American hubris, the self-satisfaction that comes from having at last made ambassador. He's a bit pompous as he stretches out his hand to say, "Hello, Craig. Heard you were in town." We shake and I nod a greeting. And suddenly in this fantasy Joss appears, looking stunning, but using a cane. No crutches today. Seeing me, her eyes brighten. The sight of her vitalizes me and the sensations I feel at seeing her again vibrate so strongly inside me that I have to look away.

"Mrs. Hazen, I'm Tom Craig," I say in my fantasy. "We met several years ago in Morocco."

Joss offers her hand with the practiced manner of the diplomat's wife, as if we may have met, but she's not quite sure and we're having fun playing our little game before the preening ambassador. "So Max tells me," she says. "We fed you lunch—en famille—it seems."

"Quite a good lunch," I say and this is the banality of polite conversation on the diplomatic circuit. Generally, it has no subtext and that's what we hope Hazen assumes. I give Joss the slightest glance. She just barely cocks me an eyebrow and I know she'll find a way for us to meet.

Then as I drive along, edging away from the city into the swanky suburbs, my fantasy changes to that moment when we're alone. We're moving along an empty hallway, Joss in the lead with her cane. I reach forward to take her arm, stopping her. She turns, grinning like a predator, and suddenly she has moved the cane behind my back and is holding it with both hands, entrapping me. I'm her delighted prisoner. We kiss passionately. She breaks the kiss and pulls away, tapping me flirtatiously on the head with her stick. "I don't really need this cane," she confides. "I use it to drive Hazen crazy." She grins naughtily, starts quickly down the hall, dispensing with the cane, and beckons me to follow.

We tiptoe along the private corridor in that family wing of the house that I imagined the previous night. We reach a door. Joss slides her fingers onto the doorknob, stops, turns and gazes at me, clearly wanting to be kissed. I oblige her and our kiss goes on and on.

"Where's a spare bedroom?" I ask her.

"What about your friend in Johannesburg?" she replies.

"You bitch! Don't tease me," I whisper. We kiss again. My hand slides to my old best friend, her breast.

I'm jarred out of my reverie by the realization that I've just driven past the residence. I turn the Cruiser around and go back. As I move into the residence driveway, I see through the gate embassy staffers frolicking beyond the well-kept lawn I crossed last night in the dark. Some play volleyball. Others lie beside the pool on towels or tanning racks sunning, gossiping as they munch goodies. Those Foreign Service officers who have spent long years in good colleges and grad schools learning that all play impedes progress along the career path swim dutiful laps in the pool while their children, not yet initiated into lives of ambition, dive for stones, play tag or launch themselves as bombshells from the diving board. Under a canopy sit non-athletic women. I look for Joss among them. I do not see her.

I park the Cruiser beside five or six Land Rovers, Chevrolets and Fords. As I start up the drive, a man— obviously an American—emerges from the residence as if to intercept me. He wears chinos, a sport shirt, and an over-eager smile. Trailing behind him is his sharp-eyed, dark-haired, full-bosomed wife, also smiling. "Mr. Craig?" he asks as he nears me. "Bill Sykes said you might be coming. I'm Roy Foresta, the political officer. My wife Dina. Welcome." We shake hands all around.

I say, "Thanks. I'm Tom, by the way." I'm a little suspicious of this display of hospitality. It looks very much like an effort to head me off at the pass or at least keep me chaperoned. But I play it cordial.

"Max Hazen wanted to greet you," Foresta assures me. "But he's swamped right now. Tied up on a call."

I smile.

"Aren't the Hazens generous to have us all over here on Wednesdays?" chirps the little wife. "And with all these murders going on!"

I act interested.

"In a small post like this," adds Foresta, "morale really goes south—unless we all work as a team. The Smash gives everybody a little weekend at midweek. Keeps everybody happy."

I nod and smile at this Stepford pleasantness and move around the side of the house with my escorts to enter the garden. I keep an eye out for Joss. Under the canopy, out of the sun, I spot a woman too old for overseas assignments in the Foreign Service and realize she's the woman who entered the kitchen while I was observing Joss. She must be Hazen's mother. Several younger women are with her. But I do not see Joss. A black man, wearing glasses and an American polo shirt and slacks pushes a woman in a wheelchair under the canopy. She wears a lightweight shawl over her head and shoulders and I am certain that the black man is not an American; he's African. The glasses mark him as educated, a professional. I don't see Pepper, Joss's daughter, and wonder if they are both inside the house. If so, how do I shed the Forestas and get inside?

Although I'm not giving him much attention, Foresta is chatting on. He says, "I do want to apologize if we at the embassy seem to have ignored you."

I shrug this off since they have neither ignored me nor given me much help.

"Max is doing a top-flight job," Foresta assures me as if I represented not the press, but a promotion panel. "This has been a brutal time for the Hazens."

"Jocelyn is so brave," chirps Dina. "She's just pulled through a car accident in Europe."

"How terrible!" I say. "Their daughter's ill, too, I hear. Can she get the care she needs out here?"

"Pepper's been depressed," Dina acknowledges. "But now she's about to go to the States with her grandmother. I'm sure everything will come right once she's there."

"She has an African doctor?" I ask.

"The doctor's here right now, in fact," says Foresta. "Come on where everybody is."

We pass partygoers: young Foreign Service officers, secretaries, Marine guards, and Blantyre-based Peace Corps volunteers, those libertines whom Banda has announced he will shortly banish from the country as a corrupting influence on his people. As the Forestas move me toward the canopy, Dina cautions, "Max says that Jocelyn doesn't remember things the way she used to."

"They have had it rough, haven't they?" I agree, growing apprehensive.

"We admire them both unreservedly," says Foresta.

Dina adds, "Her entire face had to be reconstructed."

I try to mask my concern. I'm feeling increasingly unsettled: "car accident," "incredibly brave," "face reconstructed." I'm not supposed to know this woman. When I see her, how will I react? My mind plays with an image of Joss looking up at me, in supplication rather than the usual flirtation, a hand covering her mouth and jaw. She implores me, "Don't look at me, Tommy! Please!" and I wonder what to think.

Foresta says, "She's rather fragile. You understand." And then suddenly he grins. "Here's Max now."

Max Hazen approaches, looking casual, not pompous. His hair has begun to go gray and that adds an aura of wisdom to what is still a picture of the sophisticated diplomat. He moves forward and offers his hand.

"Hello, Craig," he says. His hand is long and thin, without strength in a handshake. I feel as if I could crush its bones if I applied pressure. "Glad you got here. Please excuse the fact that I've been so busy. You here for any particular story?"

I'm on my way to Kenya, I tell him, and just thought I'd peek in. He seems relieved to hear that.

"Come say hello to Jocelyn and my mother. Then we'll get you a drink." We start toward the canopy. "We met in Morocco, didn't we?" he asks and I know that he knows we did. "You met Jocelyn there, I think."

I shrug and say, "Did I? A guy doing my job meets an awful lot of people." Despite my apprehensions, what I really feel like telling him is that one man ought not have as much pleasure cuckolding another as I have had cuckolding him. I recognize the older woman I saw in the kitchen. Pepper is now sitting on her lap. It's as if the child has been put on display to reassure the embassy staff that the grandmother's care will help her recover. But the child does not look sick so much as bored; she fusses with her grandmother's necklace. I catch sight of a woman, her back toward me. Her hair has that night black sheen. The set of her shoulders is so familiar that I confirm: Joss! She looks okay. Heat and giddiness surge through my body. Then I realize this woman is in a wheelchair.

Joss in a wheelchair? Somehow that comes as a shock—even after all the preparation Sykes and the Forestas have given me. Is she a cripple? When I saw her walk across the kitchen last night on crutches, I thought merely that her legs were not strong yet. It did not occur to me that she could be a cripple.

The child glances over at the four of us approaching the canopy. Focusing on me, she drops the necklace, sits up straight and stares. Slowly a smile of recognition appears on her face like a light going on inside her. She hails me, "I remember you!"

If she truly remembers me, this is a very bright kid. "Hello," I say to her. "And I remember you." I step away from the others and offer my hand to her, dropping to a knee so that we can look at one another on the same level.

"You told me to pray for my kittens."

"I did?" I say. "That doesn't sound like me." But she has an excellent memory. "Come to think of it, I remember you praying. I watched you."

"You said a miracle would happen."

I am certain I never said that. "And did it?" I ask.

"The kitties opened their eyes."

"But that's wonderful." I smile at her, trying not to laugh.

She gives me an accusatory look. Then she smiles. "I thought it was a miracle at first. Then they told me that kitties are always born with their eyes shut. And in a couple of days they open them."

"Are your kittens with you here now?"

"We had to leave them in Morocco. A friend of mine took our cat."

"I understand you're going to the States."

"With my Gramma."

Hazen introduces me to his mother. She's in her mid-60s, seems dumpy sitting under the canopy with a child on her lap. I rise and bow toward her, glancing around for the shiny dark head I saw. Hazen puts his hand on the shoulder of the woman in the wheelchair and confides, "Jocelyn, darling, our distinguished visitor. Tom Craig, the journalist." Joss turns toward me.

I'm disoriented for a moment. The woman gives me a perfunctory smile. Can this be my Joss? My blood turns to ice. The reconstructive surgery has taken another woman's face and placed it on the bones of my beauty. They've completely altered her face. I recognized her last night without beholding her face. Now that I see it, how can she be the woman I loved?

I try to control my reaction. But it's hard. My expression must not convey my surprise, my horror. I glance at Hazen in order to look elsewhere. His face is frozen in sociability. His mother offers her hand, having finally fumbled it free of the child. I shake it. Then

Hazen gestures to the woman he's just called Jocelyn, the woman who now, after surgery, hardly resembles the Joss I knew. The same coloring, yes; a similar manner. But—

This Jocelyn offers her hand. She's very thin now. She gazes at me, smiles blankly. There's no recognition. I take the hand with a growing sense that something is very wrong. The hand is cold. Wasn't Joss's hand always warm? I'm so disoriented I can't remember. Wasn't it larger than this one? When she caressed you in lovemaking, her hand seemed to touch you everywhere at once. "You're so good to entertain everyone!" I chirp, as banal as the Forestas. "I hope I'm not intruding."

"We're glad you're here," she says. "Welcome." Is this Joss's voice? Wouldn't I recognize it? Can reconstructive surgery alter a voice? No! I'm sure it can't. But fragility might. And Joss's eyes. I've looked deeply into them on many an afternoon. These are eyes that have never seen me before. Did the accident take some memory with it?

"And may I present Dr Chakanza?" asks Hazen. He gestures toward the competent-looking African in glasses and an American polo shirt.

"Call me 'Chak,'" requests the doctor as we shake hands. "Are you from Florida?" he asks. "I did my medical studies there."

Hazen introduces others who sit under the canopy. Then he says to me, "When you came through Rabat, didn't you have lunch with us?" He speaks as if he is trying to jog his memory, but I am certain he knows that I went to his house. If he does not remember it clearly, he has looked it up in the daily diary he no doubt keeps.

Jocelyn says, "If you did, I'm sorry to say that I have no memory of it—and I should." She looks downcast and Dina Foresta reaches forward to take her hand.

"I confess that I don't either," I say. "A journalist shakes a lot of hands. Like a diplomat."

Jocelyn smiles and relief spreads under the canopy because the journalist—and journalists are known as untrustworthy and often brash—has done the gracious thing. That's a relief to all of these diplomatic types who've been schooled in the gracious thing—even if it hides a lie.

"Will you join us, Mr. Craig?" Jocelyn asks.

"Yes," I say. "Just let me get a drink." As I hurry to the bar on the terrace of the house, I catch Hazen and Jocelyn exchanging a glance that could mean nothing, but might mean everything. When I arrive there, my stomach is churning. I have to steady myself against a wall. My head is full of silent queries: Can that be Joss? No, it can't be! How could that be Joss?

Chapter Five

As I POUR MYSELF A GIN TONIC, I TRY to get my head to stop whirling. I grab hold of the table to steady myself. What the hell is going on? I take a bracing swallow and look back at the canopy, thinking: No! That is Not-Joss. How can that be Joss?

There have been women besides Maggie since I last saw Joss in Paris. But they have not taken the edge off my memory of the woman who has haunted my dreams for years. I take another swallow and study the woman chatting with her husband, Mama Hazen, Pepper, and Dr Chakanza. As I assess her, into my memory swims my Joss. I picture her sitting there under the canopy and I am sure: That woman is Not-Joss.

But I don't want her to be Joss, do I? I came here to find my Joss again, to see if the old feelings were still—I can feel nothing for this woman. Am I resisting this situation because I don't want us to end?

I take another swallow of my drink. My teeth clench as I mull the inescapable conclusion: Hazen and this woman, whoever she is, this Not-Joss, did something to dispose of Joss. And after they did it, an event of providential revenge occurred, the accident that sent Not-Joss to plastic surgeons and into a wheelchair.

But this is nonsense. The conclusion is hardly inescapable. Hazen's a very careful guy. On a very public career path. He would never do such a thing. This broken woman has got to be Joss. I groan inside at that thought. Oh, God! She is Joss.

An African servant appears under the canopy, a woman with a scarf tied around her head. Apparently a nanny, she takes Pepper by the hand and leads her toward the house. Studying the child as they move along, I wonder: Is she truly suffering from depression?

Or is that merely a convenient excuse to keep her confined to the house? I'm impressed at how bright she seems. She recognized me because I'd played a gentle trick on her in Morocco. She remembers the trick, realizes I was joking with her. If she is suffering from depression, it's not caused by Malawi, but by the fact that her mother has disappeared. I'm back at that idea. But even if this woman is Joss, her mother has disappeared. That disappearance is undoubtedly something Pepper cannot comprehend. She must be looking forward to the trip to America.

I wonder about the grandmother. Is she torn by the same questions eating at me?

I see Roy Foresta approaching the bar and busy myself freshening my drink. Foresta sidles up, takes a glass, and pours himself what I am sure is as strong as it gets for a careful guy like him: a ginger ale. "The social chit-chat a bit much?" he asks, trying to be engaging.

I demur and wonder: Fella, do you have any idea of what's going on right under your nose? I look across the lawn at Not-Joss. She chats with Mama Hazen, glances at me and then at her husband. He pats her shoulder.

"I hope you'll have good things to say about our little slice of Africa," Foresta intones. "Leopard-man's not the only story."

I smile and shrug. I'm not about to discuss my work.

"President's a modernizer," Foresta tells me. "Doing everything he can to make positive changes."

"Like maneuvering to get himself elected life-president?" I ask. My outrage at what has happened to Joss affects my tone.

Foresta adjusts his approach, assuming I'm a tiresome moralist. "Malawi needs that to establish continuity," he tells me. "To assure development. To raise development capital for the Lilongwe project." I listen doubtfully. "Stories about murders in Blantyre are likely to scare away investors." I say nothing. Foresta smiles uneasily.

"Is Mrs. Hazen always in the wheelchair?"

"She walks short distances on crutches," Foresta says.

"Exactly what kind of accident was it?" Foresta knows there's danger in discussing this sort of thing with a journalist. He clearly wants to avoid answering. In fact, he does not respond and I don't press him. Before long Hazen joins us. "I hope your reportage on Malawi won't hit too hard on this leopard-man business," he says.

I reply, "I hope we'll have a chance to talk about it on the record." It is very hard to play it light, given my suspicions of what Hazen and Not-Joss may have done to his wife. But I smile because I must.

"On the record," Hazen begins a little pompously as if making a statement for the press, "I'd like to say Malawi's on the map at last. An Assistant Secretary of State is about to visit. The US is probably going to make an important contribution to the President's Lilongwe project. He wants to move the capital up to the Central Province, as you've probably heard." I nod. "The country may be ready to take off," he continues. "We think that American aid may make that possible. In any case, the US is bolstering democratic values and weaning Malawi away from the apartheid embrace of South Africa. That's the important thing."

Hazen is pitching me the story he wants told. If journalism were an entirely serious enterprise, my mouth would be watering with anticipation. But alas! Hazen's story will not interest my readers. Much of the coverage I offer the Big Guy is not really news. It's exotica. Intriguing reading for people who will never visit Africa except on lazy Sunday afternoons when they linger over a tale I spin for them in the fat Sunday paper. The Big Guy is ad-rich. Often it needs text to run across the top of pages devoted mainly to ad lineage.

My exotica is well researched and decently written. It allows the Big Guy to make a pretense of presenting its readers news instead of merely sales come-ons. As a result I am allowed to write at extraordinary length as long as my editors believe it will hold our readers' interest.

"What about the leopard-man murders?" I ask.

Hazen purses his mouth with distaste. "Off the record," he says, "I'll be frank with you. They've shaken the President. He and I click, fortunately. I'm just happy to be able to help him through this time of crisis."

"Max is keeping political chaos at bay," Foresta informs me.

"If you guys reported what's really going on in Malawi," remarks Hazen, "the development, I'd be glad to talk with you."

I don't much like being called "you guys," as if I were a lower life-form, focused on sensationalism at the expense of the Big Picture. It's a sensitivity I have about being a mere jester, a purveyor of exotica, and that sensitivity is exacerbated when "you guys" is hurled at me by a striped-pants cookie-pusher who may have done something very nasty to his wife. Even so, I grin. I say that sources I've talked with suggest that the American development money will mostly land in the President's purse.

"Some of it may," Hazen has the candor to admit. "I don't deny that. But less than you guys suggest. Every time you repeat that speculation—and it is only speculation—fewer aid dollars get to Africa. Why do you guys always portray Africans as ignorant, superstitious, primitive?"

"I'm not 'you guys,'" I say. "And I don't 'always.'" I keep the grin stretched across my face and raise my hands in a gesture of supplication. "I happen to like Africans." I look Hazen in the eye, still grinning. "Do you want me to leave?"

"Of course not," he says lightly.

"Sykes invited me. I thought—"

"We're glad you're here," Hazen assures me. "It's just that when the President reads your report and calls me, I'll want to say truthfully that we never talked."

I smile tightly and shrug. Hazen's not going to like it when he discovers I've roughed out a piece about the murders that quotes "informed observers"—I hate using that term—who regard the killings as politics by other means, as well as a local anthropologist who believes that men actually turn into beasts. But when he does discover it, I'll be long gone. Perhaps that qualifies me as one of "you guys." Purveyor of exotica or not, I see myself as an advocate for Africa, addressing those readers of the American audience interested in the continent. In my own way I'm serving Africa just as he is. I study Hazen closely, then look at Not-Joss. She shakes hands with Dr Chakanza, who glances at his watch and says his goodbyes. My jaw tightens. Whose doctor is he? And does this coziness assure better care?

I glance back at Hazen. "Free press is rather a new idea to our President," he says. "I hope I won't have to plead with him not to declare you persona non grata." Hazen smiles at his little joke. Foresta laughs.

"The trouble with getting booted out of Malawi," I explain, "is that you really can't boast about it. No one's actually sure it's a country." The men do not smile. "Getting bounced out of South Africa? Now that's a different matter, a badge of courage. You've been fighting apartheid." I finish off my drink. "I think I'll have a swim," I tell them. "Cool off. Excuse me. My suit's in my vehicle."

I hang around the back of the Land Cruiser, stuffing my swimsuit in and out of my duffel, waiting for Dr Chakanza to appear. At last he does and I sling the duffel over my shoulder, looking up as if surprised to see he's there. I ask him about his medical studies in Florida: when he was there, what was his specialty, and how did he find the United States. Delighted to have caught the attention of a journalist, he waxes enthusiastic about America. I tell him how incredibly beautiful I find Malawi to be. "We are making progress," he says.

"And Mrs Hazen," I ask. "Is she making progress?"

"She's very brave," he replies. "I admire her."

"Will she walk again?"

"I keep urging her to use the crutches. I'm afraid she's resigned to the wheelchair."

"She's had a rough six months," I say. "And the little girl? How is she?"

He hesitates as if suspicious that I may be asking for more information than it's wise to give. Perhaps he's concerned that his assessment of Mrs. Hazen's condition is not as upbeat as an American, steeped in optimism, would expect.

"Pepper? Isn't that her name?" I ask. "I met her in Morocco. Lovely kid."

"It's a baffling case," acknowledges the doctor. "Every time we make progress, there's a relapse." A cloud of concern sweeps over his face. "I don't want to lose her."

"Lose her! Could that happen?"

Chakanza realizes that he's misspoken. "We will not lose her," he assures me. "Progress, then relapse.

"That must be—"

"I'm sure we will not lose her," he repeats, all optimism.

The stakes in Pepper's case for Chakanza and Malawi, I realize, are quite high. If Chakanza loses his patient, his reputation will suffer; his European clientele will choose expatriate doctors or fly to South Africa for treatment. His country will continue to be regarded as an unsafe backwater.

"Kamuzu has taken an interest in this case himself," Chakanza notes. "He's also a doctor, you know."

"It must have something to do with the child's reaction to her mother's accident," I suggest. "The reconstructive surgery. At the age of— What is Pepper? Seven? Eight, maybe? To see your mother's face so altered—"

Suddenly there's a tension between us. In some way I've alarmed Chakanza. I quickly backpedal. "But I'm guessing here. Are her mother's looks much changed? I really don't remember meeting her though it seems I have."

Chakanza glances at his watch, "I'm afraid I'm late for the hospital," he says. He offers his hand. "Nice meeting you. Enjoy your visit to Malawi."

He hurries toward his Peugeot 504 and races off, leaving me to wonder if he's truly late or if my persistent questioning alarmed him.

Returning to the house, I enter a reception area that leads to the living room and the garden beyond. On either side lie wings of bedrooms with access to them through frosted glass doors. A sign has been taped to the door of the wing on my right. It says, "Family Quarters," meaning, without saying so, "Private Keep Out." Pepper's room must be down that hallway. As a journalist I want to know especially what others keep hidden. I also want another chance to talk to the child. So I enter.

I move stealthily along this forbidden hallway, wondering why Pepper was removed from the party so quickly after recognizing me. Was it to keep us apart? If so, that's all the more reason to seek her out. I glance about. I listen, sniff the air, poke into the various rooms: an office for Hazen, a library and game room, a master bedroom with a pair of crutches leaning against a corner. I'm nearing the room farthest down the hall when out of it emerges Dina Foresta. Her sudden manifestation so surprises me that my expression exposes my guilty conscience. "Mr. Craig!" she says, surprised, but laughing. "Are you lost?"

I prefer to be thought a bumbler than a snoop and so I reply, "I guess I am." I hold up my duffel. "I'm looking for a place to change into my swimsuit."

"This is all private here," she tells me, suspicious, of course, that I have been snooping. "Come to the other wing. I'll show you the room." She leads me through the entry area into the opposite wing and shows me the men's dressing room.

"Thank you for rescuing me," I tell her. I move into a guest room where duffels and jeans, sandals, briefs and tee shirts lie thrown across chairs and beds. Dina waits until I'm securely in the room, her voice trilling in laughter that shakes her bosom. Then she closes the door. I have a sense that she will wait in the woman's dressing room across the hall to be sure that I do not try to sneak back to the family quarters.

As I rejoin the party in my swimsuit, Bill Sykes hails me. He needs a third man for a three-man volleyball team that will consist of the two of us and a trim, athletic-looking woman in her 40s, Kay Kittredge. Kay, who's African American, declares herself an "old Africa hand" and explains that she's on temporary duty from a finance center in Rome. She pays me the ultimate compliment by not only saying that she has read a lot of my stuff in what seems to be a weekly compilation of Africa coverage by American papers, circulated by USIS, but by being able to quote phrases I've used, ideas I've peddled. So we are immediate pals. Our trio proves to be a whammo volleyball team.

Kittredge likes to set the ball high above the net, and Sykes and I are happy to spike it down the throats of the Marine guards and Peace Corps lassies who oppose us. Whenever we win a point, all three of us slap hands. We wipe the competition.

To salute our victories, the Marine Guards—sore losers—push us into the pool. The water is cool, relaxing against my sweating body. The three of us tread water, chatting about Sykes' family in Indiana. Sykes' wife has decided to stay Stateside this tour in order to get their kids through high school; she wants them to feel rooted in a hometown before they go off to college and develop their own adult lives. I have a hunch that Sykes and Kittredge comfort one another now and then. The combination of Malawi and the Foreign Service can be pretty grim without a partner to help you through the downsides.

As we chat, I notice that Not-Joss and Mama Hazen sit watching the volley-ball games from under the canopy. Hazen stands beside them, his hand on his wife's shoulder. The Foreign Service is structured in such a way that it is never entirely free from considerations of rank and pecking order. I notice that none of the younger embassy staffers enters the privileged precinct of the canopy. The Forestas are permitted access, as are two or three other couples, but the younger people, no. I mention this to my pals, asking if Hazen, however effective he may already be with President Banda, lacks the warmth to inspire affection in his staff. Kittredge flicks her eyebrows slightly, just enough for me to under-stand that she finds Hazen icy. But Sykes, whose job it is not to forget that I'm a journalist, insists that it's still "early days" for Hazen in this assignment. "The guy's had an excruciating six months," he reminds me. "The staff respects that. They know that he and his wife are still hurting inside. Especially with the kid sick. They're grateful to see him trying, opening up the residence for them at midweek. It'll come together." But when Sykes suggests that we join the ambas-sador, I notice that Kay begs off and keeps her distance.

Sykes and I towel off and, putting on our shirts, move in under the canopy, wrapping the towels around our wet suits. We chat with the Hazens about the Midweek Smash that the ambassador has instituted. I flatter him a bit, saying what a good morale-builder it must be and how generous the Hazens are to open their home every week. He is modest about this hospitality, saying that an ambassador he served under in Mali did the same sort of thing.

"Were you together in Mali, Mrs. Hazen?" I ask, wanting to hear her talk.

"Oh, please, call me Jocelyn," she implores.

"Yes, we were there together," Hazen says, answering my question. "You've been there, of course." He shifts the talk away from his wife and memories that this woman may or may not have of Bamako. Very soon he offers their excuses and wheels her toward the house. Sykes excuses himself as well and I'm left with Mama Hazen whom Sykes apparently wishes to avoid.

"Have you been long in Africa?" she asks. "How do you like it?"

"I love it! How about you?"

The woman sighs deeply and shakes her head. "I visited them in West Africa once. But here nothing is like I expected it."

"How is that?"

"Men becoming leopards. Joss's accident. I can't hardly cope."

I smile at her, give her my full attention. This seems to please her for she's undoubtedly felt herself an outsider in this bewildering continent. It's clear that embassy people are not interested in humoring her. "What do you know about her accident?" I ask.

She glances about and looks at me wickedly. Then she lowers her voice and confides, "I know she looks very different. I'm amazed my Max still loves her so." Then she catches herself and feigns chagrin at her naughtiness. "What a thing to say!" she whispers flirtatiously. "You never heard that from me."

I laugh; she's pleased. "I'm curious," I say to prime her. "With Jocelyn in a wheelchair and their daughter so depressed, why are they here? Shouldn't they both be getting treatment in the States?"

"Max wants me to take Pepper back to Arizona with me," Mama Hazen confides. "Not a day goes by but what he implores me to do it." She looks at me for a sympathetic reaction. "But I live in a retirement community. There's nothing there for Pepper to do."

"She might get well, mightn't she?"

The old woman looks at me woefully. "I can't nurse a child," she says. "Some days I can't hardly get myself out of bed."

"It must be very difficult for Pepper," I suggest, "if her mother's looks have changed."

"It's difficult for all of us!" she whispers to me. "Jocelyn seems like a changed woman. An entirely different woman." She shakes her head. "And there are times when Max can't hardly keep his hands off her. A tragic accident," she says. "I can almost see how that might strengthen a couple's commitment to each other. But Max and Joss have often fought. So this—" She shakes her head in total befuddlement. "It's as if this plastic surgery were—" She lowers her voice. "An aphrodisiac." She looks at me, confused. "Is that the word, I mean?"

Dina Foresta joins us and I'm not sure whether it's because she feels that Mama Hazen should be chaperoned when seen in whispered consultations with a journalist or because her courtesy to the ambassador's mother will further her husband's career. Mama Hazen explains that I had just been wondering about why Jocelyn and Pepper are here in Blantyre when the best medical help is at home in the States.

"They're serving their country, Mr. Craig," Dina replies. There's an edge in her voice that I don't like, the lower life-form business again. I say I ought to get out of my wet swimsuit and take off.

Once I've changed back into slacks, I make another foray into the family wing of the house. I move stealthily along the hallway, towel around my neck, the duffel hung over my shoulder. I again pass Max's office, the den, the library and the master bedroom—those doors are closed now—and reach yet another closed door, the final one on this hallway.

There's a small bulletin board at a child's level beside the door. Thumbtacked onto it is a folded note which reads, "For Daddy. Dictated to Mommy from Pepper." I recognize Joss's handwriting. So the accident has not altered that. Hmm. But how old is the note? Surely Pepper writes her own notes now.

I listen at the door. Hearing nothing, I slide my hand onto the doorknob and turn it silently. I lean against the door, push it open just enough to peer into the room.

I can see almost nothing. The room is dark. Curtains are drawn over the windows. Across from where I stand is a door of glass panes leading into the garden; a translucent curtain covers it. With cartoon animal figures on the wall, it's obviously a child's bedroom. And from the scent of medicines obviously a sick room. My view of the child's bed is obscured by a mosquito net partially pulled back. I see the form of matchstick legs under a blanket. Two figures hover at the bedside. One is the middle-aged African nanny, standing behind a wheelchair. In it sits the woman I cannot think of as Joss. Whoever she is, to me she is Not-Joss.

This woman leans forward from her wheelchair, holding a dish in one hand and offering a spoon of food to the patient in the other. "Pepper, Pepper, Pepper, Pepper!" Not-Joss implores. "Please get better—for me and Daddy. For Dr Chakanza."

There is no response to this plea. I push the door open a bit farther. Not-Joss entreats, "Your father needs you up and well. He needs your smile. Okay?"

With a piteous expression Not-Joss gazes at the patient. I'm not unmoved by her plea. I know I should withdraw, but I need to see how the child reacts. There's nothing for that but to push into the room. Not-Joss looks up. She's surprised at my intrusion, but not enough to drop the spoon. "Mr. Gray," she says.

"I must be lost," I say, moving into the room. "And it's Craig, Mrs. Hazen. Tom Craig." I smile, casual, but take a hard look at the woman and the room. "I wanted to chat more with Pepper."

Pepper scrambles forward to see me, peering around the mosquito net. "Hi!" she sings out.

"Hi!" I reply with a grin. I look at the woman in the wheelchair. "Pepper remembers me coming to your house, Mrs. Hazen. My ego's a bit bruised that you don't remember." It's an asinine remark, but I'm trying to evoke a response.

"I was in an accident, Mr. Craig. As a result, my memory's very shaky." She has the elegant manners of a diplomat, smiling at me, masking hostility. "I'm afraid I'll have to ask you to leave now. Pepper needs rest."

"No! I want to talk to him! Can't I—"

Not-Joss gives Pepper a withering look. The nanny steps between me and Pepper, blocking my view of her. The child lies down, her back to us, and whimpers.

"Must I ask Mama Bo to call a Marine guard?" Not-Joss queries.

I try to smile boyishly and get a look at the child; I fail in both endeavors. Not-Joss hurls me a look that would freeze boiling water. I move toward the door, watching the child's bed.

"Get well, Pepper," I say. "Have a good trip!"

I listen for a response, but all I hear are whimpers. Not-Joss stares me out of the room.

I leave the Smash and head back to the Mount Soche Hotel, wondering what in the world is going on.

Chapter Six

MY ENCOUNTER WITH NOT-JOSS IN PEPPER'S ROOM STRONGLY reinforces my suspicion that something is awry. Whatever the effect of the accident, this would have been an occasion, removed from prying eyes, when Joss would have given me some signal of recognition. But she didn't. How can this woman be Joss? No accident, I feel, could have transformed the Joss I loved—and knew so intimately—into the woman feeding Pepper.

Once back at the hotel the journalist in me demands that I subject this suspicion to scrutiny. Almost immediately I realize how outlandish it is. How full of vanity. I acknowledge that I have no real understanding of the extent to which a terrible car accident can disfigure a woman's face. Or alter her personality. Nor do I know what might be required of reconstructive surgery to restore that accident-damaged face to social acceptability. For that's what had to be done, is it not? I've always assumed, I realize, that plastic surgery meant a nose bob, a face-lift, or wrinkle removal, vanity procedures to enhance one's beauty. Yet I've seen photographs of World War I soldiers so horribly wounded, before the advent of plastic surgery, reconstructive surgery, whatever it's called, that they were forced to wear masks to hide their deformities. Could Joss's accident have caused a disfigurement so extensive that, fifty years earlier, a mask would have been her fate?

Could the accident also disfigure, transform, her personality? Of course. There have been many cases of this kind. In this case, is she so altered in her beauty, so damaged in her self-esteem, that she no longer acknowledges former lovers? Even with a flicker across her eyes? Does she calculate that the best way to deal with our affair is to pretend it never existed? That we never met? Isn't that the curse that beauties have to deal with? Contending with the loss of beauty? Could that loss have rekindled a flame between two lover-enemies like Joss and Hazen?

If Joss has suffered such an extensive trauma, then why do I expect to evoke a response in her? Or at least to see her give some acknowledgment of our former relationship? It's my own conceit, isn't it? My vanity. I assumed, didn't I, that my aura would overwhelm her? That, in contrast to the diplomat's bureaucratic caution, my charm, my glamour and verve, my foreign correspondent's boldness would still so consume her that she must somehow convey her delight in seeing me? Even in the presence of her husband and mother-in-law? I have to laugh at my own self-deceit. Somehow, all along, I've assumed that Joss must love me more than her husband, even though when I have begged her to leave him for me, she's refused.

Given the situation she's in, given the fact that she's had numerous liaisons, I must admit that it makes sense for her to call a moratorium on lovers. For her simply to be grateful to be alive. To be cared for by a husband upon whom she must now depend and who rewards that dependence—almost miraculously—with affection, maybe even passion.

Has the accident somehow helped the marriage sort itself out? Has it shaken all perversity out of her? Joss without perversity? I can't imagine it.

And does Hazen—who sees impoverished and donor-dependent Malawi as an opportunity to accomplish his ambition—regard spiritually impoverished and husband-dependent Joss as an opportunity to fulfill husbandly ambitions? That is, to conquer her? To bend her to his will? Might Hazen love Joss best when she's damaged? He just might.

And another question. Are all my suspicions about the woman being an impostor really based on an egotism that rebels against being ignored? Perhaps.

But I can't shake the notion that that woman is Not-Joss.

I go round and round on this, pacing back and forth. Finally I telephone the house in Johannesburg, hoping against hope to catch Maggie, my confidante and friend. I've never mentioned Joss to her so it would be imprudent to discuss the matter with her. Still, I'd like to hear her voice.

Even so, as I listen to the phone ringing, I wonder why I'm calling. I assured Maggie I'd call yesterday, just to check in, but I purposely avoided doing that. It smacked too much, I thought, of an on-the-leash husband checking in with wifey. Of a commitment that does not exist now and probably never will. But at last I've got a girlfriend who is actually a friend. I want to hear her voice.

I think now of the dinner party Maggie and I gave the Saturday night before I came here. When I told our guests about the leopard-man, they burst into excited conversation.

"They what?" exclaimed Clive who runs the charter air service for which Maggie does freelance flying. "They believe that men turn into beasts?"

"But they do!" said Jill who's a journalist like me. "Every woman knows men who turn into beasts."

"Righty-ho!" agreed Liz, Clive's wife. "And not just if the temperature's right." She and Jill laughed heartily together.

I often feel a need to defend Africans and their beliefs to South Africans brainwashed by apartheid. So I chimed in with, "We Westerners are so consumed with rationality that turning into beasts seems preposterous to us, primitive, savage—"

"Not to say inconvenient," suggested Clive. The others roared with laughter. They snarled exaggeratedly and clawed the air.

"We Westerners have lost all touch with the supernatural," I insisted. "But guess what: it may exist."

"Oh, it does!" affirmed Maggie—bless her!

"Sometimes when I'm flying, all alone in the clouds, I have a mystical feeling about—"

"But you don't turn into a buzzard," said George.

"Or do unspeakable things," added Jill. "Like ripping out people's throats."

They clawed and snarled again and chortled at my expense.

After the party I walked Clive and Liz to their car and put Liz into the passenger seat. As I returned to shake his hand, Clive said, "I can rearrange things to let Maggie fly you up to Malawi. Interested?"

I shook my head. Clive studied me in the light shining from our front window. "Maggie's not a serious proposition?"

"We're just two Americans in somebody else's country," I said. "Too young for 'serious.'"

The truth is: my work does not allow for "serious." Maggie's a guest, a college friend of my kid sister Sue—and now a friend of mine—who has a pilot's license and a yen to fly. She and my sis arrived six months ago, having decided to kick around Africa for a while. They camped in my spare bedroom and worked out of Joburg to explore southern Africa. After about three months, when Sue's leave of absence was about to expire, she returned to the States. Having landed freelance piloting jobs, Maggie stayed on. She pays no rent. I generally pay for the groceries; Maggie does the shopping and cooks for us. She's a capable, intelligent person, well-traveled, and an enjoyable companion. With Joss I have passion. A kind of hungry madness for the other possesses us both. With Maggie I have a friendship.

"Time to grow up, lad," Clive said. "You won't find better than Maggie. And before you know it, you'll be looking at middle-age."

"C'mon," I objected. "I'm only thirty-two."

When I returned to the house, Maggie was in the kitchen, preparing the place for the African girl who would come in to do the washing-up. As I brought the cocktail glasses and hors d'oeuvres plates in from the living room, Maggie said, "We're a sparkling couple, don't you think?"

"No question about it."

"We give delightful parties. You're fascinating. Men tell me I'm passable."

I gently rubbed her behind. "You're extremely pattable."

Maggie brought her hands out of the soapy water and leaned against me. "I don't imagine you ever think of me, do you, when you're working."

"Oh, I think so. I'm one of those guys who can do two things at once."

Maggie flicked soap at me and resumed washing dishes. "Your work's all concentration," she said. "Whereas in mine, I get the plane into the air and land it. And all the rest is course corrections. So there's time for me to think of you."

"You must yawn a lot in your work."

Again a flick of soap. "Since we're together," Maggie said, "too bad we're both gone so much. Hmm?" I wondered where this was going. It sounded like "closer relationship" talk, just when I was going off to see Joss. "Clive could let me fly you up to Malawi. We'd have a day together. Would you like that?"

I did not immediately answer. Maggie stopped rinsing dishes to look at me. I glanced away, putting glasses on the counter. "It really is very concentrated," I told her. "Let's have the week together we planned." She was going to meet me in Kenya. I nuzzled her. "And a sweet time together tonight." I gave her a kiss-kiss, not a friend's kiss. When we went upstairs we made love. Afterwards I felt like a shit because even while I was holding her, I was thinking of Joss Hazen.

And now I'm thinking of Maggie, wishing I could hear her voice. The phone rings on and on. Undoubtedly she's out flying somewhere.

I pace away the afternoon, moving back and forth across the room, from the entry door out onto the small balcony and back, puzzling about Joss, trying to figure things out. Still a working journalist, I catch the BBC World Service's Africa news program, as well as that of the Voice of America on which I'm quoted. Nice to know someone's reading my stuff. I check over the appointments for tomorrow, made earlier in the day. I'm to see a senior police detective, a man named Jika who, as an African, seems unusual in this country where whites still linger as officials. I'll also see a politician that Bakili's put me on to and an officer of the South African Legation. Since Banda has threatened to expel all Peace Corps volunteers, I may also catch the head of the Peace Corps. Perhaps I'll try to interview Roy Foresta as well. He may see me instead of the Ambassador who has a speech to give.

Professional details arranged, I go back to puzzling out this business of Joss. I order chicken-rice soup and a pitcher of coffee from room service. While eating I take a pad of paper and pencil in three columns. In the first column I write down the elements I'm cogitating. In the second column I list all the reasons why the Jocelyn Hazen I met today must be the Joss I have known. In the third column I note the reasons why this Jocelyn must be an impostor. I go down the list:

- Voice. Joss had a melodious voice that she lowered occasionally to make humorously cutting remarks. This woman's voice is without music, without laughter or humor. But... Since the voice expresses one's state of being and inner feelings, is it not possible that the voice of a damaged Joss could have lost its melody? Especially in a situation where her home is being invaded by people she does not know? Especially when she's tired? Nothing conclusive here.

- Coloring. Not-Joss's coloring looks like that of Joss. If coloring were the sole factor, one would have to conclude they're the same woman.

- Hands. Can I really remember Joss's hands? My recollection is that they were warm, lively hands with tapered fingers. Were they large? I would guess that Not-Joss has smaller hands, dry and cold. Were her fingers stubby? Or do I think that because I disliked her? Is it possible that when I think of large hands, I'm really remembering my friend Sarie who grew up on a farm?

- Eyes. Both women have blue eyes flecked with green. The truth of the matter is that I'm not a devotee of eyes. Lovers are supposed to rhapsodize about the color of the beloved's eyes. But I can tell a woman I love her and not have the foggiest notion of the color of her eyes. What I remember about Joss's eyes is that they sparkled when they beheld me. They sought mischief with me—and laughter. Not-Joss's eyes seemed dull by contrast. They no more sparkled in beholding me than they would have in beholding a potato. But here we're back to my ego. Is it not possible that a woman whose eyes once sparkled when they beheld me, a woman damaged by an accident that left her bound to a wheelchair, might no longer feel a charge when seeing me? Mightn't her eyes be dull? So. . . These could be the eyes of the same woman.

- Handwriting. If I assume that Jocelyn Hazen wrote the note I saw outside Pepper's room, then the handwriting looks the same. But is the note old?

- Manner. I'm not sure what I mean by this. I never saw my Joss acting as hostess at a Foreign Service Smash. If I had, I would have expected her to be vivacious and humorous, a bit ironic about the hypocrisies and pomposities of diplomacy. Certainly she would have been charming to men—because they interested her. Because their pleasure in her inflamed Hazen's jealousies and she enjoyed his being jealous. This woman was so subdued. But—be charitable, for God's sake, Craig!— she was in a wheelchair. She might still be in pain. She was wearing a mask of flesh that might still seem strange to her. She hardly knows her guests and one of them is a mother-in-law who is both obtuse and not supportive.

- Recognition. I did not recognize this woman as Joss. I acknowledge that I'm strongly opposed to thinking that Joss could be transformed into her. I do not like admitting to myself that if she truly is Joss I could not desire her. I would want to run. I would not opt to help her through this rough patch that might never end. Put crudely, that means that the relationship with Joss was about good sex with a beautiful woman. Probably that's often the case. But am I no deeper than that?

I acknowledge that on the plains of East Africa I sometimes felt she was several different women. Which turned out to be true. But this broken woman was not one of those I thought she might be.

I have to admit that when I first saw Joss at the house in Rabat I didn't recognize her. And she had changed hardly at all, only a matter of garments and a few pounds. She recognized me first and the flashing in her eyes sent the old siren's signal. If this is Joss, bad luck's badly shaken her. She's someone new. No longer a striking beauty. The groin-fires are probably burning low. She's no longer sending out siren signals to men like me. Maybe the best way for her to forget the old times is by refusing to remember them.

- Retribution. Was the accident an instance of divine retribution? Would my Joss have been likely to see it in such terms? As punishment for a life lived promiscuously? I hardly think so. Joss wasn't religious. She regarded enjoying herself in bed with a friend as just one of life's pleasures. And she would have considered herself lucky to have a lot of friends. She would have thought the charge of promiscuity amusingly Victorian. And regarded a God who would maim and disfigure a woman for enjoying the men He created as illogical. Why would the Creator have made sex so pleasurable if He was going to punish you for enjoying it? But if she did not see the accident as retribution, how would she regard it? As bad luck? One of the tricks of an indifferent fate? However she regarded it, would it not have subdued her?

If the woman I met is an impostor, who is she? An American, yes. One who stepped into a Foreign Service role without much difficulty. Two years ago Joss said something about her cousin being Hazen's lover. Is this the cousin then? Family hatreds run deep.

But cousins do not always resemble one another. And blood is thicker than water. Except when passion is involved.

If this woman is an impostor, how does she regard the accident that befell her? If she's an impostor, she must at least be an accomplice to a murder. If she murdered—or helped to murder—my Joss, then was hit by a car, how would it be possible to regard the accident as anything but retribution? Would that not subdue her? Make her contemplate the consequences of her sins?

I have to ask myself: What do I myself think about this retribution business? I've witnessed and reported on a certain amount of evil in the world. It's difficult for me to think that much of it gets punished— at least not this side of the grave. I guess I would have to say that Joss was a person who ran a lot of risks. She may have run them in automobiles as well as in bedrooms.

At the end of this exercise I have reached no conclusions. The exercise turned out to be more about me than about her. I like myself less than when I began it. That's something I'll get over; we all do. But I haven't decided if she's Joss or some improbable impostor.

Tired for the moment of this enigma, I find myself thinking again of Maggie. I realize this was the day she was flying junketing business executives up to Victoria Falls. They planned to spend the night there. I wonder if she's in her room at that magnificent colonial palace, the Victoria Falls Hotel.

When Maggie and my sister Sue were visiting me, they considered themselves adventurers continually encountering new insights, new exploits, new places. I insisted they were merely tourists with pretensions. I contended that they were dedicated sightseers, bright and engaging young women, yes, but nothing more than wanderers, visiting landmarks, beholding sights and checking them off: the Cape of Good Hope, Table Mountain, Kruger Park, Vic Falls, the Kalahari Desert, the Okavango delta and the ruins of Great Zimbabwe. I teased them about seeing much while understanding little. Provoked, they asked, "What, O Wise Man, should we understand?"

I suggested that they seemed not to realize that the societies they were visiting were worth as much attention as the sights. Especially in South Africa which had not one society, but a mix of them, along with a Grand Master Plan, woefully impractical, devised to allow the different societies to live side by side in peace with The White Man always on top. My job as a journalist was, in part, to make my readers aware of the complexity of South African society and of the fact that apartheid, the master plan, was at best a grand illusion and at worst a mechanism of unspeakable cruelty and deprivation. Sometimes I suggested in my reporting that it bore resemblances to the failings in our own society with its segregation in the South. I teased my sister and her fresh-faced friend, hoping to achieve some consciousness-raising, but did not press my views. In their defense, my guests insisted that travelers faced different languages, currencies and foods, as well as the pressures of schedules and disappearing funds. These factors reduced most travel, they said, to a process of floating over societies despite their best efforts to understand them in the way I recommended.

When Maggie decided to stay a while, getting freelance jobs as a pilot, I kidded her that she would be, not only metaphorically, but quite literally, floating over the societies of southern Africa. I regarded her as a creampuff, my kid sister's pal. I did not expect our relationship to move to a place where we talked seriously about things, where we shared ourselves with one another.

But on the days Maggie wasn't flying—which at first were many—she got to know Matilda, the African girl who comes in every morning from Alexandra Township to clean and wash up. She worked side by side with Zakes, the gardener who arrives three days a week from Soweto—the Southwestern Townships—to tend the yard. She heard about their families, the conditions of their lives, the strictures they endured under apartheid. Sometimes over dinner, which Maggie began to cook, we had discussions about what the National Party government's separate development scheme aspired to do for the country and what it actually did.

One evening Maggie told me about her attempt earlier that day to visit Alexandra. Wanting to see for herself what township life was like, she decided to spend the night with Matilda, only to be turned back by police at the train station. I admired Maggie's curiosity and courage, but cautioned her that the exploit was foolhardy, both in terms of her physical safety and of bureaucratic snafus. She asked me to take her along when I next did reporting in a township.

Often this kind of reporting involves taking photographs. That's something I detest doing. I'm a words guy; analysis is my trade. What I report is best perceived through words. But the Big Guy wants visuals and there's no question that provocative photos draw readers into a story. Taking usable photos, however, requires—at least of me—a degree of concentration that subordinates my efforts at reporting. I told Maggie that if she could handle a camera, I would let her accompany me into a township. She had a 35 mm camera and set to work. The photos she took did not suggest that she would become another Margaret Bourke-White, but they were often usable. She began to accompany me on stories. The Big Guy printed her photos, paid her for them, and credited them to her. In this way we became partners, colleagues. We got to know each other pretty well. She began to understand the society as well as understanding me.

Not surprisingly, my colleagues assumed I was bringing a girlfriend along on stories and passing her off as a photographer. "Sleeping with your shooter?" they would taunt me.

"Not my type," I would say.

"No?" they'd ask. "Living with her, aren't you?"

"She's my kid sister's friend," I'd say. "More a kid sister than—"

"Oh, sure!" they'd interrupt, cackling at the lameness of this assertion. "Pretty cozy arrangement. It must get hot in the darkroom."

They tested my denials when they began to ask her out.

At this time I was not seeing anyone. I traveled so much that it was not easy to maintain a relationship. Every now and then an Afrikaner woman I had met in Bloemfontein would spend a weekend with me. I had met her doing a story in the Orange Free State, that bastion of Afrikaner reaction. She exemplified for me the cage into which apartheid thrusts young Afrikaners who want to live modern lives, but are thwarted from doing so by the rigidity of the apartheid system, the domination of the Dutch Reformed Church, and the stifling expectations of their families. In Sarie's case, her father was disabled by a farmyard accident; her mother spends all her energy doing housework and taking care of him. Sarie has worked for years in a Bloemfontein department store; she's advanced to a position as a buyer now. She lives with her parents who seem, as she tells it, totally dependent, emotionally and financially, on her support. Sarie's brother, who has a wife and five children, lives in Pretoria. He sends what money he can, but refuses other kinds of help. Sarie has a quiet, unassuming beauty. Several local men have asked her father for her hand. But whenever this happens, the father's health takes a turn for the worse and the mother's strength deteriorates. Bloemfontein is not, so Sarie contends, the kind of place where a young, quietly beautiful, church-going woman with a decent job and a good reputation can carry on a long-term affair with a man willing to wait for a change in her family situation. In any case, the men who want to marry her also want her to bear their children. Sarie knows she's trapped. She understands that her parents manipulate her, but she feels she cannot ignore what she calls her "responsibilities" to them.

About two weeks after I interviewed her in Bloemfontein, Sarie came to Joburg on a buying trip. She called me. I'm sure that act demanded all the courage she could muster. Thinking that she might open a window for me on the closed society in which she lived, I invited her to dinner. I am an attentive and sympathetic listener; interviewers must be. Sarie talked to me easily and for hours. Watching her I felt like a magician. Color blossomed in her cheeks. Her eyes began to sparkle. Her beauty became more vivid. She told me about her constricted life, not complaining, but rejoicing in having escaped it for a few hours and in being with someone who paid attention to what she said. After dinner we drove around for a while; she wanted to see more of the city. She asked to see where I lived and I took her home. I offered her some wine and the transformation I was beholding—that I was working; that's how I saw it—so flattered me that I let us finish the bottle of wine together. She stayed the night. In fact, we spent most of the next day in bed together. She knew I did not love her. But she needed a friend she could trust with her body; I was that friend.

In the next months she came to Joburg several times. She did not arrange to see me. In that way she could tell her parents truthfully that staying in town happened spur-of-the-moment. She would arrive and call and, unless I was off on a trip, we would share the weekend together.

Then Sue and Maggie came to stay at the house with me. The next time Sarie arrived, I introduced her to Maggie and Sue so that she would know, when I told her she could not stay at the house that weekend, that I really did have guests. When I took her to the station for the train back to Bloemfontein, Maggie and Sue still in the car, tears ran down her cheeks. She bit her lip. I kissed her cheek, but she would not look at me. I knew I would not see her again.

Maggie and Sue being around changed the way I lived. I couldn't walk around the house naked anymore. I had to remember to shut the bathroom door. And not to enter when it was closed. And, with my tourists there, I could not bring Sarie home for the weekend. That was something I deeply resented because my having guests trapped her in the cage of Bloemfontein.

"You sleep with her, don't you?" Sue said as I drove us back to the house.

"Not when you're around," I replied.

"Why not?" Sue asked. "We're adults." This was not a matter I felt like discussing with my kid sister. I knew Sarie would not have stayed. Our being lovers was a secret known only to her and me. In that sense Bloemfontein was a cage she never really escaped.

"Sarie looked a little sorry to me," Sue said. "Is that what you go for these days?" Sue could still be a brat. "Bring her home," she went on. "We don't care."

"She cares," I told her. "She's not going to sleep in my bed with you two listening through the walls."

"We'll get men of our own," Sue taunted. "You don't mind, do you?"

"I don't mind your having men," I replied. "I just don't want to know about it. So don't have them at my house."

"I guess we'll have to move on soon," Sue said. She and Maggie laughed.

When the time came that Maggie did get men of her own, my reporter buddies, I found myself confused about what to do. I did not want to warn her off those of whom I disapproved; that seemed too brotherly and might be mistaken for jealousy. Perhaps jealousy was part of it; I had begun to find her attractive.

She was not striking, just a fresh-faced girl in her late twenties whose ready laugh you answered with a smile or a joke. She was bright and smart-tongued, confident and capable at flying those planes around, taking them up and bringing them back down. She was of medium height, had short-cropped hair that couldn't decide whether it was blonde or not. She was not seductive; she was a pal. Seductiveness was something she would have mocked. Still, after a while you realized that her body was trim and athletic, but also felt soft if you hugged it, which I did not have enough occasion to do.

One Friday evening she came home with a reporter named Gerrit Uys. We had some wine together. When I realized that Uys intended to hang around until I had the decency to retire to my room, I decided I'd be damned if I'd let him outlast me. When we'd drunk together for two hours, with long lapses in the conversation, Maggie excused herself to go to the bathroom. While she was gone, I told Uys, "I know what you're waiting for."

"I guess we all know," Uys said.

"You won't get it here," I informed him.

"No? You try to get some and she wouldn't give it to you?"

"Take her some place," I told him. "You're not getting it in my house."

"You can have it in mine," Uys said. He laughed. "You can have it from my wife. You wouldn't be the first who got it there."

When Maggie returned, I said, "Uys was just saying goodbye. He needs to get home to kiss his wife and children."

After Uys left, Maggie seemed miffed. When I asked her what was wrong, she said, "What business was it of yours to kick him out?"

"He's married," I said.

"He's also attractive."

I looked at her impatiently. "He's charming and a pretty good journalist," I said. "He's also a shit."

Maggie picked up the wine glasses and took them to the kitchen. I followed her, feeling pissed off that she found Uys attractive.

"He tells me I'm beautiful."

"Any guy can tell you that."

"Maybe. I haven't heard it for a while."

"Do you sleep with married men?"

"I don't know what business that is of yours."

"Just don't do it in my house."

She turned to me, leaning against the kitchen sink. "Let's not fight about this, okay?" I nodded and felt stupid because I did not know that we were fighting. "No, I don't sleep with married men," she said. "He led me to believe he's single, although he didn't precisely say that." I mumbled an apology. "Do you sleep with married women?" she asked.

"Uys's wife's a sweet person," I said. "She puts up with a lot." I transferred the wine glasses from the counter where Maggie put them into the sink. I began to wash them so that I did not have to look at her.

"Is it time I found my own place?" she asked. I did not reply, keeping busy at the sink. "Clive knows of a room near the airport."

"Clive should mind his own fucking business," I told her. "Do you want to pay rent?"

I knew Maggie was about to say goodnight, wondering if she ought to take Clive's room.

I looked at her. "You are beautiful," I said.

"I'm not," she said. "But it's nice to hear it."

I reached over, clasped her jaw with my wet hand and kissed her very lightly as a friend. "I don't mean to treat you like a big brother," I told her, "a brother you don't want around." We gazed at each other, but did not speak. I turned back to the sink and saw out of the corner of my eye that she was wiping water off her chin. I felt stupid again and I wondered why I'd kissed her. Then suddenly a wine glass broke in my hands. It cut the inside of my fingers. "Shit!" I exclaimed. The water ran red with my blood.

Maggie took my hand and opened it to make sure no shards remained in the wound. She pulled a dishtowel off the rack, dried my hand, and wrapped the towel around it. She stood so close to me that our bodies pressed together. I put my arm around her, pulled her to me and kissed her. "You are beautiful," I told her again.

"I heard you the first time." She slapped my chest in rebuke. "I guess I asked for that, didn't I?" I kissed her again. "Did I ask for that, too?"

I kissed her again. "If you're all hot to sleep with a man," I said, "you can sleep with me."

"What woman could resist that offer?" She laughed. "When it comes to charm, you're not in the same league as Gerrit Uys."

"But I'm bleeding and he's not."

She cocked her head and studied me. "If I do, will you boast about it to Sue?"

"You can do the boasting. Tell her all the lies you want."

So we spent the night together. The lovemaking was full of teasing and laughter and delight, two friends having fun together. Continuing to enjoy each other this way, we formed a friendship. We savored that friendship for what it was, something very good right now, but without expectations that it would last beyond its time. We were invested in each other, but without passion. Neither of us tried to bend the other's personality to our will or to plan the other's life. We were free to go our own ways.

With the help of the Mount Soche telephone operator, I put a call through to the Victoria Falls Hotel. The operator there connects me to Maggie's room. The phone rings and rings. When Maggie answers, I hear in her voice that she's annoyed, but wants to hide the fact. "Oh, it's you," she says. "Hi."

"I've called at a bad time," I say. "You thought it might be important."

"No, I didn't." She mutters a curse. "Of course, it's important. It's you." Then she swears like a drill sergeant and when I ask what's wrong, she says, "I got out of the shower to answer this damn thing. I'm standing here naked as creation, dripping water all over the carpet."

She goes off to get a towel and her string of profanities reassures me that things are right with the world. When she returns to the phone, she tells me about the flight and the passengers, grunting as she contorts her body to get it dry. I report what I've learned about the murders: that they seem actually to involve politics. I tell her about Dr. Chitambo. I say that I've unthinkingly supposed that a man educated in our tradition will accept the premises of that tradition. We agree that it is curious of me to make such an assumption, but even more curious of him not to see that, of course, my way, the white way, is correct. I tell her, too, about the morning's demonstration and the tear gas and about the Midweek Smash. I say nothing about Joss and the enigma that has made me want to hear her voice. I ask what she's doing this evening.

She pauses slightly before answering. "Having dinner with one of these business guys," she says. I think of the hotel terrace where they'll dine with its magnificent view of the Zambesi gorge and the bridge over it. And I wonder why the pause before answering. "He's a little boring, but there'll be good eats."

I tell her that I've just had soup in the room and hear myself saying that I will probably not call again. These trips tend to develop a momentum of their own, I explain, one that demands my entire concentration. We do not end the call with endearments. We sign off as pals: "Don't work too hard," she advises me. I caution her, "Don't fall into the Zambesi up there at Vic Falls."

After I hang up, I wonder about her use of the word "eats." I've never heard her use it before. And I wonder about the "business guy who's a little boring."

Adding material to the notes I've made on the leopard-man murders, I finish a second pot of coffee. By then my hair is close to standing straight out of my head. I go back to thinking about the Midweek Smash. I'm puzzled by Mama Hazen's speaking of the strong sexual attraction between Max and Joss. Why did she mention it to a stranger? Because no one pays attention to her? And she wants attention? Or was she telling me to take a close look at what everyone seems to accept as normal?

If the woman is truly Joss, she and Hazen have been married a dozen years. There's bound to be the kind of lovemaking that happens in a marriage, but the hand-holding and the touching that accompanies initial attraction should by now have mellowed into contented companionship. Actually, Joss led me to believe that she and Hazen shared discontented mutual toleration, occasionally mitigated by sex. If the accident has at last given Hazen complete dominance over Joss, would that be likely to express itself as sexual attraction? That phenomenon takes many strange forms, but I hardly believe that it is likely to take this one.

Which means that this woman must be an impostor. That she and Hazen have somehow conspired to eliminate Joss with the woman taking on her identity. Joss was unquestionably a handful. Did she and her infidelities simply become impossible? Did Hazen find another woman with similar appeal—men generally, I think, fall for the same characteristics such as dark hair—with whom he wanted to live? Did they together hatch a plan?

If this is what happened, they've set it up beautifully. Hazen has spent most of his career in the Maghreb and Francophone West Africa. He's unlikely to encounter many of the same officers in English-speaking southern Africa. Most of those he does encounter will not have met his wife—although those who have are not likely to forget her. But this woman can always claim delicate health as a reason for failing to appear at social functions. The Hazens' soldiering on in spite of their bad luck wins the unquestioning admiration of their embassy staffers—and unquestioning admiration is exactly what they want. The Forestas illustrate the benefits of this. They are both running interference for the Hazens, Roy praising the job Max is doing, Dina telling me with icy intonation, "They are serving their country, Mr. Craig."

The puzzler is this: Why not simply divorce Joss? Or, if she made trouble about that, send her back to the States with the child and, if he must, take a lover? Of course, living with a lover might disqualify him from the achievement of his ambitions. Even maintaining one discreetly might do that. Joss must have really made him believe she would ruin his career.

Another puzzler is Mama Hazen. If she knows this woman is not her original daughter-in-law, why does she stay? Her presence lends credence to the notion that the family is bravely soldiering on. But maybe she didn't much care for Joss? Certainly she does not want to make trouble for her son just at the moment when he has achieved the goal of some twenty years' work. Maybe Mama Hazen's an enabler, a woman who's never asked questions, just does what's expected. Her taking Pepper off Hazen's hands—as an enabler she will eventually accede to this plan—will complete the transformation of this impostor into Jocelyn Hazen. I'm sure Hazen has already equipped her with a passport that bears her photo and her new name. So she's certifiably Jocelyn.

All of this makes fascinating speculation. I'm almost convinced. But then I ask myself: Why would Hazen take the risk? If my speculation's accurate, he's put his career on the line. Not this careful guy. And yet he took the risk of marrying Joss. Risk was part of her excitement. She sparked passion—even in careful men.

Maybe the clue is this: Hazen possesses an intellectual arrogance. That's why he refers to journalists—we tend to think we're pretty smart ourselves—as "you guys." He hides the worst manifestations of this arrogance. Still, wherever he is, he's convinced that he's the smartest man in the room. Killing his wife and pulling off this imposture would prove it. He and his new woman would enjoy endless pleasure—while enduring Malawi—in treasuring their unexampled cunning and brainpower. More delicious because it's secret.

In fairness I have to admit that I want to think badly of Hazen. After all, Joss who hated him refused to leave him for me. Well, I've certainly succeeded tonight. When at last I turn in, I try to put this matter to rest. I do that by wondering what Maggie is up to with a business guy who's a little boring.

The next morning I arrive promptly at 8:00 at Police Headquarters. Early in the day the place is all spit and polish, policemen standing erect, walking smartly, as if Kamuzu himself were about to inspect. As a young policeman with tribal marks on his cheeks leads me to an office, I wonder why so spiffy a crew has not turned up useful leads as to the identity of the leopard-man. But that musing, perfectly rational to a Westerner, does not take account of the way things work in Africa. The man I'm about to see understands the process. As I enter, Inspector Jika sits at his desk reading reports. He hardly looks up, just enough to ascertain that I have arrived, the journalist from the paper in faraway California. He gestures for me to take a chair, but I find every chair stacked with official files. When I do not sit, Jika looks up. He grunts as he recognizes that I, a man of discretion and delicacy, will neither move nor sit upon his files. "You journalists keep turning up like corpses that won't die," he says. "Just put them on the edge of the desk."

Which I do, observing, "We don't know who the leopard-man is yet. How can we die?" Jika leans back in his chair and examines me. I explain that I'm a friend of Bakili who suggested I interview him.

"Will you promise to die when we find him?" Jika asks dryly. Then he glances at his wristwatch and announces, "I can't talk to you now."

"Too bad," I tell him. "Because I had an interesting question to ask you."

He studies me, wondering if this can possibly be true. He is a very rumpled African with an Oxford accent, with curls of white among the tight black springs of his hair. He wears horn-rimmed glasses, wrinkled chinos that have toured many crime scenes, a plaid sport shirt, and a split-seamed UCLA sports jacket with a body of thick felt, blue and gold in color, and leather sleeves. His clothes offer an explanation of who he is: an individual in a society that discourages idiosyncratic individuality, a man who respects his own opinions even while keeping them to himself. A police inspector leading an investigation of importance to the government, he is undoubtedly well-connected, probably a confidant of Kamuzu Banda. He undoubtedly suspects who is behind the leopard-man murders; he may very well know who is committing them. He also knows that the time is not yet ripe to make arrests. He tells me, "There are no more interesting questions about the leopard-man. I've been asked them all." He rises and announces, "I'm off to do a turn around the site of the latest of these murders."

"May I tag along?"

"So that people in California will cluck about us over their coffee?"

"I wanted to ask you something entirely different."

Jika has not stopped studying me. Now he nods an assent, pulls a pair of dark glasses out of his desk, exchanges the horn rims for them and starts off. I follow behind.

As we drive out to the brothel where I stood some thirty-six hours before, he consents to my asking him questions about the murders. However, he specifies that he not be quoted by name and refuses to allow me to use a tape recorder. He seems a straight shooter, understands that I have a job to do just as he does. He's not evasive, but refuses to consider some questions, mainly those exploring the political implications of the murders.

"Is it possible," I ask, "that there is more than one leopard-man murderer?"

"Have pity on me, man," he replies. "Always the same questions. What's this 'entirely different' question you were going to ask?"

"I'll get there soon. But first: is there more than one leopard-man?"

"There might be several," he acknowledges. "Occasions like this are always attractive to copycat artists and revenge killers. Your paper must be full of such things."

"Then the police don't know yet? Is that an accurate—"

"My dear fellow," Jika interrupts, "you must know the rules of this game. The perpetrators must regard the police as omniscient. Of course, I know— We know. But you must say that we are unwilling to compromise an investigation."

When pressed, Jika readily acknowledges his doubts that the murderer actually transforms himself into a leopard, but he won't comment on whether or not he thinks such transformations are possible. "How," he asks, "can I arrest a murderer for turning himself into a leopard if I tell you that no murderer can do this?" Jika proves a fascinating interview subject, but his cleverness guarantees that I learn little more than I've already gleaned from Bakili and others.

It's early for a visit to a brothel; its inhabitants are still resting from their nocturnal exertions. But we walk through the place together. Jika assumes that both the leopard-man and the victim were inside the brothel at the same time. His detectives have already interrogated the girls who work at the place, those who did not disappear between the time the murder occurred and the time the detectives arrived. We enter the second floor room at the front of the house. A balcony off it overlooks the street below. According to the testimony of the chauffeur, the leopard-man leaped from this balcony to attack the victim. Jika paces about the room, past an overstuffed chaise longue and lounge chairs, around the enormous playground of a bed, peering into closets and bureaus and behind the floor-length curtains, through the French doors and out onto the balcony itself. As I observe him, he seems everywhere in the room, for mirrors are mounted throughout so that a client may both perform and observe his performance, watch the movie in which he is enacting the star role.

As we arrived at the brothel in the police Land Rover, I asked the inspector my entirely different question. At the time he made no comment about my query. Now, returning from his inspection of the balcony, he asks, "An unidentified white woman? Thirty-five, thirty-eight?" I realize that he's been puzzling over the matter ever since we entered this establishment. "Why would a woman's body be dumped by a roadside?"

"They have to get rid of it. And in a hurry."

"Would you do it that way? How many women have you murdered?" I smile at this question. So does Jika. "Why not dump her in the forest?" he asks. Then, with a dry smile, "Why not eat her?"

"They're dieting," I suggest. A small smile plays at the corners of Jika's mouth. "And they don't have much time. They have to keep moving."

Jika rubs his chin. "But they've planned the murder, whoever they are." I nod. "Where did they murder her?" Jika asks. "Your murderer usually does his work in an environment he controls." He points to the balcony and says, "Our leopard-man, for example, waits on the balcony in darkness. His victim leaves the building and the leopard-man pounces. Makes his kill and runs into the night. Witnesses are too terrified to follow him." He continues to rub his chin, turning his thoughts to the more immediate crime. "Do you suppose our leopard-man entered this place in his animal get-up? Or did he change into it once he was here? Did he open the door of the room where the minister was enjoying himself? Is that why the minister was trying to leave in such a hurry?"

Interesting questions, but I want to bring him back to the other case. "My woman's not been found in Malawi?"

"Not that I know of. And I would know." He smiles at me roguishly. "If such a woman is discovered soon, I will certainly arrest you."

The proprietor of the establishment enters, a large, black woman of considerable presence. "Madame," Jika says to her with a slight bow.

"Your Grace," replies the woman. They shake hands warmly and I excuse myself. "Please have some coffee and refreshment on the way out," the woman says to me.

As I return to the main floor, I encounter one of the inhabitants of the place, a slight child/woman of about fifteen. She takes me by the arm, leads me into a parlor and pours me a cup of coffee. As I sip the stuff, I ask her questions about the murder and her belief in leopard-men. She smiles shyly and beckons me to a room down the hall. Although we do not speak the same language of words, I understand from the language of gestures what she intends in terms of refreshment. Meaning no offense to her personally, I make my apologies and walk back toward town.

Chapter Seven

I HAVE AN 11:00 O'CLOCK APPOINTMENT WITH OPPOSITION POLITICIAN Charles Makanga Musopole, the dominant figure of the Malawi National Union, a grouping that serves as an umbrella for all those of the educated elite who bear a grudge against the good doctor Banda. Musopole enjoys a position of prestige in Blantyre and Zomba where the national elite gather— waning prestige, it must be acknowledged. Even so, he's consulted by reporters like me who feel that "objectivity" requires us to flavor our reportage with comments from oppositionists. But because the president has been an astute and successful mobilizer of the Malawi peasantry and because Musopole lacks the skill, the appetite or the resources—perhaps all three— for grass roots politics, Musopole's MNU party has always lagged at the polls.

Having some time before this appointment, I drop by the Blantyre Star to pick Bakili's brain. I have the good luck of finding him bent over his Royal standard typewriter, beating out a story. I pull him away from work. In fact, the piece is not going well, he confesses. He's happy to leave it; closer to deadline he'll be more focused. We repair to a street vendor's pavilion and, sitting in the shade of a palm frond roof, consume beer and fried plantains in a spicy palm nut sauce. I tell him what I've picked up in my interviews. He grunts responses. When I ask for background on Musopole, he says the man has inherited the mantle of Henry Chipembere, an independence activist of a decade ago, who fled the country a few years back after being ousted from Banda's cabinet for defying the old man and threatening to become his rival for power.

I lean close to Bakili and in a whisper ask, "Is our friend Muso instigating the leopard-man murders?" Bakili glances about to see if anyone has overheard the question. He shrugs. Then he grins. "He and Banda are playing a game," he whispers. "Shortly after the murders began, our friend's house was firebombed. My hunch is Banda's people did it. The police never turned up any suspects."

"Will he have to flee like Chipembere?"

"The old man wants him where he can watch him."

"Even if the murders continue?"

Bakili shrugs. "Your ambassador is trying to mediate between them. Maybe something will come of that."

"I keep sensing that these murders are being committed by more than one leopard-man," I tell Bakili. "When I ask about that, people evade the question. What gives?"

"They are sensitive about being portrayed as savages." He says this with a grin. "Everything about your honest white man's face proclaims that you will not do this. But they do not trust white. Furthermore, they see you thinking, thinking, thinking, behind those innocent questions."

"I'm a well-known thinker," I acknowledge, "a philosopher-journalist. And are you evading the question?"

Bakili sucks on the long neck of his beer bottle as if considering whether or not to respond. To encourage a reply I say, "If Banda and Musopole are truly playing a game, I would suppose there'd be losses on both sides."

Bakili smiles. "You are a philosopher-journalist," he says. "A much more penetrating thinker than the man I knew at the Daily Nation."

"I knew nothing then."

"We didn't want to tell you." Now Bakili leans close to me and speaks in a voice hardly above a whisper. "Musopole has also lost people," he says. "Some of them to a leopard-man, presumably sent by" —he glances about and whispers so softly I can barely hear him—"Kamuzu or his loyalists. Other of Muso's people have simply disappeared."

"Do you report such things?"

"Not the Blantyre Star. We don't all want to be out of jobs."

—*m*—

When I arrive at his office, Makanga Musopole rises from a much-scratched wooden desk and steps forward to greet me. Reporters like me affirm, contrary to reality, that Musopole is a player in Malawi. He welcomes me with a firm handshake and a grin so predatory that I wonder if I will leave his office minus body parts. The office is small, its shelves overflowing with files, books, and newspapers. A movie projector sits on the desk, pointed at the only stretch of wall not covered by ancient election posters showing Musopole's benign, aged, and wily face. It is there for my benefit. Musopole means to implant ideas in my mind with the aid of visuals.

An assistant soon appears with two mugs of tea. At a signal from the politician—the interview has not yet begun—the man moves to the movie projector.

Musopole sits in a recliner, the leg rest raised. One hand holds a flywhisk; the other languidly moves a palm-leaf fan. I quickly activate my tape recorder, aware that he is studying me. He moves his flywhisk in an arc, his arm never leaving its rest.

A black-and-white nature film begins. Suddenly moving across the wall is a superb leopard. Ah ha!

Musopole knows that it is easier to talk about leopards while watching them. The animal glides along a tree branch, then races across parched plains.

"Beautiful, no?" says Musopole. He observes me, not the wall. The operating lights of my tape recorder glow red as I watch footage of leopards.

Musopole says, "You Westerners think: What a lovely zoo Africa is! Am I right? But I'm a politician. I live with these beasts! My people live with them, too."

On the wall the leopard's prey comes into view: a gazelle almost as beautiful as the leopard. Inside I cringe. While I wish the leopard a long and happy life, I do not want to see this magnificent gazelle turned into bones. Musopole says, "These beasts terrify me. And you? They don't terrify you?" He smiles, then laughs. I continue to watch the film.

"The President accuses his enemies of carrying out these murders," Musopole comments. "He says we are leopards. Do I look like a leopard?"

The old rascal! You have to admire the chutzpah of a fellow who denies complicity in the leopard-man murders while just happening to show you nature movies about leopards. "These leopards deeply upset our people. Some of the workers in the Malawi National Union have been lost to these beasts."

"Who commits these murders?" I ask.

Musopole turns toward me. "It is said: a leopard- man. What do you think?"

"Are they political?"

"I have no idea," says the old scoundrel. "And you?"

"How do you think the leopard-man picks his victims?"

"Interesting question! Wouldn't we like to know."

"Government officials seem to be the principal victims. And associates of the President. Some people I've talked with fear the leopard-man might get to the President himself." Musopole stares at me and slowly moves his palm-leaf fan. "Do you have any thoughts about that?"

"I'm sure the leopard-man will be apprehended soon. It's only a matter of all the people working together. I'm sure Kamuzu understands that."

Is this a sentiment I'm supposed to deliver to the President via my story? Is he suggesting to Banda that they negotiate?

I pose questions about the state of Malawi. I make notes as Musopole lists all the country's ills, the chief of which, he claims, is the lack of real democracy—which translated, of course, means rule by Musopole.

As the interview progresses, the politician asks, "If I speak frankly to you, may I trust your judgment and discretion?"

I assume this wily operator will not tell me anything he does not want quoted. Still, I'm not entirely sure what this means. I gesture my assent. Musopole leans closer to me.

"It is the President who is killing people," the politician declares. "He robs them. Rigs elections. Keeps the people poor. The South Africans need our labor for their mines. So they decide that our President is an honorary white man. He can stay at their best racist hotels, eat in their best racist restaurants." Musopole looks at me for a reaction. I do not react. He continues, "Since Banda's always wanted to be a white man, he's flattered. He's vain and, by getting into bed with South African racists, he enriches himself. What can Malawi's true democrats do? What would you do?"

I tuft my lips as if considering the question, but say nothing.

"You are American," he observes. "You would take action."

"What action?" I ask. "Turn into a leopard? Or a vulture?"

Musopole cackles. "A vulture!" he shouts. "Why not? Be like him!" He gestures toward the leopard film. It continues to run. Obediently the leopard makes a dash for its prey, snatches and overcomes it. After a quick moment the gazelle lies motionless, dead. "The leopard knows his job, see?" Musopole says.

I watch the leopard pull the gazelle's body into a tree. The politician studies me and laughs. I ask, "This American development project. Will it help the country?"

"It will help our President," replies Musopole. "Ambassador Hazen is naive about this." He looks at me carefully. "Why is that?"

"What do people say about Ambassador Hazen?" I ask.

The politician grows cautious. He wonders: Why this question? Then: "That he is cunning, alert, secretive. A leopard." He chortles heartily.

"What about his wife?"

The old rascal wickedly licks his lips. "Ah, the wife!" he says. "If she were not his wife, I would make her mine. One of them." I am unable to mask my surprise.

"A woman of passion," pronounces Musopole. "I know women. I tell you my hunch." He tosses me a salacious wink. "A great fook."

"She's crippled," I say. "Her legs hardly move."

The politician strokes his chin. "But I move. Even at my age I could do better for her than that husband does." He laughs lasciviously, confident in his masculinity. Then suddenly he turns serious and asks, "Why is it that he so craves position, this Ambassador Hazen?"

"You tell me," I answer lightly, a little offended frankly for Hazen's sake. "You crave it, too."

"But only to help others," Musopole quickly proclaims. "And I have women—out of love. Not out of anger." I look surprised, interested that the politician sees anger in Hazen's passion for his wife. Musopole declares, "He enjoys running our country, Mr. Hazen."

I ask, "Might the leopard-man come after him?"

"How would I know?" responds Musopole. "I do not consort with leopards."

As I move to the door, carrying the tape recorder over my shoulder, my notebook in my pocket, he says, "When you see Mr. Hazen, give him Musopole's regards. Tell him Musopole feels sure the murders will end soon."

So I am supposed to carry a message. I thank him for the interview.

Chapter Eight

Returning to town, I drop by the Malawi Information Office. Van der Merwe, the South African who runs the place, informs me that Dr. Banda's schedule does not permit him to fit in even twenty minutes for an American journalist. "I urged him to see you," Van tells me. "The old man should talk to journalists. He can sound positively visionary about building a new capital at Lilongwe." Van der Merwe gives me a tape of the President's most recent speech. "Perhaps you can draw some nuggets from that." He expects that I will pull quotes from the tape and craft the story so that, unless a reader studies the wording carefully, he will think that I've had an interview with Kamuzu. But this is not my style. Nor that of the Big Guy in California. I'm beginning to feel it's time to push on.

I pass by the American Embassy, hoping that Hazen might be inclined to chat. I'm told he's tied up. I encounter Roy Foresta who agrees to speak with me though not for attribution. "I know you've got a job to do," he says. "We want to help you do it."

"The Ambassador's speaking at a meeting tomorrow," Foresta says. "Would you like to sit in?"

I tell him that I expect to be on the morning plane for Nairobi tomorrow. I've just about got everything I need here.

"Pity," says Foresta. "You'd see how impressive he is. He'll blow them away. And when people see Jocelyn Hazen committed to this assignment even though she's in a wheelchair, they begin to understand what an amazing couple we've got here, what commitment means to Americans."

In his office Foresta serves me coffee. He gives me a "tour d'horizon" of issues in Malawi: the possibility of US aid money to help with the Lilongwe capital, the peculiar problems of a donor-dependent country, and the brake that donor-dependence places on local initiative and entrepreneurship, the leopard-man murders and the knotty questions they pose about the contending traditional and Western systems of justice. I tell him I've just seen Musopole and convey the message he gave me. I can't judge if it means anything, but wangle from Foresta an agreement to quote him on a couple of matters. It's unlikely I'll use the quotes, but I'll have them in reserve. The request feeds his ego.

I make another stab at getting him to talk about the Hazens. "I think a profile on the Hazens would make a compelling story." I suggest. Foresta immediately grows wary. "So many Americans think of diplomats as partygoers and cookie pushers."

"It doesn't sound like Max," Foresta replies. "He doesn't want publicity."

"It'd be good for readers to understand the kind of dedication some folks are giving their country, the kind of sacrifices they're making."

"That's out of my bailiwick," says Foresta. "Try that out on Bill Sykes."

A knock comes at the door. Before Foresta replies to the knock, the door opens. Hazen pokes his head inside. "Sorry to interrupt," he says.

"No interruption," Foresta assures him. "Come in, come in. I was just telling Craig about your talk tomorrow." Hazen's in his shirtsleeves and seems to have walked down the hall to consult with Foresta. He appears uncertain about interrupting our talk. My hunch, however, is that the interruption is intentional, a way of getting a better fix on what I'm up to. "Come on in if you can spare the time, Mr. Ambassador," Foresta urges. Hazen enters and lifts a haunch onto the edge of Foresta's desk as if he will stay only a moment.

"What's the topic of your talk?" I ask. "Basic Principles of American Democracy.

Simple stuff, but when your audience has been socialized in a chieftaincy system, it's worth going over."

"The Ambassador tries to give Malawians a hint of what might be in store for them," notes Foresta.

"Sounds subversive," I suggest. "What with Kamuzu angling for life presidency."

Hazen shrugs this off. "Just out of college I taught civics to high school people," he says. "I've brushed up some of that for the locals."

"Will Banda maneuver the life presidency?" I persist.

"Very possibly. He wants to be the new Mzilikazi," Hazen says, tossing me the name of the nineteenth century founder of the Matabele nation, one of southern Africa's great chiefs. He's testing to see if I can hold my own. I'm unwilling to be enticed into matching wits on his ground. "Chieftaincy is the only model he's had. So he twists the democratic forms the British left in place in order to conform to African norms."

"I understand he calls you when these murders happen. And you go and talk him through them, is that right?"

Hazen and Foresta exchange a glance. "Who told you that?" Foresta asks.

"Sources. Is it true?" I look at Hazen.

"On the record it's not true," Hazen specifies. "And off the record?"

Hazen measures me, remembering his telling me that he would not talk to me to retain deniability if questioned by Kamuzu. But perhaps his deniability is flexible—as most of them tend to be. "We're off the record?"

I lay down my ballpoint.

"You agree not to report this at all? Not as diplomatic sources. Not as informed observers. But not at all."

"I agree. I'm trying to figure out how things work here."

"What's your background anyway?" Hazen asks.

He smiles, hail fellow, well met. "Do you answer questions as well as ask them?"

"Why not?" I say. The smartest guy in the room wants to know just how smart I am. I have been in Africa for almost a decade, I tell him. As a high school student I read books of popular anthropology. Colin Turnbull's *The Lonely African* and *The Forest People* especially intrigued me. As an undergraduate at UCLA, I studied anthropology with professors who'd done field work in Africa. I trot out their names so he knows I'm not making it up: Daniel Biebuyck in the Congo, M. G. Smith in northern Nigeria, Hilda and Leo Kuper in South Africa, Hilda in Swaziland. After graduating I bummed around Europe and North Africa for a year, then returned to Los Angeles to start a doctoral program in anthropology. After that first year of grad school I did field work with— here's another guy's name for them—David Brokensha, an anthro professor at UC Santa Barbara, who was studying the Mbere people of central Kenya. That summer, I confess, I discovered several things about myself. The first was that I flat-out lacked the necessary linguistic skills for anthropological fieldwork.

Even with training, my ear resisted learning languages quickly enough to make fieldwork practical. Secondly, I lacked patience for the minutiae that fieldwork required: noting down the intricacies of the smallest cultural practices, detailing tools, houseware, rituals, charting kinship relationships. And, most importantly, I'd had enough of school.

While in Mbere I wrote pieces about African life and sent them to American newspapers. Several of them were published. When classes resumed that September, I stayed in Kenya. The truth is my grandfather wished he'd done the same kind of thing as a young man; he offered to finance my wanderings for a couple of years. But I don't go into that. I say merely that I passed myself off as a freelance journalist and eventually landed a job on Nairobi's Daily Nation. That spot made it possible for me to pick up stringing assignments for American newspapers and that led to working for the Big Guy.

"I'm sure we've all read some of the same books," I say in conclusion. "But that's not why Kamuzu Banda has you talk him through these murders."

Hazen slides off the edge of Foresta's desk and sits in a chair opposite me. "At first the murders seemed random," he says. "The leopard-man wrinkle was something tossed in to get Joe Muntu excited."

"I guess it did," I say, smiling at this reference to the African man on the street.

Hazen elaborates. "As the murders of Banda loyalists increased and the challenge became more serious, Banda began to worry that he might be assassinated. He needs someone to talk with whose loyalty is not suspect. He knows I'm not trying to take over his country. So he talks to me."

"Did he call you the other night?" I ask.

Hazen nods. Foresta begins to take notes on what's being said so that, in case I welch on my word, there will be a State Department memo of conversation. "And what did you two talk about?" I ask.

"I tried to reassure him that he would not be assassinated. That he'd survive these attacks against his government." Then he adds, "If that's what they are. And we're not at all sure of that."

"Do you tell him he's the new Mzilikazi?"

"I tell him the truth: that he's a strong leader, the father of his country. But I try to suggest that being the real father of a country moving into the modern world involves allowing opposition elements to have a voice."

We all smile knowing that African chiefs do not encourage opposition or dissent, although they have ways of testing the winds, of gauging tribal opinion.

"Of course, I also stress how important it is to keep Communism out of Africa," Hazen adds. "That's one of our main policy goals."

"So," I say, "you advise him to give voice only to non-Communist opposition elements."

"And," Hazen says, anticipating me, "he claims it is impossible to distinguish the Communist from the non-Communist opposition."

"He tends to think all opposition is Communist," interjects Foresta. "Which is how the South Africans regard it."

"The President is not always happy with my advice," Hazen notes, "but he can receive it from me. In a sense we are equals as chiefs. He accepts it from me in a way he cannot accept it from his underlings." Hazen looks at me. "Have you talked with Musopole?"

"Yes, I have."

"I encourage Banda to consult with the man. But this is hard for him. He doesn't want to talk with Musopole; he wants to crush him."

"Banda must know," I say, "that in some African groups chiefs are ritually killed when they outlive their usefulness? Or stray too far from—"

"He knows that better than we do," Hazen says. "But he feels with some justification that Malawi is his creation. So he wants to control everything, mold every opinion. I keep trying to fortify him for the truly modern way: democracy. I encourage him to construct an independent judiciary, a free and responsible press, an opposition that has a voice. He has to hold free elections. I say he's the only man who can do it. He says he's too old, the country's too poor, underdevelopment's too great a burden. If he's Life President, he says, he'll try, but otherwise…" Hazen shrugs.

Watching him, feeling some sense of the good he's doing Malawi by espousing the right kind of nation-building, it's almost impossible for me to believe that he could have killed my Joss. A man of intelligence and capacity, one with a promising future of service, does not do such things. Even if his wife were a handful like Joss. He'd divorce her. Perhaps abandon her. He might become involved with another woman, one with a strong personality who would push him to get free. But he would not murder his wife. Unless some momentary passion overwhelmed him, something I cannot imagine.

"Banda's options aren't easy," Hazen continues. "Democracy hasn't worked well in Africa. So he's reluctant to trust it. He says he'll give it a chance if I guarantee to sustain him in power. Obviously there's no way I can do that."

"Will he be assassinated?" I ask.

"We hope not," Foresta interjects.

"I think it's unlikely," Hazen says. "We'll do everything appropriate to sustain him in power. An assassination will only play into the hands of the apartheid ideologues in South Africa. If Banda's assassinated, they will push their claim that blacks cannot be trusted to act except as savages. That doesn't further our interests."

Suddenly Hazen throws up his hands. "I've got to get back to work," he says. He stands. I rise as well and thank him for his insights. "Everything I've told you is deep background. We're in agreement on that. Am I right?"

I assure him that I understand the rules. We shake hands. Leaving the office, Hazen moves off down a hall while Foresta walks me as far as the reception desk at the entrance to the embassy.

Driving back to the hotel, I reconsider Hazen. He's a little pompous, it's true, with a touch of intellectual arrogance. But I return to the assessment I made of him in Rabat, before I knew that he was married to Joss: that he's a valuable Foreign Service officer, conscientious and dedicated, a diplomat the United States can feel proud of.

But how can that woman I met be Joss?

At the hotel I make arrangements for tomorrow's flight and have a sandwich and a beer brought to the room. I work polishing the story I've already roughed out about the leopard-man murders. Although I suggest that politics is the murders' subtext, I go light on that analysis and drench the story shamelessly with exotica, just short of that point where my editors will reach for their red pencils. I lay it aside to read again before I take it to the telegraph office this evening.

Feeling I've earned my keep, I have a swim. The pool's empty except for a couple of young African women, the wives of government bigwigs probably, and their children. The day's running around, as well as the humidity, has put a heavy stickiness on my skin. The water's cool. As I swim a first lap entirely underwater, I can feel the liquid's soft coolness pulling that stickiness off me. I swim laps in sets of three, one of breaststroke followed by one of freestyle followed by a third on my back where I can enjoy the tumbling billows of late afternoon clouds. I try not to think, merely to exercise my body.

But I keep musing on the possibility that Hazen snookered me at the embassy, putting on display the impressive side of himself in order that I discount the likelihood that he has a murderous side. How can I follow up on this? I'm not a detective. Nor am I in a position to set a trap for Hazen in order to catch him. He's clever. He remembers my visit to the house in Rabat. He's trained to remember things and knows that I am, too. He's already wary, wondering what I'm wondering. Without strong evidence—which I do not possess—there's no way I can publish anything that will flush him out. If he has murdered Joss or had the deed done by someone else, I will not be able to catch him.

While I'm swimming, Kay Kittredge, with whom I played volleyball at the Midweek Smash, arrives. She waves to me, her dark skin stunning in a yellow bikini.

She dives in nearby to do laps of her own. After we've swum side by side for a while, I ask if I can buy her a drink.

"How do you find this little sliver of a country that no one's ever heard of?" I ask her once our drinks arrive. She demurs and I realize that, with a journalist, even the most innocent of conversational gambits sounds like preparation for picking your interlocutor's brain.

Then she offers, "I find it very beautiful. And very sad. As far as I can see, there's no way out of its poverty."

"How is it as a place to live?"

"I don't really live here," she says. "I'm here from the Finance Center in Rome. Temporary duty." Then she asks, "What brings you here? Smelling out a scandal?"

"I try to stick my foot in here every couple of years." She looks at me carefully. I perk up. "Is there a scandal I should know about?"

She guffaws. "Next question. The talk is: you're the enemy."

"Li'l me? Who told you that?"

"Bill Sykes is an old friend. We served together in Nairobi."

"He says I'm the enemy?"

"He'll probably turn up here shortly. We sometimes have drinks together." So that I don't think they're a couple, she adds: "We talk about his wife in Indiana. He misses her tremendously."

Kittredge has kept herself in good shape, swimming those laps, and I think it is probably nice to have an old friend like her around when your wife is far away.

"I'm an old Africa hand," Kittredge reminds me. "Been reading you for years. I guess lotsa women tell you that, don't they?"

"Not many. No one reads anymore. Is this American-financed development project for real?"

"No idea. I've only been here a month." Then she says, "Let me ask you a question. I served in a post where the wife of one of the officers swore that foreign correspondents were fantastic in bed. She was in a position to know. Is that true?"

The lady wants to flirt. Okay. "Where was that?"

"West Africa."

"I'll tell you this: I prefer that reputation to the one that says we're all drunks." Bill Sykes appears across the pool from us. Kittredge raises her arm and signals him to join us. "The truth is," I tell her, "it's hard to be good both in bed and in print." Sykes circles the pool, ordering a drink from a waiter.

"And if you're not good in print," says Kittredge, "you don't stick around."

"Exactly."

She turns toward me, her back to Sykes, and flashes me an enigmatic smile. "There is a scandal story here," she says. "I hope you're digging."

"What scandal story?" I ask.

She turns toward Sykes and greets him cheerily. "You better rescue me," she says. "My brain's being picked by a pro."

"Actually, I haven't found much there," I jest. Kittredge puts on a mock-pout, touching Sykes' arm familiarly.

"All Foreign Service people are dull," Sykes says. "And you know why? Because they can never remember what they know that's secret. So, they pretend to know nothing at all." We all laugh.

Sykes asks how my news-gathering has gone. I suggest that stories date-lined Malawi pose a special problem: Most readers don't even know if the country exists. I explain that the leopard-man murder story is all of a piece with a country readers aren't sure exists. It gives them something to daydream about as they drive to work or sit on their chaises in the Sunday sun. But stories of substance—the problem of the donor—dependency, for example—don't seem to stand up.

That's because, for my readers, Malawi itself lacks substance. So, I tell them, I've decided to push on to Nairobi. I'll be going there on the early morning plane.

Sykes feigns distress the way a hostess feigns it at a guest's announcement of departure. But I sense that he's relieved. With Hazen as ambassador, I suspect, no coverage is good coverage. By contrast, Kittredge looks distressed. "There are stories here," she says. "You really ought to dig them out." I'm uncertain what her game is. Am I a ploy in a minuet she's dancing with Sykes? That seems unlikely. Or is she actually trying to inform me of a story she can't talk about? Could that story be Hazen and his wife?

I disregard her comment and inform Sykes that I expect to file the leopard-man story before I leave and will file background on both the Lilongwe project and Banda. That could prove useful to other reporters on the paper. Shaking hands with them both, I tell them I look forward to seeing them down the road.

In my room as I take another look at the story I've written, there's a solid pounding at my door. When I open it, I find van der Merwe standing at the threshold. "You're in incredible luck," he tells me. "Kamuzu's agreed to see you." He smiles at me enormously, very pleased with himself. "Get dressed and grab your tape recorder and notebook. We need to get to Kamuzu House before he changes his mind."

I don a clean shirt, a tie, and a coat and jump into Van's South African-made Chevrolet. As we drive to the interview, Van lays out the rules. Banda will entertain questions about the Lilongwe project that needs foreign aid support and about Malawi's external relations, especially those controversial ones with South Africa; they need to be understood from a Malawian perspective. Questions about internal politics are off limits; they will give offense. "The President is accustomed to having his way. But he's not autocratic," van der Merwe insists. "I'm sure your President operates the same way."

As we drive along, I wonder if, after our embassy conversation, Maxwell Hazen telephoned Kamuzu to say that I might usefully serve as the messenger for his views on South Africa and Lilongwe. Perhaps I should feel pleased, having passed whatever test it was that Hazen put me through. But I feel as if I'm being used to serve Banda's purposes. There's always some of that in this game and I am using Banda for my purposes. But I'm uncomfortable. "Van," I say, "I don't mind disseminating Banda's philosophy. But I can't ignore the leopard-man murders. Or the issue of life presidency which may be the cause of them."

"The old man will regard that as interfering in Malawi's internal affairs."

"That's nonsense," I say. "When did he last talk to a journalist he couldn't put in jail?"

"Don't go there," van der Merwe advises. "That's all I'm telling you. Your ambassador keeps talking to the old man about a free and responsible press. You can help us take him there by emphasizing 'responsible.' In this context that means playing by his rules and leaving 'free' for a later occasion."

Hastings Kamuzu Banda is a very small man sitting behind a very large desk in a very large room. He's a stern, grey-headed grandfather with penetrating eyes that take my measure as I walk toward him. It's the measure of a professional medical man. After receiving his degree in the States at the age of twenty-five, Banda practiced medicine in England and Ghana until he was called home to lead Malawi to independence. As I approach him, I have the uneasy feeling that his scrutiny tells him things about my personality and my physical condition, both present and future, of which I myself am totally unaware. Van der Merwe stays with me—he will make a record of the interview—and introduces us.

Banda, who has been reading documents, does not rise to shake my hand or make any other gestures of courtesy. He points me to a chair. He watches without speaking as I set up my tape recorder and prepare to take notes. Then, without benefit of questions, he launches into a discourse on his views about Lilongwe and Malawi's external affairs.

My interview technique seeks to make possible a conversation between interviewer and subject. That technique does not work well for television but allows a print journalist to pursue topics until they yield insights instead of canned statements. I do not interrupt Banda: that also seems to be one of the rules, perhaps the primary one. When he stops talking, I begin to ask questions.

He generally answers by remarking, "I have already covered that," or asking, "Didn't you understand what I said?" and giving me a stare fairly dripping scorn. In short, he is a difficult interview. He makes it clear that I am testing his patience while it is expected—another of the rules—that I am not to show that he is testing mine.

Finally American egalitarianism gets the best of me. I ask, "Is it true, as some people have suggested to me, that you want to move the government to Lilongwe in the Central Province because the leopard-man murders make it impossible to operate efficiently from Blantyre and Zomba?"

My question completely non-pluses the old man. Possibly because of its audacity and insolence. Possibly because of its content. He turns to van der Merwe. "That question is outside the boundaries we set up," he says.

"Is it?" I ask van der Merwe. "We're discussing the Lilongwe project, aren't we? This is a question about Lilongwe." I turn to Banda. "Certainly that project cannot be realized as long as these murders continue. When will the government get this problem under control? There was a murder just two nights ago."

"End of interview," Banda announces. He looks at van der Merwe. "Get him out of here." He turns to the documents he was reading when we came in and ignores us.

Van der Merwe rises, slides a hand under my right arm and lifts me off my chair. He ushers me out of the office. "Why did you do that?" he asks once we're outside. "It was going well. You agreed to the rules."

"I asked a question about Lilongwe," I plead, although even I do not believe it.

"You guys always have to be provocative," Van says. "What is it about American journalists that they must always be insulting?"

Feeling the sting of Banda's irritation, I walk back to the hotel chastising myself for feeling compelled to act the probing journalist and break the rules I've agreed to, thereby insulting a Head of State and betraying the trust of his Director of Information. Because Malawi is tiny and remote, this behavior will not damage me professionally. Still, I'm pissed off at myself. I wonder if I would be equally annoyed if I had docilely played by the rules, not seeking comment on the leopard-man. Probably.

I append a note to my story of the murders, informing my editors that I had an interview with Banda during which he refused to comment on the killings. If the editors want to add that bit of information to the story, that's their call.

About 9:00 o'clock I drive into the town center, to the Malawi telegraph office. I give the only attendant on duty my account of the leopard-man murders and educated speculation as to their probable function as part of a political dialogue. "Any possibility," I say, "that you could send this immediately?" The attendant scans the text, pauses to glance up at me, and then reads on more carefully. Is it my style that tweaks his interest? Undoubtedly the subject matter. I lay a ten- rand note on the counter. "Could it go out within the next hour?" I ask. The attendant places his hand on the note and keeps reading.

"I can send it right away," he says when he's finished the piece.

"What did you think of it?" I ask. "Is it accurate?" These are not questions I ordinarily pose, but why not?

"You will not be staying in Malawi, I think," the man tells me.

I offer my hand. We shake. He pockets the rand note and I repeat my request, "Within the hour." He assents. It's about noon in California. Even if the piece goes into tomorrow's paper, it will be several days before any news of it reaches here. But surely I'm kidding myself if I think it will cause anything more than a momentary stir. In any case, I'll be in Kenya well before anyone in Blantyre hears of it.

Leaving the telegraph office I want to tell Bakili I'm taking off. He's not at the Blantyre Star. Neither he nor Beryl are at home. I tear a sheet from my notebook, scratch out a farewell, and slip it under his door.

Back at the hotel, packing my duffel for Kenya, I find myself thinking, of all people, about Pepper. The kid is in a terrible spot. I wish I could do something for her. But what? I'm leaving tomorrow. Fortunately she'll depart soon for the States with her grandmother. So, really, there's no need to worry about her.

I sleep fitfully. I dream. In the dream I'm moving surreptitiously down a long, dark hallway full of doors. It's like the hallway in the Hazen residence, only infinitely longer. It's cold and wind whistles through it. I have to lean against the wind, wearing only pajama bottoms. They flutter around my frozen legs and I hug my chest with my arms.

Whenever I reach a door, I struggle to pull it open. When I succeed, the wind catches it and bangs it back and forth. Whenever I look into a doorway, I see only darkness, nothingness. The sound of the wind becomes that of terrified weeping. The sound makes me work more frantically to open doors.

I push open a door and find beyond it a room that resembles Pepper's bedroom. There is a glass-paned door leading outside. Against the far wall stands a four- poster bed with the curtains drawn. The wind tugs at them.

I move to the bed. The weeping grows louder. I lift my hand to part the curtains, then hesitate. Finally, I master my fear. I pull open the curtains.

Joss stares out at me. Her head is gashed. She's weeping and dead.

I wake with a shout. I sit up. It takes me several moments to remember where I am, to realize that I've been dreaming. I stumble into the bathroom. I push into the shower stall and turn on the water. Its coldness jolts me fully awake. Only then do I realize I'm standing in my pajama bottoms in a cascade of water. I have not even remembered to turn on the bathroom light.

Chapter Nine

TOTING MY LUGGAGE TOWARD THE TERMINAL THE NEXT MORNING at Chileka Airport, I see the American ambassador's black Cadillac pull up before the departure terminal, the small flags fluttering at the tips of the fenders. I wonder where Hazen's headed. As eager baggage-carriers flock to the car, the chauffeur hops out and speeds to the right rear passenger door.

When the chauffeur opens that door, it's not Hazen who emerges. It's his mother, puffy eyed with tears, her mouth clamped shut in bitterness and anger. She swings her feet to the pavement and, gripping the car door, moving like a woman older than she is, hoists herself erect. Hazen appears on the other side of the Cadillac and hurries beside her. The chauffeur withdraws to the trunk. Mama Hazen starts toward the terminal, paying no attention to her son. Looking grim, Hazen hurries after her. Obviously Mama's leaving Malawi. So where's Pepper? Still in the Cadillac, embarrassed by her elders' argument? Examining the Cadillac, I slip behind a palm near the arrivals entrance. Pepper is not in the car. I turn back to see Hazen take his mother's arm. She stops walking, but refuses to look at her son.

There on the sidewalk the mother and son assail one another in high wasp dudgeon. Neither person raises their voice. Even so, the long knives are out: in angry looks, in stinging words, spoken in curt whispers. It's the posture that reveals their passion. They hold themselves under such rigid control that a fellow wasp observer suspects that one or the other may explode.

Mama turns her head away from Hazen. He stands even more erect. Now he does not bother to mask his exasperation. Mama bites her lips. She swallows the cries in her throat. Tears flow down her cheeks. Hazen removes a handkerchief from a trousers pocket, reaches to blot her tears. Again she moves away, her back to him. He bends close to her, whispers through his teeth. She turns, wiping tears off puffy cheeks with the back of her hand. She pushes into the terminal. Hazen starts to follow, then draws himself erect, his face a mask, and starts back to the Cadillac.

To hide from him, I slip inside the arrivals terminal. Approaching the check-in counters in the departure area, I see the chauffeur tipping Mama Hazen's baggage-carriers. Mama huddles in a waiting area, trying to compose herself.

There's only one flight leaving at this hour.

Mama Hazen and I are both traveling to Nairobi. On a flight of several hours she may want to talk, to let slip what's going on. If the plane is not full, perhaps I can arrange to sit beside her. When she enters the line to check in, I take the place behind her. Feigning surprise, I say, "Why, Mrs. Hazen! Hello!" I introduce myself and remind her that we met at the Midweek Smash.

"Are you going to Kenya, too?" she asks.

"Yes, I am. Is your family here to see you off?"

"Max just left me at the door. He's not happy with me."

"I'm sure that's not the case," I say. "He must be very pleased you've come all the way out here to visit."

She cocks her head, assessing me. Her wasp training militates against her unburdening herself to me here. But I sense she needs someone to talk to.

"You must be very proud of him!" I say. "It's not every son that can rise to the rank of ambassador!"

She sighs. "I'm leaving in the middle of a spat with him."

"Oh, no!"

"I've been crying." She daubs her eyes with an embroidered handkerchief.

"I'm so sorry." I leap where no gentleman should go. "About what?"

She stands forlornly, like someone abandoned. She knows she should keep silence, but she needs to talk. "I told him I couldn't be a party to what he's doing." I want to ask what it is he's doing. Instead I move her luggage closer to the check-in counter. She feels under my protection. "He wanted me to take my granddaughter home and raise her. But how could I do that? I'm an old woman."

"Old women don't come out to Africa," I say.

"If I do that, I'm a party to what he's doing. I can't do that."

"What is it he's doing?"

Once again she stands forlornly, staring off. "Africans really seem to believe that a person can transform himself into a different body. Do you believe that?"

"You mean like men becoming leopards?" I shake my head.

"That's what Max wants me to believe. That his wife can have had an accident and then come out of it in an entirely different body. I can't believe that."

I give her a sympathetic smile. No wonder she's found Africa difficult.

"I'm too old to believe such things." I start to object about her age, but her flow of words continues. "No, it's true. I'm old. I live in a community for retirees. That's no place for an eight-year-old child. Where would she go to school? Where would she find friends? But Max insisted that I must do it."

"I do see your point," I say.

Mama Hazen lowers her voice. "I think she may die, poor child. I'm not sure he cares." This statement chills me. Mama Hazen shrugs. "I'm not sure either one of them cares."

"She's such a sweet child!"

"Well, I don't want her dying on me. Or being sick for years on end."

"Do you really think she'll die if she stays out here?"

"She might, poor waif. I told Max he should bring them both home from Malawi and keep them in the States until they're well. But he wants to be Mr. Ambassador!" She sighs and looks at her luggage. It's her turn to check in. I place her bags on the scale.

As I wait behind Mama Hazen, I hear a child's giggles. Glancing around, I see an African girl, seven or eight. She's dressed in school clothes and laughs with her parents. Her father, who must be a government official, bends down. He lifts the child into his arms.

She laughs, delighted with the attention. Watching them, I wonder how long it's been since Hazen picked Pepper off the floor and held her in his arms. I wonder if he ever did that.

When the agent returns her ticket, Mama Hazen lightly taps my back. She smiles at me. "Thanks for being so nice," she says. "I'll see you on the plane." She starts off briskly as if she had no cares. I watch her go off, thinking about Hazen and Pepper, hearing the child behind me laugh. I wonder if Pepper will die.

The ticket agent says, "Next." I hardly hear him.

He calls, "Next, please. Sir!" I step out of line and gesture for the African family to take my place.

—⁓—

Driving back to town in another Toyota Land Cruiser, I think about Pepper. Would Hazen and his consort really let her die?

At the Mount Soche Hotel I reclaim the room I vacated only hours earlier. I call Kay Kittredge at the embassy. I was so intrigued by her contention of a scandal brewing in Blantyre, I tell her, that I decided to stay over a day or two. I ask her to have a very late lunch with me beside the Mount Soche Hotel pool. "I'm not sure I should be seen with you," Kay says. "Not after what happened yesterday."

I ask her if I'm famous now at the embassy. She says infamous. We fix a date for two o'clock.

—m—

At the Blantyre Star I catch Bakili just as he's leaving for an interview. "What's going on?" he asks. "You're still here."

"I need some help late this afternoon," I say. He gestures for some background. I shake my head. "Why so mysterious?" he asks.

"I'll tell you about it this afternoon."

At the USIS library Bill Sykes is equally surprised to see me. "The word is you got into a balls- up with the President yesterday and managed to insult him."

"I'm the injured party," I say on the principle that offense is the best defense. "He insulted me. Does he think I work for his information ministry?"

"It's tricky with Kamuzu," Sykes acknowledges, escorting me to his office. Once again we have coffee and he sits at his desk, his feet resting on the open drawer. "I thought you were leaving this morning," Sykes says.

I reply that pulling quotes from my tape-recorded interview with Banda proved to be more time-consuming than I expected. Moreover, I knew I'd get swept up in Kenya stories if I went to Nairobi. Then I add, "I was tossing an idea around with Roy Foresta yesterday. I decided to follow it up." I outline for Sykes a profile on Max and Joss Hazen. It would detail the sacrifices Foreign Service couples make to further American interests overseas. "My readers need to know about this sort of thing. They think FS life is all hobnobbing with Glamorous People in Paris."

Sykes gives me a rueful smile. He takes a long sip of coffee, staring at the American travel posters on the wall behind me. "Why that story when you can write about African development? Or an Assistant Secretary's visit?"

"You don't think my readers deserve a story about Foreign Service life? They think it's all cake and champagne, you know. What about heat and dust, mosquitoes, dysentery and bad food?"

Sykes grins. "Do my story. I could use the publicity."

"The Hazen story sings. New ambassador, crippled wife, sick kid."

"I'm out here without my wife. That's no fun."

"I'll do a sidebar on you."

Sykes rises from his desk to pour us more coffee.

In fact, he's trying to decide if I've laid out an opportunity or a minefield. "I'll run it past Hazen. Don't expect a lot."

"I'd need photos of the Hazens. Maybe a photographer from the Star could help me." Sykes ponders this. "Or maybe," I suggest, "I could use stuff you already have. Wouldn't need to bother the ambassador."

Sykes goes to a file cabinet, withdraws a folder, and hands it to me. I finger through the contents, finding both posed portraits, probably taken by an embassy photographer, and informal shots taken at a Midweek Smash.

"What if I took this folder and brought it back tomorrow?"

Sykes' eyes narrow. He studies me for a long moment. "What's between you and Max Hazen?" he asks. This query catches me off guard. I try not to let my surprise show and say, "Nothing. I assume he set up the Banda interview for me."

Sykes gazes at me. "Hazen called me at home this morning. Asked me to check at the hotel to be sure you'd gone. Why is that?"

I think: Well, well. Sykes must have reported to Hazen that I planned to leave. I wonder if he saw me at the airport. "And did you check?"

Sykes nods.

So he knows I've just been bullshitting him. We regard each other. I suggest, "Maybe he's super-worried about Banda's throwing me out of his office."

Sykes continues to measure me, wondering if Hazen and I are playing some kind of chess game or if, as he suspects, Hazen's just extraordinarily cautious. "Hell!" he says finally. "Take the photos. My job's to encourage coverage of American activities in this shitass country. Goddamn Hazen wants everything checked with him first." Sykes throws up his hands. He mutters, "Fucking control freak." He grins. "That's off the record."

Despite this outburst, Sykes tries to assess the dangers I represent. "Hazen says you were snooping around his house at the Midweek Smash."

"'Snooping'? I got lost." Sykes grins at this and I'm suddenly on the defensive. We watch one another. I relent. "I might also have wanted to get another look at the daughter. To gauge how sick she is."

"What business is that of yours?"

"I'd already thought there might be a story here about the sacrifices of Foreign Service life."

Sykes presses the tips of his open fingers together, mulling what to say. "You're wondering what kind of a guy Hazen is not to send his kid home to the States." A pause. I say nothing. "Aren't you?" I shrug. "He was hoping his mother would take her home."

"Is she still here?"

"Left this morning. Didn't you see her at the airport?"

He knows I'm trying not to admit what I know. I wonder how much of this he will report to Hazen. "Pepper? Is that the daughter's name? What's 'acute depression' mean in Malawi?"

"You better ask Hazen," Sykes says. "I'll try to set up an appointment."

Sykes and I rise at the same instant. I thank him for his help. We both know that Hazen will not agree to an interview, that he will not allow a profile to be written. But I have the file of photos. They will help.

At the hotel I spread the photos in Sykes' folder across the bed. There are half a dozen of the ambassador's consort. If she is Not-Joss, she could, indeed, be her cousin. Studying the photos, I decide that Hazen must be one of those men who has a singular taste in women. No blondes for him. Brunettes with curves are his preference. Especially if they are 5' 7", 5' 8", and carry themselves with the self-assurance so characteristic of Joss. I sense that same self-assurance in the posed portraits of Not-Joss, even though she has purportedly been through an accident and reconstructive surgery. I wish I could make a timeline of her life since that surgery took place. She seems to have recovered very quickly. Perhaps the surgery never happened. No, that kind of lie would trip them up. It must be that the surgery was not as extensive as everyone thinks.

Room service brings me a tall bottle of beer and a mug. I pace the room in chino shorts and a tee shirt, sipping from the mug, studying Sykes' photos and comparing them with the photos of Joss I have with me.

Looking at Joss's photos, I can't help wondering what happened to her body. I decide that if my questions were good ones for Jika, they should be asked of others. Hazen and his woman had to dispose Joss's body. So where did they do it? I call contacts in South Africa: Johannesburg and Cape Town police, wire service editors and police reporters. They offer no help and are as amused and scornful as Jika. "What's wrong with your readers, laddie, that they got an appetite for things going wrong in Africa?" asks a Durban wire service guy.

"Does she have to be nude?" queries a reporter pal in Port Elizabeth.

"She's nude because that makes her hard to identify."

"You never heard of scars, moles, tattoos, deformities?"

"So put her in a parka," I suggest. "You heard anything about her?"

"A dead woman in a parka in South Africa! Now that's a story!"

"Why pick on us?" asks a police official in Windhoek. "You got no kicky murder stories at home?"

"Your murderer admires sloppy police work," I kid him back, "especially since they're new at the game."

"It's not sloppy if she's white," he reminds me. "Who's your killer anyway?"

But there's no going down that road and I come up empty.

As I'm dialing a contact in Lourenco Marques, Mozambique, a knock comes at the door. "Hello. Who is it?"

"Maxwell Hazen," comes the reply. "Ambassador Hazen."

"Just a moment, please." I grab several photos and hide them under my pillow. I gather the rest into a pile and set them conspicuously on my worktable where Hazen will see them.

I open the door and offer my hand. I say, "This is an unexpected honor, Mr. Ambassador. I'm afraid you've caught me barefoot." Hazen is dressed for Foggy Bottom, not for Central Africa. He wears a lightweight suit, blue-grey, with a white shirt and a tie, dark as the night sky, through which tumble tiny American flags.

"Come in, Mr. Ambassador."

"I was at the hotel," Hazen says, "and remembered that Bill Sykes said you had not gone to Nairobi, after all."

"Come in, come in," I say. "Have a seat. Would you like to share my beer? I'm afraid it's all I can offer you to drink." Hazen glances about the room. He notices the photos on the table, but does not mention them. "I can get a glass from the bathroom."

"Is anything going on?" Hazen asks. "What's to stay around for?"

"I had a funny hunch," I say, "that the leopard- man might take a bite out of Banda. I could spare a couple of days. So I decided to hang around."

The smoke I'm blowing alarms Hazen. "Have you had a tip?"

"Not a tip. A hunch. No more than that."

Hazen senses that I am improvising. He watches me through those narrowed eyes, then glances again at the photos on the table. "Have you filed anything about Malawi? May I ask?"

"Does it matter?"

"Will it cause us problems? The President is extraordinarily sensitive about coverage of Malawi."

"So I discovered."

We stare at each other, hostility behind our eyes. "I'm afraid you've made the President's list of bad white guys."

"I was doing my job," I contend. "I was wrong to accept Banda's rules. I acknowledge that. I thought maybe we could help each other." In making this mea culpa I try to put a smile on my face and warmth in my voice for hostility will only deepen Hazen's distrust.

"I wouldn't want the President to declare any American journalist persona non grata."

The threat of getting booted out of a pipsqueak Malawi makes me yearn for a swallow of beer. Because being deported will make it almost impossible for me to discover what happened to Joss. Feeling constrained about drinking in front of my guest, I go into the bathroom and fetch a glass. Returning, I pour beer for Hazen. "That's for you," I tell him. "I don't feel right drinking unless you have some."

Hazen bows slightly, but does not take the glass. I have a bracing swallow and note, "If the President PNG's me and tosses me out of Malawi, the world press may descend on Blantyre to find out what the hell's going on."

"The world press," says Hazen, "does not even know Malawi exists."

"I may help them discover it."

Hazen ignores this. He says, "Sykes mentioned you asking questions about Jocelyn and me. Something about a piece on the rigors of the Foreign Service. Is that what these photos are about?" Hazen gestures to the photos on the table.

"Right. I'll need to take some of you two as well."

"Sykes gave you these?" I acknowledge that he did. The ultra-controlled Hazen tightens his lips in anger.

I ask, "Can we set up a time for someone to take some photos of you and your wife?"

"No coverage, thanks. No photos."

"No? Fame beckons, Max." His name slips out unexpectedly. He detects a hint of derision in its use and scrutinizes me. "I hope you don't mind my using your first name. If we're going to do a profile together—"

"Fame does not beckon me, Mr. Craig," he says. "I'll stay faceless. Promotion panels don't advance publicity hounds."

"In you they'd see an exemplary American. We all see that."

Again the narrowed eyes. "They'd see divided loyalties," Hazen replies. "So I'll take my chances on a solid record that does not call attention to family problems."

"You've run through a bad patch all right," I say. I place a sympathetic hand on his shoulder. He moves off. "Your wife's quite a beautiful woman. Has reconstructive surgery altered her looks? It must—"

"You fellows really stop at nothing, do you?"

"I'm sure readers would admire an attachment so deep that—"

"I assert our right to privacy. And I'll take these."

Hazen gathers up the photos on the table. I make no objection. "I'm afraid I've offended you, Mr. Ambassador. First Banda, then you. I'm sorry. I'm having a bad run. The truth is we're usually besieged by people who want their names in the paper. That validates them. I thought I was doing you a favor." "No stories, no photos." I hand Hazen Sykes's file. He stuffs the photos inside it. I examine him. He turns away from my scrutiny.

"In my business most of those who want their names in the paper are without interest. Those who don't are interesting because they're so unusual. Is your wife sensitive about what—"

"I find this insulting," says Hazen. "I don't come from Old Money. But I come from Old Wasp. We feel it's never a good idea, outside of official duties, to have your name in the paper. Now excuse me. I've got honest work to do."

"Believe me, Mr. Ambassador, I did not mean to insult—"

Before I complete my apology he is gone.

—⁓—

Half an hour later I drive out to Ambassador Hazen's residence and turn up the murram access road across from it. A quarter of a mile up, I park the Land Cruiser well off the murram. Africans passing nearby will see the vehicle—they seem to see everything in a landscape—and will know that it does not belong in the neighborhood. They will undoubtedly investigate the vehicle's sudden appearance and so I make certain all the doors are locked. But what is important to me is that the Americans do not see it.

As I retrace my steps toward the residence, carrying binoculars, I wonder what in the world I am doing. Is it my reporter's curiosity that pushes me to get back inside that house? What do I expect to find there? Do I suppose they have Joss's body hidden in a closet? Or will I discover that the ambassador's woman is Joss, after all? Is there story potential in discovering how Pepper is reacting to her grandmother's departure? I scramble into a stand of banana trees and watch the house through the binoculars. A man works in the garden, repairing the damage done by the Midweek Smash. He works at a leisurely pace, his head hidden by a broad-brimmed sun hat. He sings to himself, and now and then bits of the tune float across the road to me on the warm, sunny air. Now I hear a motor fire up. The sleek, shiny, and very black Cadillac I saw two nights ago pulls into the porte cochere.

A black chauffeur in a black suit leaves the car, opens the trunk, and takes out two small flags attached to tiny standards. He inserts the standards into sockets at the end of each fender, the American flag on the right, on the left the ambassadorial flag which sports a blue field with thirteen stars circled around the Great Seal of the United States. Apparently preferring a low profile two nights ago—not that many people drive black Cadillacs in Blantyre—Hazen did not fly his official flags. Now that he is on his way to give a talk, he's instructed his chauffeur to see that, when the Cadillac moves along at the hurried clip required by Very Important Persons, the flags flutter charmingly. The chauffeur also checks the sheen of the fenders and buffs the gold embossed decals of the Great Seal on the passenger- and driver-side doors.

Hazen emerges from the house. Now the ambassador's wife appears, seated in a wheelchair, and pushed from within the house by the African woman I saw in Pepper's room. I focus my binoculars on her. Is she Joss? No. Maybe. No. The wheelchair stops at the driver-side rear door. Using the arms of the chair, the woman pushes herself to her feet. Hazen's quickly at her side. She maneuvers herself into the car. She seems able to lift her legs and I wonder what exactly happened to them. Foresta said she could walk short distances on crutches and I saw her do it. The African woman pulls the wheelchair aside; the chauffeur closes the car door. Hazen enters the car through the passenger-side rear door. The African woman and the chauffeur fold the chair and hoist it into the trunk. By now the gardener has run to the gate. He swings it open. As the Cadillac moves down the drive, the flags on the fenders already beginning to flutter, I crouch in the thicket of banana trees. I wait till the car passes and moves beyond earshot.

Standing again, checking the house, I see that the African woman has returned inside. I wonder what she knows. About Joss? Probably nothing. Although I've asked Inspector Jika if Joss's body has been dumped in Malawi, that seems most unlikely. If Hazen's consort is Not-Joss and she and he killed my girl, they would not have waited to arrive in Malawi to do it. If this Not-Joss met her accident in Europe, as Sykes claims, they must have killed my Joss before arriving in Africa.

But the African woman might have some idea of what is troubling Pepper. How can I induce her to tell me? Telling me must not, of course, threaten her employment. In Malawi working for the American ambassador is a very sought-after position, a job she would protect.

Watching the Cadillac depart, I noticed that the gardener opened the gate without a key and casually let it slide shut. It proves easy enough to do as I did the other night, that is, reach through the bars of the gate and fiddle with the latch to open it. Once inside the grounds, I remove the notebook from my jacket and circle around the house, pretending to check off items on a list. The gardener waves at me; he assumes I'm official. I wave back. The door to the room where I changed into my bathing suit stands ajar, a screen door covering the entrance. This door opens easily. I enter the house. I tiptoe across the room and open the door to the hallway. I listen, holding my breath. Once again I wonder what I'm doing here. I'm not a detective. I'm not even an investigative reporter. The Big Guy in California does not expect me to get stories by entering places like a thief.

But I am here. I do a quick survey of the hall. It contains bedrooms prepared for guests, an exercise room with an exercycle, barbells, and contraptions for Not-Joss's therapy, a kitchen and a utility room.

Someone's humming in this last. Peeking around the doorjamb, I see the African woman standing at an ironing board. She's ironing the ambassador's undershorts.

I tiptoe across to the family wing of the house. In the ambassador's home office I look through papers on the desk; they are without interest. Because Hazen is a careful man, the desk drawers are locked. In the Hazens' bedroom I poke through the closets. The ambassador and his wife have many more clothes than a journalist needs. In her closet I recognize no outfits as belonging to Joss. I find no bodies, but discover an extra pair of crutches. In their bathroom I search the medicine cabinet and the drawers beneath it. I feel a guilty intimacy in knowing his brand of shaving cream and aftershave lotion, her preferred lotions and mascara, perfume and contraceptive pills. My conviction grows that this Mrs. Hazen is Not-Joss. Her products are not those Joss used during our week together in Paris. But that was two years ago and Joss is not the kind of woman who would feel bound by brand loyalties.

I quickly check Hazen's den. The room smells of pipe tobacco, has shelves of tomes about Africa, apparently written by academics, copies of Foreign Affairs quarterly and The Economist. On a coffee table before a Naugahyde couch lies a thick file labeled "Family." It might have interested Mama Hazen. Was she leafing through it? Or has it been laid out specifically for my perusal? That seems unlikely. But my suspicions are aroused. Even so, I take a peek. The file contains family memorabilia: photos, letters and postcards, press clippings, exactly the items a visiting mother might linger over, savoring through memorabilia her son's overseas experiences. From what I have seen of the mentally disheveled Mama Hazen, I can well imagine that she would leave the file lying about. No doubt her son would prefer that after every use it be returned to its place in the file cabinet.

Unless it's a trap. My suspicions are ringing alarm bells. It must be a trap. Hazen needs evidence that I am on to him just as I need evidence that his woman is Not-Joss. He has undoubtedly been told that I have snooped around his house. He intuits that I may return. And so, a master of deviousness, he sets the file in a place where he knows I'll find it. But do these thoughts exaggerate the craftiness of his mind? Or give evidence of the twistedness of mine?

I sit quietly on the sofa. Despite mounting concern that I'm moving into a trap, I pore through the file. It contains Pepper's letters from Switzerland. "Dear Mommy and Daddy," starts one of them. "The montains here are très beau. I fond a friend here, but most kids are fou et mechant. The food is okay. The staff is not frendly. I can't want to see you! How is Malawi? Are there monkeys in the backyard? I love you SOOOO much!! XOXO Pepper." I read two others of her letters and decide she's a super kid.

I scan a letter of commendation from the ambassador at Hazen's last post. He praises Hazen's work as deputy chief of mission and congratulates him on his appointment as ambassador to Malawi. I look over several letters from Foreign Service friends, concerned about Joss's accident, hoping she recuperates fully. There are several photos of Not-Joss—or is she truly Joss?—standing beside a man in doctor's whites before the entrance of a building. Their figures partially block a sign over the entrance. It starts "Clin—"— which could be "clinique"—and ends "de Rhone." Is this the plastic surgeon? Certainly I am invited to suppose so.

I come upon a clipping from page three of a provincial newspaper, La Voix de Bourg. It includes a photograph of a Citroën crashed against the abutment of a bridge. The accompanying story identifies "la victime" as Mme Jocelyn Hazen, "femme de l'ambassadeur-designé des Etats-Unis à Malawi" and mentions serious facial injuries ("blessures serieuses du visage") and possible internal ones ("lesions internes"). But there is no photo of Mme l'Ambassadeur.

I remove the clipping from the file and test it with my hands. The paper has the feel of newsprint. Ads appear on the reverse side; I wonder if they would be easier than news stories to fabricate. Since I know that Hazen is meticulous, I'm certain that Bourg is a town in or near the Rhone Valley. But does La Voix de Bourg actually exist? And how can I trace it from here?

I thumb through other contents of the file. There are photos of my Joss. I compare them with those of the woman standing beside the doctor. They could be the same woman. Could be. But are they? The clipping could be authentic. But is it? Some kind of reconstructive surgery happened. Or did it? And to whom?

I slip the two photos into my pocket. I'll compare them more carefully at my leisure. I start to fold the clipping, then stop myself. If Hazen discovers that the clipping and the photos are gone, he will know I visited his den. If he notices that the clipping is folded, I will have allowed him to trap me. I return the photos and the clipping. I reorder the file and position it just as I found it on the table. And I acknowledge how adroitly Maxwell Hazen is playing with my head. And that of his mother. For, seeing the file, who can doubt his account of the accident and the surgery? It's simply not credible that he faked all this. If he did, he truly is the smartest guy in the room.

I close the compartment of my mind that wants to linger in the file. I move to the door, open it a crack, and listen. Silence. I move into the hallway and soon find myself at the end of it, outside the child's room. I take hold of the doorknob. Silently I turn it, push the door open and peek inside. As before, the room is dimly lit. I hear no sound, no breathing, but the curtains are drawn on the large bed as they are at the window and at the door with the glass panes leading outside. I enter an atmosphere that is close, stuffy, medical. Depressing. I stand, allowing my eyes to accustom themselves to the gloom. I wonder if the child is here. I close the door and move to the bed. Cautiously, I push back the thick mosquito net and look inside.

Out of the dim cave that is her bed, Pepper stares at me. She's very pale and holds a doll close to her. Her eyes look out from dark circles. She lies motionless, as if lacking the energy to move.

I watch her, alarmed at how sickly she appears, much more sickly than at the Midweek Smash two days ago. But I do not want to show my concern. I give her a smile. "Hi, Pepper," I say.

Pepper says nothing. She stares at me, wide-eyed.

She's apprehensive.

"Remember me? I was at the Midweek Smash."

But she does not seem to remember me. Someone has put this child under heavy sedation.

"I came to lunch at your house in Rabat," I tell her. "A servant brought you home from school. Mamadou, maybe?"

The slightest smile flickers in Pepper's eyes. "Was Mamadou right?" I ask. She smiles more fully.

"You showed me your kittens. Their eyes had not yet opened."

She watches me and a softness comes into her eyes that suggests she may remember me.

"I'm a journalist," I go on. "Recalling names is one of those things you learn how to do." I kneel beside the bed and cock my head to look at her. "I don't like coming here and finding you sick," I say. "You going to get well for us?"

Pepper lifts her shoulders in a shrug and bites her lower lip. I smile and slowly, gently, reach forward to touch her cheek and then brush her forehead. Her forehead is hot and that concerns me. Why can't Dr. Chakanza heal her fever? "That day I came to your house," I say, "you told me—You started to say you hated maths. But your father was with us and you said that you 'did not care for them.' Like a perfect lady."

I've spent a goodly part of my life trying to win smiles from females, and I want to win one as much from Pepper as from any of those whom I've tried to charm. She rewards me with an attempt to grin.

"Do you remember my being there?" I ask. Pepper shakes her head.

"I was with your father and you came in. He asked about your mother and you called out, 'Mommy!' very loud. 'Ladies don't shout,' your father told you.

And then your mother joined us." I was about to say that I had seen her father here, but not her mother. But I could not get the words out. I did not want to disturb her. I wanted to see her up and moving about with the same joyfulness she had shown in Rabat. "Are you going to get well for us?" I ask again.

The child stirs. She holds the doll away from her body, showing it to me. I nod encouragingly, smiling, wondering if I am supposed to speak to the doll. Then Pepper reaches out her thin, pale hand and slides it beneath the doll's dress. She starts to pull something from beneath the dress, but lacks the energy to withdraw it completely. She moves the doll toward me and I sense that I am to remove the object from under the dress.

I take the doll and remove the object. It's the family photo Joss sent me at Christmas, the complete version with Hazen standing beside Pepper and Joss. I glance at the photo, then look up at Pepper. She gazes at me beseechingly.

"Your mother," I say. "A beautiful woman."

Pepper whispers, "Where is she?" Her voice is so soft that I have to lean closer to hear her. "What happened to her?" She takes the photo and stares at it.

Tears begin to fill her eyes. They spill over her eyelids and run down her cheeks. I reach out with a handkerchief to dry them.

Outside I hear a car toot at the gate. Can that be the ambassador and his party back so soon?

"Can you stand?" I'm not sure why I ask this question. Do I expect to take her to a hospital? Maybe it's because I don't know how to answer the questions she's asked me. What if the woman I think of as Not- Joss turns out, in fact, to be her mother? I feel— strangely since I'm here—that this is a matter I should not interfere in. I watch Pepper struggle vainly to sit up. When she cannot manage it, more tears flow down her cheeks. As I reach up to dry them, she falls back onto the bed with a whimper. At this moment we hear the sound of the door to the room opening.

Pepper's eyes grow wide with alarm. I take the photo from her hand. I shove it back into its hiding place under the doll's dress. As I place the doll back against Pepper's shoulder, tears are streaming down her cheeks. She bites her lips, fearful that being caught with me can only bring her difficulties. I rise and turn toward the room.

The African nanny stares at me. She holds a small bundle of ironed clothes and watches me with an expression of hostility and panic. I stare back.

"What you do here?" she asks.

"Why is this child so sick?" I demand. "She should be in hospital."

"You go now." The woman places the laundry on a bureau and points to the door with the glass panes. "You go now. Mrs. Foresta, she come."

"We should get this child to a hospital!" I tell her.

"You go," she repeats.

"What makes this child so sick? What are they giving her?"

Suddenly we hear Dina Foresta's voice. "Yoo hoo? Mama Bo? Mama Bo?" Her voice grows louder as she approaches the room.

Mama Bo stares at me in a panic, fearful that she will be thought complicit in my presence here. She starts toward the door. I grab her arm and reach for my wallet. I pull two $20 bills from my wallet and push them at her. Mama Bo shakes her head, afraid of being caught with my money in her hand. "Mama Bo? Where are you?" calls Dina Foresta, her voice coming closer. I pull more bills from my wallet and shove them at the African woman. She glances at them. Her eyes widen. I ask again, "What makes this child so sick?"

"Juju," she says. She snatches the bills from my hand and stuffs them down the front of her dress. She points to the glass door.

But there is no time to use the door. I squeeze behind the head of Pepper's bed where I'm hidden by mosquito netting. Mama Bo moves to the bundle of laundry, adjusting the bills inside her dress, and busily refolds pillowslips that she has already ordered. There's a sudden silence. I hear the door pushed open. I feel Dina Foresta's presence in the room.

"Ah, Mama Bo!" I hear Dina whisper. "There you are."

"Yes, Madam."

"Is everything all right? Mrs. Hazen wanted me to check on Pepper."

I feel, more than see, Dina approach the bed. She leans over and peers down at Pepper. Craning my neck around the thick mosquito net at the head of the bed, I see that she's close enough for me to touch. I hold my breath.

"Please get well!" Dina says softly. "Please, Pepper, please!" I assume that in order to absent herself, Pepper has closed her eyes. Dina reaches up to pull the mosquito net closed. Her hand lies inches from my face. I hold my breath so as not to breathe on her skin. As she draws the net closed, I hide myself farther behind the bedstead. I feel Dina moving across the room.

"Has anyone been here?'

"No, Madam."

"An American journalist is in town. Be sure he doesn't come nosing around."

"Yes, Madam."

"The Hazens have enough to contend with. They don't need journalists badgering them."

"Yes, Madam."

"I'll get some coffee and stay till Mrs. Hazen gets home."

"Let me make you coffee, Madam. I know just how Madam likes it."

"Thank you, Mama Bo. That's very kind."

Mama Bo ushers Dina from the room. As I slide out from behind the bedstead, Mama Bo steps back into the room to shut the door. She throws me a panicky glance and points toward the door with the glass panes. Then she's gone.

I listen at the door to be sure they're leaving. Then I return to the bed. I open the heavy mosquito netting and peer down at Pepper. She gazes up at me, her eyes as large as moons. I smile at her reassuringly. "I'll be back, Pepper," I tell her. I touch her cheek very lightly. She manages a smile and I feel that a bond of trust has been formed between us. I close the mosquito netting and tiptoe across the room to the glass door. I unlock it. When Mama Bo returns to the room, she will lock it once again. Suddenly I'm outside in the bright sunlight. I hurry across the lawn.

Chapter Ten

HAVING A FEW MINUTES TO SPARE WHEN I RETURN to the town center, I pass by the USIS office. Fortunately, Sykes is out, attending Hazen's talk. Using an atlas in the USIS library, I locate the town of Bourg in eastern France. But the library's resources do not permit me to track down La Voix de Bourg. Since there's no French embassy in Malawi, I'll have to do that in Nairobi.

Now back to the hotel for my lunch with Kay Kittredge. Having sweated in the sun at the Hazen residence, I take a quick shower. I've positioned the photographs of Not-Joss against the wall. I feel uncomfortable as they watch me change clothes.

As I escort Kay Kittredge across the Mount Soche's pool terrace to a table shaded by an umbrella, she mutters, "Oh, shit!" On the other side of the pool Max Hazen appears, pushing his consort's wheelchair, followed by Dr. Chakanza and an African couple.

Hazen spots us. "Double shit!" says Kay. "He's seen me with you. There goes my next promotion."

"Am I a leper?"

"Worse. You're a journalist."

After the exchange with Hazen in my room, I can well believe that being seen with me will damage Kay's reputation at the embassy. "You're an old Africa hand," I remind her. "Pretend we're old friends."

"Not a good time to be your friend," Kay says. "It's that polecat smell." She mutters that she's glad she's not permanent staff in Malawi. To defy Hazen, she insists that we sit facing his table. As if our presence vexes him, Hazen calls for an umbrella. When it's erected, he asks that it be tilted so that it blocks our view of his party's faces. We order wine and salads and, just so that Kay understands that I will not be following up on yesterday's exploratory flirtation, I drop into the conversation the fact that a friend from South Africa is coming in late today for the weekend. We discuss the best places to stay at the lake. The waiter brings our glasses of wine. We raise them to one another and take our first sips. As we relax, I say I want to try an idea out on her. She's flattered by my consulting her in my reportage. I explain my notion of a story about Foreign Service sacrifice.

"You mean the sacrifice of lunching with a foreign correspondent on the pool terrace of a four-star hotel in Nowhere?"

"I mean the kind made by an ambassador whose wife's had an accident and whose kid has— What exactly is the matter with the kid?"

Kay smiles enigmatically and plays with her glass of wine. At length she takes a sip and holds the glass before her face.

"What's the story you're all sitting on?" I ask. "You talked about a scandal."

"I was trying to be mysterious. That's all."

We measure one another. My hunch tells me that Kay is not merely flirting. She has something she needs to tell me, but she also wants to be coaxed.

"Something's going on," I say. "Nobody will talk to me. The Forestas are like robots. Sykes doesn't like Hazen, but he's very careful."

"Smart to be careful. I served with them once." This bit of information intrigues me as it's meant to. Kay stares into the silvery gold liquid in her glass. Then she smiles at me. "I'm Foreign Service staff," she says. "Eyes open, mouth shut. I live by that and it's kept me out of trouble."

Our salads arrive. As the waiter arranges them before us, we stare at the Hazens' table. Chakanza is standing, adjusting the umbrella. Sunlight sparkles off the chrome wheels of Not-Joss' wheelchair.

When the waiter moves off, Kay remarks, "Yesterday you said you were better in print than in bed—"

"I'll deny that quote," I say, "if I ever hear it repeated."

"You were supposed to leave this morning," Kay says, "but you didn't. Why'd you stick around?"

"The climate? The friendly natives? You tell me."

"You must have a hunch what the story is," she replies. "Don't you?"

"Where did you know them?" I ask. It's the right question.

"In Senegal. We overlapped for about six months." Kay nibbles at her salad. I sense her being pulled by two impulses: by her desire to tell me whatever it is she knows and by her understandable caution about doing that. We eat in silence.

Finally Kay clarifies. "I knew her. Didn't really know him. He never mixed with staff people. Despite the Midweek Smash, he still doesn't."

I nod. Now she feels ready to talk.

"I liked Joss," Kay goes on. "She could be very funny. Also malicious and willful. Had a wonderful laugh."

This sounds like my girl, I think. I recall how attracted I was to Joss' laughter that first night we met on the terrace of the Norfolk Hotel.

"She was gone when I first arrived," Kay continues. "People at the post doubted she'd come back. The marriage was ending, they said. She'd had a Senegalese lover; that was the story. And before him a French anthropologist. I took it Hazen played around, too. Then she came back and before long she was pregnant. She was radiant, beautiful, and he even mellowed a bit. They did everything together. They were the post's happy couple. But gossip chased them."

"How so?"

"People started whispering it wasn't Hazen's baby. Couldn't have been."

"Why not?"

"Hazen's semen carried less sperm than a glass of water. That was the gossip."

At these small posts, I take it, gossip is like a disease. And the urge to gossip is undeniable. Personnel live too close together. They have too few outside contacts. They socialize with the same people they work with. And the pecking order is very rigid. No wonder Joss got away when she could.

"How would anyone know?" I ask.

"The post nurse knew. Or said she did. Swore us to secrecy, of course." I look at Kay doubtfully. "He'd gone to a urologist and that was the report." Kay takes a sip of wine. "That means Joss got pregnant elsewhere."

Kay raises an eyebrow and gives me a wicked smile. She claims that she liked Joss. But I wonder. I can well imagine that Joss's physical beauty and vividness, her impatience with fools, and her outspokenness would have drawn malicious gossip. "Isn't it more likely," I suggest, "that she was artificially inseminated? If he did have low sperm count."

"More likely," Kay says, "that when she'd come back from her trip—she was in France doing some sort of research, I think—they felt like newlyweds.

Couldn't get enough of one another. His semen got peppy and suddenly she conceived." Kay takes a forkful of salad and talks with it poised halfway between her plate and her mouth. "I thought people should stop talking about them," she says. "They were obviously happy about the baby. But, in a place like that, if you're happy, you stand out. You get talked about."

We eat in silence for a time. We watch the ex- colonials who've come to the pool for their early afternoon swim and the African professionals who sit at the poolside bar, enjoying the perks of government jobs, the chief of which involves not bothering to work. I think about what Kay has said and ask casually, "When were you in Senegal?"

Kay gives me the dates. Her arrival there coincides with the time when Joss and I were together in Nairobi. Can it be possible, when we were together, that Joss was looking for someone to give her a child? I take a sip of wine. What I'm thinking gives me pause. I tell myself that such a notion is crazy. The child has to be Hazen's. If Hazen truly had a low sperm count, artificial insemination was the obvious solution, something they would have decided about together.

Even so, I glance across the pool at the ambassador and his wife. Suddenly I hope very much that the woman beside him in the wheelchair is Joss.

Kay dispenses with her salad, pushing the plate aside, and finishes her wine. She gazes across the pool. She takes out a cigarette. "Do you mind if I smoke?" she asks. She lights up, inhaling deeply, and watches the smoke curl off the tip of her cigarette. "If I tell you something," she begins, her eyes moving from the smoke trail to me, "can I be sure you'll never tell anyone you heard it from me?"

"Scout's honor," I say.

"This is serious," she says. She takes another drag on her cigarette. "It sounds like small post gossip, but it's not. I have to be sure the tip can never be traced to me. Because I need this job."

I explain to her that a journalist often has confidential conversations with informants. That's how he does his job. If he does not keep those confidences, he's out of business. Which is why a number of journalists have gone to jail rather than reveal their sources. As I say this, trying to build Kay's confidence in spilling her story, I wonder if it's really something I want to hear. Confidential conversations have a way of dredging up wrongs, some real, some imagined, that a journalist has no way of righting. As well as personal grievances and information that he can't check. Not infrequently you wish you hadn't gotten involved.

Kay stares across the pool for a long moment. Finally she says, "That woman is Not-Joss Hazen."

"Pardon me?"

"The woman sitting in the wheelchair over there is using the name of the woman I knew in Senegal. But she is not that woman."

I lean forward and peer at Kay as if I have not heard.

"I've been watching her for weeks. We're both on a committee to put together a post cookbook. We meet every Saturday morning at the Colonial Club."

Kay draws again on her cigarette. Then she states, "This is not the woman I knew as Joss Hazen." I continue to look at Kay, uncertain how to respond. "Bill Sykes says you met Joss somewhere."

"I guess I lunched at her home in Rabat two or three years ago. But I have no recollection of her." As this lie leaves my mouth, I think of Joss and our hurrying together to her bedroom after I returned that afternoon for my notebook.

Kay says, "Then you know what I'm saying is true."

There is a long moment while I listen to the sound—and sense—of what she has said. "How can it be true?" I ask. "You said they were happy together."

"They fell out of happy. Once the baby was walking. Out of happy into infidelity again. That's what I heard."

"Have you told all this to Bill Sykes?"

Kay shakes her head. "Only to you."

I wonder if I believe her. I examine Kay and I decide I do not like her. "Eyes open, mouth shut," she claims. I assess her as badly ill with the disease of gossip. Her working life of temporary postings to remote embassies fuels her susceptibility to that malady. Right now she feels important, enjoying the attention I give her. I wonder if what I do not like in her is what I sometimes do not like in myself, the grubbing for tidbits of news. The difference is that I do it professionally and many people think highly of me, whereas she is a diseased amateur, a bottom feeder on whisper, rumor and idle talk.

It is instructive to hear what I have been thinking coming out of someone else's mouth. "What you're suggesting is preposterous!" I tell her. "He'd just divorce her."

She shakes her head. "Messy divorces damage your prospects in this business. And if you'd known her, you'd know it would be messy."

"Hazen's too smart. Too careful."

"He's smart, all right." Kay shakes her head out of admiration for his cunning. "People who've served in the Maghreb almost never come down here. When they do, they say nothing. They're just grateful their spouses have not been in accidents that changed their looks."

"You think there was no accident?"

"I've been trying to track the medical benefits he receives. Because he's too smart to defraud the government. He keeps those records locked in his office safe."

Listening to Kay say things I've been thinking, I realize how obsessive and eccentric they sound. To a reasonable person Kay appears to be a crank, the victim of an idée fixe who succeeds in arranging every strand of life to fit a preconception. This is why I cannot possibly approach my editors about this story—if it is a story—until I have discovered incontrovertible evidence.

"The man is devious," she says. "He puts his daughter into a so-called summer camp for psychiatric observation. So if she comes down here and tells anyone, 'That's not my mother,' they think, 'his little girl can't handle what's happened to her mom. She even denies her.'"

"And bringing the mother out," Kay continues, almost talking to herself now. "What a master stroke! Africa confuses the old dear. So does this Jocelyn. But what can she do? She feigns knowing Jocelyn and so everyone accepts her." Kay drags on her cigarette again and tamps its ashes onto her salad plate. "You have to hand it to Hazen. That's truly masterful!"

And even if Kay is obsessive, I have to agree that Mama Hazen's acceptance of this Jocelyn credentials her beyond question.

"You must really have it in for Hazen."

Kay ignores this. "But in the end the mother let him down. Because the child is not his. If she were his, the mother would have taken her back to the States. They really pressed her about that, I understand. But she refused to take responsibility for a child who was not kin. She left today, by the way."

"Did she?"

Kay reaches across the table and takes my hand. "Do something about this," she implores. "Write something."

"Why don't you write the Inspector General of the Foreign Service?"

"I've got retirement to think about."

The waiter takes our salad plates and I order coffee for us. Across the pool sunlight now spills onto tables that had been in the shade. Dr. Chakanza stands to adjust the umbrella at the Hazens' table. From our vantage point we see the Hazens clearly. The ambassador has his hand resting on his wife's thigh.

Kay glances over, then turns away almost embarrassed. "Look at his hand," she says. "On her thigh. Do you really believe that people who've been married fifteen years behave that way in public?"

Our coffees come. Kay watches me, awaiting my reaction. Although I usually take coffee black, I stir cream and sugar into my cup to avoid her gaze.

"You think I'm crazy, don't you?"

"No," I say. Still, I think, a woman of her experience should know that the world is full of puzzles that can't be solved, of wrongs that cannot be righted.

"Don't lie to me," she says. "You've been looking at me as if I had a social disease." Then she leans toward me again. "Let me assure you. I am not full of hatred for my betters. I am not some dreadful gossip-merchant. I am concerned about what happened to Joss. And about what's going to happen to her child. Because Pepper has no one. I don't trust Hazen to take care of her. If he intended to, he'd have gotten her out of here a long time ago."

Kay stirs sugar into her coffee, drinks, drags on her cigarette, and looks at me imploringly. "Will you do something about this? Check into it?"

I say nothing. The woman is a gossip. I cannot possibly lead her to believe the story interests me. If I do, she will tell others.

Holding herself under tight control, she finishes her coffee. She tamps out her cigarette with the vengeance she'd like to take out on me. "What in the world's the matter with you?" she asks in a whisper that reaches my ears like a blow. "They did something terrible to that child's mother and they may do something very terrible to her." She glares at me. Once again I offer a milquetoast shrug.

"Thank you for lunch," she whispers. She pushes back her chair and is off.

Across the pool Hazen watches her go. He shifts his gaze to me. Our eyes meet. He pats his wife's leg.

—m—

Back in the room I return to making calls to reporters and police officials, this time in Rhodesia and Zambia, inquiring about any news of an unidentified white woman who'd been murdered. No leads. I conclude that if the accident happened in France, the murder must have occurred there, too. And even if French detective work is more professional, the French police are unlikely to suspect a diplomat murderer, especially one hiding in Malawi.

Tiring of this, I get out the Christmas photo Joss sent me of her and Pepper. I'm suddenly struck by the resemblance of Pepper to photos of my mother as a little kid. That could mean nothing, but it might mean everything.

I sit staring at the photo, Kay's urgent words stinging in my ears.

When I met Pepper in Rabat, she was a joyful, exuberant child, eager to please her father, delighted to show me her kittens. She seemed well-adjusted, in no need of tests at what Joss described as "a summer camp cum psychiatric boot camp." Now Pepper is in a country where she knows no one except her parents.

Ever since arriving, she must have been wrestling with the very questions about her mother that I've been mulling. Would the boot camp have strengthened her sense of identity? Or undermined it, suggesting that something was wrong with her? Could it be that "something's wrong with her" is exactly the impression Hazen wants to construct?

Staring at the photo, I keep wondering how arriving in Malawi must have felt to Pepper. In my mind I see her flying alone from Paris to Blantyre under the watchful eyes of stewardesses and airlines reps who made sure she got the right connections. I see her on the final leg of the journey, the one that brought her to Malawi. She is sleeping curled into a fetal ball under a blanket, her head on an inadequate airlines pillow on an armrest. Because she's dreaming, her face is contorted with fear. Her tiny body pulls her legs tight up against her chest. She's heard about leopards in Malawi and knows she'll encounter densely wooded country. She is herself accustomed to the coastal plains of the Maghreb and the parched openness of the Sahel and probably expects to find jungle in Blantyre. In her dream it's the middle of the night. She runs for her life along a moonlit path through jungle vines and foliage. In a nightie, barefoot, frightened, she glances behind her.

She hears animal panting; it sounds like cosmic breathing, and there's also the thud of paws rhythmically hitting the path. In her backward glance she sees the leopard growing ever closer. She increases her speed. Tears fly from her eyes. She stumbles. Regains her footing. Races on. Reaches a door of glass panes.

Fumbles with the handle. Looks behind her. The leopard is almost upon her. It pants heavily. Pepper flings open the door. Darts inside. Slams the door behind her. Locks it. Dives into bed. Hides in the covers.

In the darkness under the covers Pepper hears the leopard's panting. Its thunderous scratching at the door. Pepper peeks out. The leopard circles at the door. Claws at the glass panes. Hurls itself against them. Pepper's eyes grow enormous. The leopard bounds toward the closed, locked door. Leaps clean through it. The huddled form sleeping in the airplane seat cries out. In Pepper's dream the leopard paces the room, panting. Bounds onto the bed. The bed shakes.

The sleeping child screams again. A nearby passenger signals for a stewardess. As the leopard's open jaws bear down on Pepper, a stewardess crouches beside her, takes her shoulder, and gently shakes the girl. "Were you dreaming, honey?" she asks. "We're about to land. Out the window is Malawi!"

Pepper says nothing. She rubs her eyes and looks out the window. The African landscape flashes past below: tea plantations, lushly green; villages of huts with people working outside; bicycles moving along earthen roads. The stewardess takes Pepper's blanket and makes sure she has fastened her seat belt. Then the plane is on the ground. The stewardess instructs Pepper to wait in her seat; her father will board the plane to fetch her.

She sees her father enter the plane. She stands on her seat to wave to him. He's in a dark suit and tie and has come from the embassy. He grins broadly at his girl, waves and hurries toward her. "Daddy! Daddy!" she cries.

"She told me all about her summer camp," the stewardess says as Hazen arrives. "Was it really in Switzerland? She's a brave little girl to fly all this way alone."

"My girl's a traveler!" Hazen cries, taking Pepper in his arms to squash her with a hug. "Hi, Pep! We missed you! How was camp?" Pepper hangs on to her father. She's so pleased to see him, so relieved to have escaped the leopard and to have the solitary traveling end.

"Where's Mom?" she asks.

"Mom's out on the tarmac. She's dying to see you." They walk along the aisle together, Hazen holding her hand. He reminds her, "But you remember, don't you, Pep? Mom's in a wheelchair—because of the accident. She's still your Mom. She loves you very much, but she looks a little different than she did."

Hearing this, Pepper hesitates. "We're all going to bounce back just fine," Hazen assures her. "It may be a little hard at first. Don't say anything to hurt Mom's feelings, okay?" Pepper nods, but she's queasy inside.

As Pepper and Hazen descend from the plane, the child is uncertain what she'll find. When she reaches the tarmac, she scrutinizes the two women awaiting her, one in the wheelchair whom she does not recognize and an African woman, Mama Bo, standing behind her.

Pepper hesitates. Something's amiss. She stops. Her father leans down to her ear and whispers, "C'mon, Pep. Give Mom a smile. She needs that." Pepper tries to smile. She walks toward the women, holding her father's hand. The closer they come, the slower she walks. Still trying to smile, Pepper finally stops. She inspects the woman in the wheelchair.

"Pepper, sweetie, come give Mommy a kiss," says the woman in the wheelchair. She stretches out her arms. But the child cannot bring herself to move forward. She manages a smile, but stays where she is.

Finally Hazen lifts her off the ground and places her on the lap of the woman in the wheelchair. This woman gives her a mighty hug.

This is where my imagination falters. What does Pepper know the minute she's encircled by the woman's arms? That, yes, she is her mother? The embrace is the same, the voice, the smell, the kisses, the pet names? Or does she know that this woman is not her mother? Does she wonder why her father is telling her that she is?

When it is time to meet Bakili, I slip the Christmas photo back into the envelope and go out to the Land Cruiser. As I drive into town, my mind is still with Pepper out on the tarmac the day she arrived in Malawi. I ask myself: If the woman in the wheelchair is, indeed, her mother, then why isn't Pepper swept by an intense gratitude that her mother is still alive? But that's not what happened. She fell sick, into deep depression.

My mind plays with another possibility. If Pepper recognizes the woman in the wheelchair as her mother, then her depression must stem from an overwhelming sense that fate has treated her mother unfairly. And if Pepper had truly been in a state of fragile mental health, she might easily have been overwhelmed. Especially just after making a trip alone from Europe, a trip during which she might have wondered if she would ever see her parents again.

But why would a child in a fragile mental state be required to fly to Malawi alone? Because her mother's condition was even more fragile? If that's the case, one's heart goes out to the whole family. And poor Hazen! Despite his having just become an ambassador, he's hardly able to care for his dependents.

It's a story to move one's heart.

If, on the other hand, Pepper knew that the woman in the wheelchair was not her mother, but rather an impostor, the case for her depression is undeniable. The child arrives in a country where she knows no one except her parents. Is there anyone she can tell that the woman claiming to be her mother is an impostor? No one. Any American she turns to will have heard that she has spent the summer at a psychiatric clinic. That person will have heard that, due to an automobile accident, her wheelchair-bound mother has had extensive plastic surgery. That person will feel an inordinate sympathy for the girl—but refuse to believe anything she says. Any Africans she turns to—Dr. Chakanza, Mama Bo—will understand that their own economic interests will be damaged by making accusations against the American ambassador, a man of consummate prestige in this community. And no accusation can be proved.

I park across the road from the Blantyre Star. Waiting in the vehicle for Bakili, I ask myself: If the woman is an impostor, what can I do about it? If she is one—and that's my hunch, one I trust—it's a fascinating story. But to whom can I tell it? Unless I have irrefutable proof of the impostor, my editors will, quite properly, go nowhere near the story. And I see no way that I can obtain irrefutable proof. Even reporting the story, not for publication, but simply for insider delectation might cause my editors to question my judgment. They understand, of course, that reporters have affairs with women they encounter in their travels. But if one of them, apparently jilted and without solid proof, reports, even as gossip, that his lover's husband has murdered her, they'll assume he's been too long on his beat. Especially if he claims that her child may be his. Time for a change. And so, like Dr. Chakanza and Mama Bo, I have an economic reason to go along with Hazen's explanation of events—even if my hunch says otherwise.

In any case, I have always thought that whistle- blowers are punished, rather than rewarded, for their revelations of wrongdoing. People applaud righteous indignation only when it does not affect them. But if it's your alma mater that is charged with turning a blind eye to campus rapes... Or the company in which you are heavily invested that is accused of defrauding the government of taxpayers' dollars... Or a sentimental story ruined by a professional skeptic... Well, in those cases, you tend to grumble that life would go along just fine if only people would mind their own business.

So there's nothing that I can do. And little that I should do. But the girl may be my daughter. That makes everything different.

Chapter Eleven

EAVING THE RESIDENCE AT THE END OF HER WORKDAY, Mama Bo walks to the main road, waits beneath a tree, and eventually flags down a jitney, a Volkswagen minibus already filled with passengers. Bakili and I are in the Land Cruiser, trailing her. She leaves the jitney at its hub in the heart of the African section of Blantyre, adjacent to the central market. Bakili slips out of our vehicle so that we do not lose Mama Bo in the market crowds or in the narrow passageways between stalls. I steer the Toyota onto a curb, parking half on the roadway, half on the sidewalk, locking the doors. When I catch up to Bakili, he points out Mama Bo, stopped at a food stall, bargaining for rice. The babble of the market and its smells of cooking food surround us.

Nearing Mama Bo, we feign interest in a vendor's pineapples. Bakili keeps her in view. With my white skin a curiosity in this market, I turn my back to her so that she will not recognize me.

After she makes her purchase, we follow her into an alleyway between the canvas walls of vendors' booths. Bakili calls to her in Chichewa. When she turns to look at us, we overtake her. Bakili runs ahead of her to block her escape. She turns to confront me. "What you want with me?" she asks.

"Mama Bo, please," I implore. "Could we talk?" She looks at me apprehensively, then turns to Bakili and hurls at him a volley of offended Chichewa. Bakili answers soothingly, as he might to calm a child. I take it that he assures her that I mean no harm, that my desire is simply to ask some questions. She turns back and examines me with distrust.

"You said the girl was sick because of juju," I explain to her. "I must know what kind of juju."

Mama Bo looks to Bakili for help. Again they speak to one another in Chichewa. "If people see her talking to you," Bakili tells me, "she is afraid she will lose her job."

Assuming that we have now entered a negotiation, I start to withdraw my wallet from the front pocket to which I transferred it before leaving the Land Cruiser. Bakili gestures me to keep it hidden. "If you show your wallet, Whitey," he says scornfully, "people will think you are buying sex."

Bakili and the woman talk again. "She could use some money," Bakili informs me. "Her husband's sick and she must pay her children's school fees." We are now negotiating and Mama Bo indicates that her information will not come cheap. "But not here," Bakili says.

We follow Mama Bo out of the market to a roadside stand selling warm beer. I buy a bottle and we sit in its pavilion, shaded by a roof of banana fronds.

We pass the bottle around. Bakili resumes the bargaining. I remind him, "I'm not made of money."

"Is it your money?" he asks, incredulous.

"The paper's money," I say.

Bakili and Mama Bo continue to talk. Bakili reports the ongoing negotiation. In talking to me, Mama Bo is afraid for her job. I must pay her accordingly. I take out five $20 bills and show them to her. She shakes her head. I take out two more. This time she nods. I give her four of them and withhold three, waiting to hear what she has to say. She sticks the four bills into her bodice. I tell Bakili, "I need to know why the child she cares for is sick and does not get well. It's not normal for a child to be sick so long."

Bakili relays the question to Mama Bo. He and the woman talk back and forth. Finally Bakili says, "The child has problems in her head. At one time she claimed that her mother was not her mother. Now she says nothing."

"When I saw her before," I tell Bakili, "Mama Bo said there was juju. Why did she say 'juju.' It's a Nigerian term. People here don't use it."

Bakili consults with Mama Bo. "She says juju is what white men always call it."

I accept this explanation. "What is the juju?"

Again, the long conversation. Bakili says, "Some kind of poison, she thinks. She doesn't know what kind."

I look directly at Mama Bo. "Does the doctor give her poison?" I ask.

She shakes her head, turns to Bakili, and speaks at length to him.

"The doctor does not give the poison," Bakili states. "The child gets better, and Mama Bo is relieved. Then when she returns in the morning, the child is worse."

"Does the mother give the poison?" I ask.

Another exchange. "She doesn't know who gives the poison," Bakili says. He drops his translator role for a moment and becomes an interpreter. "You understand that she doesn't know if it's actually poison."

I ask Mama Bo, "Does the doctor know what's happening?"

Bakili clarifies what I've asked. The woman lifts her shoulders and moves her head back and forth. She will not implicate the doctor, but I take it he is aware of what's going on.

Bakili takes the remaining twenties from me and hands them to the woman. She buries them in her bodice and hurries off. We drink a bit more of the beer, giving her time to disappear.

As we drive back in the Land Cruiser, Bakili cautions me, "You understand that in her own way of thinking the problem is not poison, but witchcraft.

Someone is using witchcraft to make the girl sick. She knows you do not believe this so she tells you it is poison. That's something you will believe."

"She can't think the parents are using witchcraft!" I declare. "That's inconceivable. They know nothing about it."

"They know enough to consult a sangoma."

"Does she think they've done that?"

Bakili stares at the road as if looking for an answer there.

"Do you think it's witchcraft?" I ask.

He continues to stare at the road. I cork him on the shoulder. "If I tell you it's witchcraft," he says, "you think I'm a savage."

"It can't be witchcraft!"

"My friend," he says, "you think like a white man."

"Help me to think like an African."

"Why would one use poison which leaves a trace when one could use witchcraft which does not? If one uses witchcraft, white people will say the death resulted from 'natural causes'."

This conversation disturbs me because we are discussing two different views of causality, of reality. There's no bridge between them. Hazen and Not-Joss must be poisoning Pepper. He's very knowledgeable about Africa, but he cannot know how to practice witchcraft. I cannot believe that he'd seek out a sangoma. Or that, if he did, it would make a difference.

"It must be poison," I tell Bakili. "Probably. I know you cannot believe it's witchcraft."

"Which is what you believe it is?"

Bakili does not reply. After a moment he adds, "Your Mama Bo wants the money, you realize that, no? And she knows what you want to hear. It's possible she just says what she knows you want to hear."

"You think the doctor knows what's going on?"

"The doctor is being squeezed like an orange. It is good for his practice that he doctors the American ambassador and his family. Also good for his wallet." Bakili rubs his fingers across his palm. "But he can hardly accuse the ambassador of poisoning his own daughter, can he? Yet if the child dies, he knows who will get the blame." Bakili shakes his head. "I wouldn't be surprised," he says, "if the doctor has gone to his own sangoma and asked him to make sure that the child does not die."

—⚹—

When I pull into the Mount Soche grounds, I feel vexed and badly in need of escaping these puzzles that have their grip on me. I see a woman leaving a taxi stopped before the hotel entrance. I recognize her; I'm sure I do. I park quickly and hurry toward the lobby, feeling disoriented about my perceptions of women. I can't decide whether or not Hazen's woman is Joss. And now I've just seen another woman I'm sure I recognize… I think. I'm getting hot flashes at the maybe sight of her. But how can it be that she's here?

When I reach the lobby, her back's toward me as she stands at the reception desk. Joy leaps unexpectedly into my heart. She recognizes the sound of my footsteps and turns around. We grin at one another. I enfold her in an embrace and give her a hungry kiss. "Lady," I say, "can I carry that bag for you?" She giggles and I take her metal pilot's suitcase and lead her out onto the exterior balcony that leads to my room. "What're you doing here?" I ask.

"A girl oughtn't to admit it," she confides. "But I got randy."

"Randy? That Randy?"

"Un-hunh."

"You know him, too? He was just vexing me."

"Really. He gets around."

We get to the room. A little overanxious, I fumble with the key, manage to get us into the room, close and lock the door, draw the blinds. My readiness amuses her. While she uses the bathroom, I open the bed, straighten the room a bit. I put the leopard-man story I telegraphed the Big Guy on the desk beside the photos of Joss; she can read it later. I peel down to my shorts. She comes out of the bathroom in a robe, spots the story on the desk, asks, "Is this your piece on the murders?" Teasing me, she begins to scan it. I take the story from her, toss it on the desk. Amused at my urgency, she picks up the photos and thumbs through them, less interested in them than in teasing me.

Standing behind her, I nuzzle her and kiss her neck and ear and chin and urge her out of the robe. Finally she stops the teasing and we dispense with the imprisonment of undergarments and enjoy ourselves happily in bed.

Afterwards, holding each other in bed, Maggie says, "You needed that."

"Yes."

She asks about the woman in the photos. I tell her about being with Joss for a few weeks nine years ago and about the week two years ago in Paris.

Maggie shifts away from me. "As I remember," she says, "you have strong feelings about unmarried people sleeping with married people."

"Those were strong feelings about you sleeping with Gerrit Uys." I move to her and kiss her nose. "Do as I say, not as I do. My best advice."

Maggie gets a photo of Joss that I took on the Serengeti plains and compares it to one of Not-Joss taken at a Midweek Smash. After studying them, she says, "So the story is: This love goddess walks out of the Nairobi night and casts a spell on you. She likes sleeping with a man. As what girl wouldn't if the man is you."

I give her a modest shrug. She goes back to studying the photos.

"Goddess doesn't want to pay for a bed," she notes. "And doesn't mind free meals. After a month you suggest dragging her off to South Africa. Which sounds like more than a fling. Goddess doesn't want to break your romantic heart by saying you've begun to bore her—"

"Bore her? But I'm fascinating! You've always said so."

"Or that more-than-a-fling also bores her. So, she tells you she's married. And you spend the next years yearning for What Might Have Been." She studies the photo of Joss. "Sounds like quite a manipulative little number to me."

"You're certainly worldly-wise."

"Oh-oh. I've said the wrong thing."

How skillfully she's punctured my romantic dream. She continues her comparative examination of the photos.

"They could be the same woman," she decides. "Why would they lie? There's so much to lose."

"Why is the daughter so sick if this is really her mother?"

"She's a little girl, Tommy. These are terrible adjustments for her. For all of them. Sheesh!" She studies the photos, cocking her head this way and that. "She's mid- to late- thirties now. Everything's different. Her husband's important. Her child's very sick. Life has bitten her badly. Broken her spirit. All she wants is to hunker down. Why would she remember you?"

I do not reply to this question. In fact, it annoys me a little. She senses this annoyance; she's always read my reactions well.

"You must be hungry," she says. "God knows, I am! Some girls can live on love, but I'm not one of them. Let's have some dinner."

—⁂—

In the dining room we sit at a table near French doors. They open onto a balcony and a garden below. I tell Maggie how delighted I am that she's here and ask why I'm in such luck. She says she came on a whim.

She gives me a wicked, teasing grin and assures me she'll return to Joburg tomorrow if that's what I want. "I can go back to feeding on your romantic fantasy."

I give her a disapproving look.

"Can't I tease you?" she asks. I say nothing. "We both survive on that, you know." She plays the friend pointing out my faults, but I'm not into that game. "Oh, c'mon! Foreign correspondent? That's romantic fantasy. You dash around the world in a trench coat. With a notepad. Dancing on the pulse of history."

"You won't catch me in a trench coat."

"There's one in your closet." She laughs accusingly. "You're living a fantasy."

"So are you, Amelia Earhart."

Our waiter comes to the table to refill our water glasses.

"I don't deny it. But Maxwell Hazen is not living it. Not living it," she repeats as a second waiter sidles up beside ours. "So be careful. The last thing he'd do— " As water splashes onto our table, Maggie stops in mid-sentence. Our waiter has let his grasp on the pitcher slip. As I look up to complain, both waiters hurry away, ours spilling water as he goes. Maggie and I exchange a frown. Other dinner guests look about, mystified.

Suddenly all the waiters flee the dining room. Maggie and I and the other guests glance about in surprise. We get to our feet. There's a commotion outside, people shouting in a language we do not understand. We move through the French doors onto a terrace. It overlooks a garden lit by torches. Beyond a hedge there's a road.

People hurtle along it in a panic. Some push through the hedge into the garden. Others look behind them.

Someone points to movement on the road. "It's the cat!" someone whispers.

We see something moving behind the hedge. Is it a leopard? Or a man? Some guests flee. Others crowd beside us on the terrace. We peer into the gathering darkness. A leopard-like creature slides behind plantings, sometimes an animal, sometimes a man in a leopard costume. And then the creature is gone.

Africans flee before it. Others follow after it.

"Is it the leopard-man?" Maggie asks. I have no idea what it is.

Back in the room I telephone Bakili. He's heard nothing about another murder. I fill him in on what we've seen. Maggie sits on the bed, her arms wrapped about her, knowing that a man cannot transform himself into a leopard, but wondering nonetheless what it is she's just witnessed. I go to her, kiss the top of her head. "Lock the door," I tell her. "Don't let anyone in but me."

"Are you going out on this?" she asks.

"I won't be long."

I rush through the dining room, out through the garden, and onto the road. People who've taken refuge in trees watch me pass. I come upon a group of young men. They're too excited to question. Excitement like theirs can suddenly turn violent. I make my way back through the garden. The hotel lobby is full of guests. No one seems to know if there's been a murder.

Making my way to the room I realize I've been excited, too. Now suddenly I'm tired. I've been gone about half an hour. I move along an outside passageway, open to the air. I'm aware of movement in the garden shrubbery below me. I stop and look around, holding my breath. I see nothing, hear nothing. My senses are alert, but they're over-stimulated. I continue along the passageway. Foliage grows close to the railing. The passageway light has burnt out. As I move along, foliage rustles behind me. Something is following me!

I turn and in the darkness I see—I'm not sure what. A body of some kind. With a rank animal smell. As I peer at it, a chill grips me. My skin prickles. The hair on the back of my neck stands up. The body moves toward me in a crouch. I'm sure it's an animal.

Suddenly the eyes of my memory see blood, the head of the victim at the brothel, claw marks on his face, the throat gashed open. I hurry along the passage. The creature races toward me. Low to the ground. An animal. I run. It rushes after me. Its footfalls, its rhythms: they're those of a cat. I glance back. My arm is up to protect my throat. The creature races toward me. It leaps. I cover my face with my arms. Its weight hits me. Pushes me against a wall. Its claws scrape my face. Its fangs— That smell! It glances off me. I push it away. Its claws rip my jacket. It falls away. I kick it. Again, and again. I yell at it.

The creature lunges again. I fend it off. My hands grip animal fur, animal muscle. Its breath assails me.

It's on the floor again and I kick, my hands over my groin. Kick! Kick! It falls off the passageway. I race to my doorway. I shout, "Maggie! Maggie!" I'm afraid it will return.

I reach our door. I beat on it. "Maggie! Maggie!" "Tom?" her voice finally asks.

"It's me! Open up!"

She opens the door, a narrow slice. I force my way inside, scaring her. I push the door closed, lock it and lean against it, breathing heavily. Maggie stares at me aghast. She runs to the bathroom, brings a wet washcloth and a towel. Holding the washcloth to my jaw, I stumble to the bed. She helps me pull off my jacket. I kick off my shoes. I hold my head in my hands, the washcloth to my cheek. I'm frightened, panting. My body is sore from exertion.

Maggie stares at me. "Your jacket's all cut up. What happened?"

I don't know what to say. An animal attacked me. But can I tell her that?

"Are you hurt anywhere else?" She inspects my head, my arms, my torso. "It just looks like your face," she says. "It certainly tore up your jacket. Should you see a doctor?"

"I'm not leaving this room."

She sits beside me on the bed, her arm around my shoulder. "Was it him?"

"I don't know what it was. An animal, I think."

She stares at me. Because we both know that it cannot have been an animal. When I collect my wits, I realize that an animal—a leopard—would have inflicted more damage. Its claws would have buried themselves in my flesh. Its fangs would have sunk into me. And leopards don't hang around hotels. So it had to be a man, a small man. But I felt fur. And that smell! No, it was an animal!

But I know that, if it was an animal, I have been too long in Africa.

I lie back on the bed and pull Maggie down beside me. We lie together, holding one another, until I've calmed down. Finally I tell her, "I guess someone sent me a warning."

"A warning about what?"

"It really felt like an animal. Smelled like one."

We say nothing for a time. "Now I know why people are so superstitious about this leopard-man business."

We order sandwiches from room service. As we lie together on the bed, waiting for them to arrive, I feel a strange after-fighting nervousness that causes me occasionally to tremble. At these times Maggie holds me close. When I'm myself again, she suggests, "Let's go to Kenya. You've filed the leopard-man piece."

"How can I go to Kenya?" I ask. "That child may be my daughter."

Before we sleep, we make love again. Although much farther away now, Randy is still in the room. This lovemaking is very different from that of this afternoon when we enjoyed the sheer animal pleasure of being together. Maggie holds me now as if I were mortal, a man of diminished capacity, one to be husbanded. She is tender with my scratches, concerned about me with the concern of a wife. I'm not used to that; it scares me a little. I feel damaged, a guy with wounds. A guy whose body still trembles involuntarily. A guy who may have a daughter. I lie wondering what has become of me, a man usually so sure of his opinions. Have my analytical capacities gone kaflooey? I do not know for sure what attacked me: an animal or a man. I do not know for sure who Hazen's woman is: my Joss or an impostor. I do not know what it is I want from Maggie. Or what Maggie wants from me. Am I Tom Craig? Or Craig Thomas, some befuddled alter ego? Who am I anyway?

Chapter Twelve

THE PHONE RINGS ME OUT OF A DRUGGED SLEEP. It's an effort to pull my eyes open and I realize that morning sunlight is sliding into the room at the edge of the blinds. My first conscious thought is that my face hurts. When I sit up, Maggie slips from the bed and disappears into the bathroom. The phone continues to ring. I answer and it's Bakili. "My friend," he says, "what did you write about us? The President's people are chattering like monkeys about your story. Even the Blantyre Star has heard about it."

"Helluva a story, right?" I say. "You know I'm a fantastic writer." But I wonder how news of the story has traveled all the way from California.

"Rafiki, you learned reporting in Kenya," Bakili says, laughing. "You write like shit." He says, "A friend at the hotel tells me you have a woman with you now. With you there's always a woman."

"Look who's talking! I don't have two wives."

"I have wives. You have money. And you don't sleep alone."

"How many leopard-men are running around this town?" I ask. "I got clawed by one last night."

There's silence on Bakili's end of the line. "For real? You okay?"

"I'm not beautiful. But I'm okay."

"You were never beautiful."

"Who would have sent a leopard-man after me?" "Guess Who's people. Who else?"

"Whoever did it scared the shit out of my girlfriend."

"And you!" Bakili cackles. "I called to tell you you're a celebrity in Malawi."

"Malawi? What's that: a social disease?" "Hoping to see you again," Bakili says. It's an old line between us. "Hoping you don't get thrown out of the country."

As I hang up, Maggie emerges from the bathroom in a bathing suit and a long tee shirt, her hair pulled back in a ponytail. She comes to inspect my cheek. "I guess you'll survive," she opines. "I may go back to Joburg this afternoon." I shake my head. "Right now I'm going to swim and have some coffee."

She wants some time away from me and I don't blame her. I'd like some time away from me, too.

A knock sounds at the door. "Who's there, please?" I bellow.

"Bill Sykes," comes the answer. "Could we talk?"

I holler for him to hold on and I get out of bed. I slip on a pair of jeans and go into the bathroom to quickly brush my teeth. The claw marks don't look too bad on my face; they're healing well. Good thing the leopard-guy didn't get a real whack at me. Returning to the room, I grab Maggie and give her a kiss. I whisper, "Don't drown." When I open the door, Sykes is standing there. I introduce Maggie, but before anything's said, she darts away.

"If you two had a fight last night," Sykes jokes as he enters, "I'm glad everything's friendly this morning."

"If you mean my face," I say, "a leopard-man did that. It's a good thing the hotel could provide a nurse."

"I must get her name if I need nursing." Sykes looks at me intently. "You're not kidding about the cat?"

"No. There's a whole litter of them. Who might have sent one after me?"

Sykes seems genuinely puzzled by the claw marks on my face. He has an interest in—maybe even some responsibility about—protecting American journalists. He seems to have no idea who might have sent someone to terrorize me.

"I hear the President's got his balls twisted about something I wrote."

Sykes holds up a handful of xeroxed pages; they look very much like the text I telegraphed two nights ago. "The President's balls are twisted, but it's Hazen that's screaming. He hopes you'll change some of this."

"If that's my story, how'd you get hold of it?"

"The telegraph office sent the story to the President's office. He read it last night and hit the ceiling."

"This really is a half-assed country. Was it sent to California?"

"Hazen wonders if you could cut some—"

I shout, "Did it get sent to California?"

"Yes."

"No! I won't cut shit!"

"At least tone down the language."

"No! Double-fucking no! A chickenshit ambassador to a chickenshit country!" Sykes deflates as if I've hit him. He knows enough not to make such a request. That means Hazen has insisted. I feel sorry for the guy. "What offends the ambassador's delicate sensibilities?"

Sykes and I sit down at the worktable and go over the story line by line. Banda, it seems, is irritated that there should be any coverage of the murders. He and Hazen are particularly disturbed by the story's assertion that the murders constitute the kind of political dialogue necessitated by the dictatorship of a headstrong moralist who stifles all dissent. "What does it mean," Sykes asks, "when it says: 'Observers believe that the murders will continue until a political resolution occurs?' Who are these observers? Are you just giving us your own opinion?"

"I'm not about to justify my story to you or Hazen. Those are not merely my opinions, but if I identify the sources, Banda will punish them. We both know that. So do my sources."

"How about toning some of this down?"

"You're outta line here, Bill. Isn't Hazen reporting the same thing in his cables?" Sykes looks perplexed. "If not, they oughta kick his ass out."

Sykes looks at me as if I were a wild man. "It must be nice to be able to say whatever the hell you feel like." I shrug. "Can't you at least tone it—"

"No! Goddammit no!" Sykes must know that Hazen, through him, is asking me to invite my editors to distrust my judgment. I won't do that, particularly since I'm convinced the judgments are sound.

"If this gets published," Sykes says, "congressmen and their constituents will think what you've just said: 'A chickenshit country.' They already think we 'give away,' as they call it, one quarter of our GDP in foreign aid. In fact, we donate way less than one percent. The upshot of this piece may be that the Assistant Secretary cancels his visit."

"Bullshit!"

"The upshot of that is that our aid for the Lilongwe project gets put on hold. Less aid means fewer jobs for Africans. You've seen the poverty here. Contrast that with the abundance at home and all those affluent, obese, self-satisfied 'Murcans squealing about their taxes."

We look at each other. Sykes seems to diminish before my eyes like a balloon with the air going out. "I've appreciated your help here," I say. "But don't lay this on me. I'm just the messenger. If Hazen wants to put pressure on someone, let him put it on Kamuzu."

Sykes smiles weakly, with frustration. Now he must return to the embassy to tell Hazen that he has failed in his mission.

"I realize it's not easy for you to ask me to do this."

"Sorry to get you out of bed," he says. We shake hands and he's gone.

As I'm shaving the phone rings again. I wonder if it's Maggie and answer to find that it's Kay Kittredge.

She must talk with me right away, but insists she cannot discuss the matter on the phone. Since she's passing the hotel on her way to the Colonial Club, I suggest we meet in the coffee shop for breakfast. "What I have to tell you can't be said in there," she insists. Like secret agents we'll meet in the parking lot in fifteen minutes.

At the appointed time a black woman with sunglasses and a scarf, elaborately knotted above her head, cruises up before the hotel and toots her horn. It's no African; it's Kay. "I do solidarity with locals on the weekends," she explains through her open window. "Get in." When I obey, I see that she accessorizes her head cloth with a tan safari suit, tailored for a woman, and local sandals. She drives us to the far end of the lot and parks under a tree. Its shade will obscure our identities from anyone passing by, although no one will mistake me for an African.

"What happened to you?" she asks, looking at my face. I wave away her question the way I'd wave away a fly. But she doesn't want to think about me. "You're going to think I'm crazy," she tells me.

"I'm not sure I don't already," I reassure her.

"I got a message in a dream last night. Very vivid." I've expected a tip of some kind, but this is new. I've never had a tip from a dream. "I trust dreams," she says. "Dreams like this tell you stuff you need to know. You interested?"

"I'm not sure. But I'm up. So tell me."

"It was revealed to me how Hazen and that woman, that purported wife, intend to kill Pepper." I meditatively pat the facial scratches, hoping to quell— or at least cover—my strong urge to laugh. But Kay seems certain she's on to something. They will take Pepper outside Malawi, the dream revealed, to a hospital, maybe a clinic, in South Africa, Rhodesia, or even Zambia, a carefully chosen facility where the nursing sisters are African. The ambassador will return to his post, leaving his wheelchair-bound wife and child. Then the child will be found dead.

"Of what?" I ask. "Who kills her? And how?"

"The purported wife," Kay says. "Maybe with poison. Or an overdose of pills. Maybe she smothers her."

Kay relates the dream less disjointedly than she dreamt it. In the dream apparently an African nurse found the child in the dark of night, dead and alone, well after visiting hours had ended. Suddenly in the dream several African nurses huddled around the child's bed, trying to revive her. Appearing in her wheelchair, the child's mother put on a display of grief that neither doctors nor nursing sisters would ever forget. Anguish-stricken, she demanded an accounting for what happened. But no one really knew how to explain. The mother accused the nurse who found the child of negligence, even foul play. The African nurse fell into a paroxysm of panic similar to the reactions, so Kay claims, of a villager who realizes he's the victim of witchcraft. This paralyzing panic so disturbed Kay that she sat up in bed, crying and bathed in sweat.

Kay pauses to let the impact of this dream sink into my consciousness. But the truth is: I don't know what to make of it.

"You understand the dynamics of it, of course," Kay says to me. But what dynamics does she mean? The dynamics of her dream?

"The white wife of the white dignitary. He's influential and rich and she's educated and unable to move in her wheelchair. Most importantly, she's a mother and so above suspicion. She accuses a black person of the lowest rank of this horrible crime. The black person has little education, no prestige, no means, no recourse. As a woman she has no credibility." Kay's eyes narrow as they bore into me, this African-American woman in her strange head cloth. "That's how these things have always been done."

I feel on one hand that she's right and on the other that she's as cuckoo as she said I'd suppose her to be. If she believes that her dreams forewarn her of what will happen, I wonder if she's been too long in Africa.

"The doctors who own the hospital will never know for sure what happened," Kay says. "Especially if the powerless African who's been accused runs off, as will probably be the case. The doctors will want to mollify the ambassador's wife; they'll try to keep the child's death a secret so that the hospital's reputation— and their own—is not compromised. And, regardless of what they think, they will not accuse an American ambassador's wife of killing her own child. Not on their property. Not on their watch. So she'll get away with it scot-free. She'll come back here grieving and the embassy staff will be more sympathetic and supportive than ever. And she and Hazen will giggle about it when they do the wild thing in the dead of night."

We sit in the car for a long moment, neither of us speaking. I watch Africans pass by on the nearby road, some on bicycles, others trudging along, yakking with friends. I'm distressed that the woman beside me is so consumed with hatred for Hazen and his woman that her subconscious mind concocts wild schemes that come to her as dream-messages demanding action. Yet I've concocted some myself. But I cannot deny that, if they have killed Joss, in a curious and ruthless way killing Pepper will make sense to them and could seem to set them free.

"That's how it's going to happen," Kay finally says.

"Thanks for telling me." Before I leave the Ford, I ask, "Will the ambassador's wife be at this meeting at the Colonial Club?"

"She's been there every other time." Kay studies me. "You cooking up something?"

"Why don't you suggest to her that someone must be poisoning Pepper. She gets better, then relapses. Nothing else makes sense."

"Think about my dream," Kay says. "That's what makes sense."

Leaving Kay, I make myself walk meditatively across the parking lot as if I am considering what she's told me. But my instinct is to flee from her dream and her crazy premonition of Pepper's death. I have to maintain rigid control of myself not to start running.

When I return to the room, Maggie is still gone. I'm glad. I don't want to talk about what Kay told me, but if Maggie were in the room, I would. I'm not able to escape the Hazen puzzle, however, and as I shower, I argue with myself about the Colonial Club. My reckless side boisterously pesters me that the Club offers what may be my only chance to observe the consort up close, possibly even to confront her one-on-one. It tells me I must not let this opportunity escape. My fastidious side quietly reminds me that Hazen has already threatened to have me expelled. If I'm ejected from the country, my freedom of action against the Hazens will be lost.

Caution seems the keyword. Little in the way of smarts is required to figure out what I must do. The Colonial Club is a relic of a bygone era, the preeminent bastion of white colonials. Unlike most leaders of independence movements, Dr. Banda retains an admiration for things British. And so the Colonial Club remains an outpost and a haven for whites who have stayed on in Malawi after their time has passed.

Because of the good doctor's strait-laced ways, the bar—exclusively for men—does not open until noon. Its dining room serves lunch and dinner to those homesick for bad English food. This Saturday morning the Club has the musty atmosphere of a museum. As I enter, a uniformed retainer greets me with a bow and says, "Good morning, sir. I am Mijoga, at your service." He inspects my face but does not comment on the fading wounds. I have been careful to dress appropriately in a tie and sports jacket, the one not carved up by my attacker. My clothes and skin provide sufficient credentials.

"Good morning, Mijoga," I reply. "Is Mrs. Hazen here?"

"Indeed, she is, sir," says Mijoga. "The Malawi Benefactors are in the card room, working on the new cookbook." He points me into the interior of the club and I thank him for his help.

Moving along a hall I hear voices. I spot five women gathered about a table in the card room. Three of them are known to me: Kay, still wearing her head cloth, Dina Foresta, and the woman known as Jocelyn Hazen. I slip into a small library across the hall. From there I can observe the women without their noticing me. I sit quietly in the dark and watch them discussing recipes to be published in a cookbook that will be sold to raise money for good works.

Once I'm settled in the library, my fastidious side asks: What are you doing here? But my reckless side notices that this morning the ambassador's consort seems less withdrawn than when I observed her at the Midweek Smash. I watch her, comparing her in my mind with the Joss I knew.

Then I hear her say, "You all decide. I've gotta spend a penny." I see her move the wheelchair toward the hall. I rise, possessed by a realization that my moment has come. The hair on the back of my neck is standing straight up. I move out of sight and wait. "I don't need any help," she says. "I'll be right back." I listen to the wheelchair move across the hallway's wooden floor. Through the library door I see the wheelchair roll toward the ladies' lounge. In the library's darkness I wait to see if anyone follows the woman. No one does. The women across the hall begin to chatter about dessert recipes.

I tiptoe into the hall and move out of sight of the women in the card room. My social training rebels at the idea of what I'm doing. As I stand at the door of the ladies' lounge, I can hardly breathe, so overwhelmed am I by the conventions I am shattering. Soundlessly I open the door. I slip inside. The entry room boasts comfortable chairs covered with flowered prints, long faded, and a pair of vanities with mirrors. Through a swinging door I hear a toilet flushing. I wait several moments—one must be a gentleman in these situations—and then push my way into the bathroom.

Jocelyn Hazen stands with her back to me as she washes her hands at a basin. The wheelchair is directly behind her. I feel nervous, hesitant, as she glances in the mirror to see who has entered. When she sees a man, she freezes. One hand grabs the edge of the basin for support. I feel a wave of sympathy for her. I would like to assure her I mean her no physical harm. I want only to examine her face. She fortifies herself for the encounter. Then, surprisingly, she turns with a strength and self-possession totally lacking in the woman I saw at the Midweek Smash. "Mr. Craig!" she says, almost banteringly, "are you lost again?"

I do not answer. I move to her side and stare intently at her in the mirror. Then quite close beside her, but not touching her, I inspect her face. If she has felt in command of the situation, the wheelchair providing her immunity from threat, panic now sweeps across her face. She opens her mouth to scream. I place one hand over her mouth and with the other grip her jaw. I feel her tremble. She's very frightened. She begins to struggle. My hand moves from her jaw to her throat. I pull aside the fall of dark hair that covers her ear. She stops struggling.

"Reconstructive surgery," I say. "Where? When?" She does not answer. I feel her tremble again. I turn her face toward mine. My eyes drill in on hers.

"You aren't Joss Hazen," I whisper. "Who are you?"

This challenge restores her courage. She bites my hand. I jerk it away. She screams.

The scream alarms me. My time with her is short.

Surprised at what happens next, I shove her shoulders sharply. She whimpers. I bend her over the counter.

With my right hand at her neck I hold her down. My right hand lifts her skirt over her back. My right elbow pins it against her. "Don't! Please, don't!" she whispers. She begins to blubber. My right hand snags the top of her panties. I pull them down over her right buttock. I lean over, looking for— And there it is: the small tattoo of Africa at the center of her buttock.

I'm baffled, uncertain what to do. I was sure there would be no tattoo.

I pull the panties up around her waist. I push down the skirt. But I keep holding her down. Finally, very tenderly, I pull her back up to a standing position. I turn her to face me. She looks terrified. I stare at her, bewildered. "Is it you?" I ask. "Why don't you recognize me?"

"It is me," Joss says.

I stare at her, hardly able to believe her. "I've been through an ordeal. There were so many lovers, too many to remember." I continue to examine her. How can this be Joss? "Whoever you are," she says, "it was in another country. A thousand years ago."

I scrutinize her. "Is Pepper my daughter?" I ask. She screams at the top of her lungs. "Help! Help!"

Her scream chills me. Now I'm the one who trembles.

"Help! Help! Rape!"

I flee from the women's room. Dina Foresta comes running to help her friend. We collide. She screams at the sight of a man coming from the women's sanctuary. I hurry past. She rushes inside the women's room. No longer in danger, Joss is bellowing now.

"Rape! Rape!"

I force calmness on myself as I approach the reception area. I move through the glass and wood doors to find Mijoga standing outside his office, baffled by what he's heard. "Sir," he inquires when he sees me. "Is everything in order?"

"Everything's tiptop, Mijoga," I tell him. "The women seem to be celebrating."

"Very good, sir," he says.

Once I'm in the Land Cruiser, I race out of town on the Mulanje road. When I'm fifteen miles out, I pull onto the shoulder. I leave the vehicle and pace up and down. I keep asking myself, "What have I done? What have I done?" Before long, children gather at the side of the road to watch me.

Chapter Thirteen

B Y THE TIME I GET BACK TO THE HOTEL, I'm convinced I've been conned by a pro. The woman is Not-Joss. Instead she and Hazen are formidable adversaries.

Playing against them, I'm a yokel, a pigeon, a dupe—all the more foolish for assuming that professional skepticism will enable me to see through their deceptions. How could I have supposed that, because there were no obvious evidences of facial surgery, there would be no tattoo? No impostor would over-look the tattoo! It was necessary for Pepper. And I should have realized that the only person likely to investigate Joss's murder was one of her lovers. Now I've allowed "Jocelyn Hazen" to send me fleeing the Colonial Club with her cries of rape when, in fact, the occasion was ideal for unmasking her, especially with Kay Kittredge there to support my accusation.

I return to the hotel room, looking so jangled and annoyed with myself that Maggie emits a gasp. She exclaims, "Are you all right?"

"I've done something very stupid," I say. I toss my jacket into a chair and sit on the bed, my head in my hands. "My judgment's gone schizo."

Maggie looks at me, thoroughly puzzled. "This is something about the god-dess, isn't it? This Joss."

"She isn't Joss," I say. "She's an impostor. I know that now." Maggie watches me, her puzzlement turning to annoyance. "Maybe it was that attack last night. Or witchcraft." This last is ironic, but Maggie does not smile. "My head's a blur."

"What's happened to you?" Maggie asks. "You've always seemed so in con-trol. Then you come to this nothing country no one cares about and you turn into a basket case." I cannot look at her. "What happened?"

I shake my head. I'm too embarrassed to admit what I've done.

"I think I'm going back to Joburg," Maggie says. "I'm not sure what I thought would happen if I came here." She stands looking at me while I stare at the floor. When I say nothing, she pulls her metal suitcase off the luggage rack and swings it onto the bed beside me. I look up at her. I know that if I allow her to leave, she will move out of the house in Joburg before I get back. "Don't go," I say.

"I expected to go back today anyhow," she replies. When I glance up at her, I see that she's about to cry. I rise to embrace her. She runs into the bathroom and locks the door. Once she's inside, I hear muffled sounds of crying.

I pace up and down the room. After what seems forever, she emerges, her face freshly washed, her eyes still red from tears. I go to her and embrace her. She stands stiffly, her head averted, her arms at her sides. "Hey," I say. "We were so good together yesterday. Let's be careful here."

She pulls out of my embrace and walks to the door, as far from me as the room allows. She crosses her arms over her chest. She stares at the floor. "I was a fool to come here. I didn't come to be your easy afternoon fuck."

"Don't talk that way." I go to her and embrace her again. Once more she goes stiff. I kiss her hair. "You mustn't leave," I say. "Please stay."

After a time she puts her arms around me. She leans her head against my chin. I continue to kiss her hair. Finally I lead her to the bed. We lie down together, fully clothed, and kick off our shoes. After a while she asks, "What did you do that was so foolish?" I do not reply. We stare at the ceiling without talking, holding one another.

—⁂—

The hotel coffee shop is almost empty when we arrive for lunch. We each order a bowl of soup and find conversation difficult. Maggie has not yet agreed to stay and neither of us wants more negotiation about that.

Maggie stares at her placemat. I gaze over her shoulder at African waiters whispering to one another. "Do you suppose they're yakking about the leopard-man?" I ask. Maggie glances at the waiters. She does not reply.

Maybe, I think, they are yakking about me. Can knowledge of my being thrown out of the President's office have spread to waiters in hotels? Or perhaps they are whispering about my exploit at the Colonial Club. Is it possible that gossip about that has already traveled here? When our soup arrives, we eat without speaking.

—ɯ—

Suddenly Max Hazen strides into the coffee shop.

He's dressed for Saturday in a sport shirt, chinos, and deck shoes. Two Africans in business suits, no doubt government officials, enter behind him, followed by police. When Hazen spots me, there's fury in his eyes. He at least has heard what happened at the Colonial Club. He moves toward me with the measured, deliberate strides of a man who has his anger under rigid control. I rise. Maggie looks up.

"I was at fault," I say. "I apologize. It was unpardonable."

Hazen turns to the African officials. "This is the man." African policemen with truncheons take up positions around us. Hazen looks back at me. "A word of counsel, friend," he says. "Go back to California where they welcome hippies and weirdos and swine like you who have no clue how to behave." His words are meant to cut like shards of ice. "I speak as a friend, a compatriot. Go back where you belong before we find you in a gully somewhere with your throat cut."

These extravagant words cause me a glint of amusement.

Hazen notices the fact. "You guys are always flippant," he says. "You breeze into town, make your little messes and we have to clean them up."

I say nothing.

"It was foolish to insult the President," he says. "Provocative. It feeds his distrust of the press and undercuts his confidence in me. Because I encouraged him to see you."

I mutter, "Thank you," although I realize Hazen set up the interview as a quid pro quo. For arranging it, I was to lay off his personal life.

"Believe me," Hazen continues, "there are countries where insults to the President do not go unpunished."

I will not plead my case on this one. I stand there, feeling like an unrepentant little schoolboy suffering the principal's tongue-lashing. Hazen must have treated Joss this way; that makes her wanderings understandable. I wonder if he tongue-lashes Pepper.

"As for my wife—"

"I said I was sorry. What I did was inexcusable."

Hazen turns to Maggie. He appears in total control of himself, but he's frigid with rage. "Your friend attacked my wife."

Maggie's expression does not change. She rises to stand beside me. She's with me on this, bless her. She observes Hazen with disdain.

"You don't believe me?" Hazen says. "Ask him. He entered the woman's lounge of a downtown club."

Maggie glances at me. She wonders: Is this true? "He listened to my wife use the toilet, then attacked her while she washed her hands."

Maggie keeps watching me. "I did not attack her," I say. I can't let Maggie think this charge has validity. "I apologize for what I did do. I'll apologize to her in person if you like."

Maggie's expression changes. She now realizes that Hazen's accusations have some merit. "What happened, Tom?" she asks.

"He bent her over the wash basin counter," Hazen tells her. "Lifted her skirt over her back. Pulled down her panties. He'd have taken her from behind if she hadn't screamed for help."

A silence. Maggie stares at me.

"What I did was unacceptable," I acknowledge. "But I did not try to rape your wife. I did humiliate her. I'm sorry."

"I'm sorry, I'm sorry," mimics Hazen, losing his control.

"What happened, Tom?" asks Maggie.

"I'll explain it later." Maggie purses her lips and turns away from me.

Hazen signals to the African officials. One of them steps forward. "Thomas Craig?" he asks. I acknowledge my name. "You are persona non grata. No longer welcome in our country. We are escorting you to the airport. We'll put you on the first plane out of Malawi."

Hazen turns to leave with a tight smile on his face.

At the airport we're told I'm being deported for libelous reporting about Malawi. That's the official charge, but this expulsion is clearly Hazen's doing. Maggie's not being PNG'd, but she will also leave. She has not yet declared whether she will return to South Africa or accompany me to wherever the next plane is headed. Since I seem to be persona non grata with her as well as

Malawi, I assume she'll return to Joburg. To my surprise she asks, "Should I come with you?"

"We did plan a trip together."

"Will you tell me what this is all about?"

"I'll tell you on the plane."

"Where are we going?" she wonders.

The immigration official who processes us takes my passport, thumbs through it, then pounds each page with a stamp drenched in red ink. It declares: "RE- ENTRY FORBIDDEN IN MALAWI." Page after page of the passport, over old visas and some not yet used. "RE-ENTRY FORBIDDEN IN MALAWI." All I can do is watch.

We are put on a plane headed for Dar es Salaam, the Tanzanian capital. I like Dar. I'll get us into a luxury class hotel overlooking the Indian Ocean. We'll put Malawi behind us. When we reach our cruising altitude, Maggie asks again what provoked my deportation. I explain that Hazen engineered our expulsion from Malawi because I know that his wife is an impostor. Because I understand that the two of them did something unconscionable to Joss. An impatient expression settles on Maggie's face; she has heard enough about Joss.

"Why does he accuse you of trying to rape her?" Maggie asks.

"He knows I did not try to rape her."

"You admit you humiliated her. What was that?"

When I say nothing, she asks peevishly: "How can you know she's an impostor? Did you interview her?" When I do not reply, she says, "How did you humiliate her?"

Under this questioning there's no way to escape mentioning the tattoo. The explanation requires talking about the afternoon in Rabat when I discovered it. As I unfold the story, Maggie stares straight ahead, a look of irritation in her eyes. I say that I went to the Colonial Club hoping to talk with the purported Mrs. Hazen in order to get a close look at her face. The opportunity to do that presented itself when she went to the ladies' lounge.

"You really did follow her in there?" Maggie is dismayed.

I shrug.

"Do you know how vulnerable women feel everywhere they go?" There's an unforgiving edge to her voice. "Their restroom should be inviolable. And she's in a wheelchair."

"She killed someone," I say quietly.

"You don't know that," she replies. Finally: "What did you do?"

I say that I examined her face close up and found no traces of reconstructive surgery.

"Are you an expert on that?"

I acknowledge that I'm not. But I am certain some sort of surgery occurred. I say that I peered deeply into the woman's eyes and she did not recognize me.

"Does she have to recognize you?" Maggie taunts. "Are you so extraordinary that she has to recognize you?"

Now it is my turn to be peeved. "Yes, I'm that extraordinary."

"What about the tattoo?"

With all the delicacy at my command I explain. "You pulled her panties—" Maggie is horrified.

"Just down on one side."

"And the tattoo was there!"

"She got tattooed to confuse the child!" Listening to this come out of my mouth, I realize I sound as irrational as Kay Kittredge.

"You fool!" Maggie explodes. "She's the woman she says she is. She's Joss!"

"She is Not-Joss!"

"She is Joss, very damaged. But also very brave. In a wheelchair. After an accident that's changed her face and erased her memory. She has a daughter who may be dying. And you trap her in a bathroom and do that to her!" Maggie leaves her seat, hurries down the aisle, and sits in the back of the plane.

—⁓—

When we arrive in Dar, Maggie will not speak to me. I take charge of her suitcase so that she cannot go off on her own. In the taxi driving to the hotel she hurls an accusation at me, "Isn't it possible that you're wrong?"

"Not about this."

"You damn journalists. So sure of yourselves. Haven't you ever been wrong?"

"If she's Joss, why doesn't she recognize me?"

"Why should she? Because you're such an unforgettable lover?" After a moment she adds, "You've made love to me and I can assure you—"

"I shouldn't have told you. You're jealous." This remark infuriates her.

"I am not jealous! And don't you wish I were!"

—⁓—

At the reception desk she insists that we have separate rooms and that she pay for her own. I hope that the clerk will assign us adjoining rooms, but only one room is available on the Indian Ocean side of the hotel. I take a room overlooking the garden and the city beyond it.

As we follow the bellman to our rooms, Maggie is elaborately polite to the man. We walk on opposite sides of the hallway. As the bellman takes the bags into her room, I gaze pleadingly at her. I ask, "Can't we make this up?"

She says, "Don't call."

Chapter Fourteen

THE NEXT MORNING I HAVE COFFEE WITH A LONG-AGO fellow story-chaser at the Daily Nation. He now works as a spokesman for the Tanzanian government. "Tom, my friend," he confides to me, "I know nothing of such a woman. But I would not want to tell you about her even if I did. We have a tourist industry in East Africa and we are hungry for hard currency. Your story about a visitor who comes here and gets killed? It will only scare off visitors."

A reporter friend is no more helpful and the police tell me to come back tomorrow. I decide to turn my attention to the wildlife situationers the editors are always happy to receive. Those stories may also be a way to wangle my way back into Maggie's good graces.

The young consular officer at the embassy laughs out loud when he sees the condition of my passport.

"Re-entry Forbidden in Malawi," he says. "My, my! Who'd you piss off?" He thumbs through page after page defiled by the red stamp. "Never seen anything like this. I guess they mean it."

"Or they've never used the stamp before." I hand the man two small photos for the new passport he's agreed to give me.

Twenty minutes later he returns with a new passport. "Here you are, Mr. Craig," he says. "I bet you can even go back."

"Maybe I will," I tell him. "I was working on a murder story worthy of the National Enquirer."

"And you write for the respectable press. What a dilemma."

"Maybe you could help me with the story," I suggest. He looks interested, flattered. "You haven't heard of a woman's body being found, have you? White woman. Probably unclothed. No identification."

"American citizen?" I nod. He stares at the ceiling for a moment, then shakes his head. "That is a story for the Enquirer."

"You heard it first here." We shake hands and I wish him a good tour in Tanzania.

An hour later as I sit on the hotel terrace, thumbing through newspapers while I consume a sandwich and a beer, Maggie walks out onto the terrace. I stand and gesture for her to join me. She shuns me as if I carry the plague. As I watch her walk away through the knick-knack vendors at the curb, someone calls my name. I turn to see the young consul approaching along the terrace. "I hoped I'd find you here," he says.

I invite him to join me for lunch. He agrees to have a beer. We chat about Dar and the up-country game reserves he's recently visited, Ngorongoro and Manyara. Once he has his beer, he tells me, "After you left, I remembered something I'd read in the cable traffic from Kenya. A woman's body was found up there in one of the game parks."

"When was this?"

"Six months ago. I'd just arrived. I hunted up the cable. Unclassified—so I copied it for you." The guy hands me the copy of the cable. I scan it. An unidentified white woman, mid-30s. I nod. The consul grins. "If you write a bestseller about it," he asks, "would you put my name in the acknowledgments?" I assure him that I will.

In the hotel I write Maggie a note and stick it under her door. I grab my toothbrush and a change of underwear and head out to the airport.

It's after dark by the time I get into my room at the New Stanley Hotel in the heart of downtown Nairobi. I walk around the old haunts, being careful to stay away from the Norfolk Hotel and its associations with Joss. I have a curry dinner at the Three Bells. A few of the waiters still remember Bakili and me. I greet them and say that I've just seen Bakili in Malawi. I wander back via Bazaar Street. Mr. Patel's shop is still there with its room in the back where Joss was with me for a month. But instead of thinking about Joss, I'm wondering about

Maggie. Has she returned yet to her room in Dar to find my note stuck under the door? "Maggie, if you need me," I wrote her, "I'm at the New Stanley in Nairobi." Maybe she's even now standing on her balcony looking out across the tops of palm trees at clouds above the Indian Ocean. Maybe she's thinking about my message. "I miss you," I told her. "I don't like having this rift. I like having you with me."

—⁓—

At the Nairobi Police Headquarters the next morning I receive questioning looks when I offer my business card and explain that I am seeking a missing American woman. I realize, I say apologizing, that it would have been better to call for an appointment, but I have just arrived in town. In fact, I feared that, since business tends not to be done by phone in Nairobi, a request for an appointment would have been met with an assurance that no appointment could be granted for at least several days. Arriving in person will require me to cool my heels, but it's preferable to being fobbed off on the phone. I understand, I say, that an unidentified white woman's body was found in Tsavo National Park some months earlier; I have a hunch this is the person I'm seeking. The police officer on duty asks me to wait. There are no chairs. I stand against a wall, watching police station traffic come and go. Occasionally an officer peeks around a door to scrutinize me. I smile and nod at the officer, who then disappears.

After two hours of waiting I am taken to a cubicle occupied by an Inspector Kamau. As I enter, he sits at his desk, studying my card, a folder before him on the desk. He's a young Kikuyu, perhaps thirty-five, with smudges of brown in the whites of his eyes. There's an absence of expression on his face intended to prevent people like me from reading him. He glances up at me. He nods to a chair. When I sit, Kamau examines me as if I were a suspect. "How do you know this woman?" the inspector asks.

"I am not here as a journalist," I say, hoping to defuse that concern. "I'm not doing a story. The woman I'm looking for is a friend." As an African, Kamau will assume—correctly, in this case—that my friend and I slept together. "I haven't seen her for some years, but she wrote that she was coming to southern Africa. I expected to see her there. But she's disappeared."

Kamau studies me, assuming, despite my disclaimer, that I am a reporter chasing down a story that will reflect badly on Kenya and the Kenya police. Tourism is a huge foreign exchange earner for his country and stories about white women thrown dead and naked into game parks will not encourage tourism. I take my most recent photo of Joss, the one where she's with Pepper, and place it before the inspector. "This is the woman I'm looking for," I say.

Kamau takes the photo and studies it. Then he opens the folder on his desk, turns his back on me and, I assume, compares the photo I've given him with photos in the folder. After a moment he turns back. He asks, "What is her name?"

"I knew her as Jocelyn Bennett."

A change of expression flashes across Kamau's vacant eyes. He says, "Wait here." Taking my photo and the folder, he leaves the cubicle. After ten minutes he returns to say, "Follow me."

Kamau leads me to the office of his superior, Commander Jenkins, a Brit of perhaps sixty with graying, sandy hair over a deeply tanned face and penetrating eyes, obviously a former colonial who stayed on after independence. He rises to greet me. We shake hands and he gestures to a chair. I notice the folder and Joss's photo on his desk. Once I've sat, he watches me with even more intensity than Kamau. I explain my mission. Jenkins listens without comment. I offer some background: that I once worked as a reporter in Nairobi, that the missing woman and I were together a short time years ago and have remained in touch.

"You are not here in a professional capacity?" Jenkins asks.

"No. I need to find my missing friend. Because of our friendship I have no desire to publicize the circumstances of her death."

Jenkins leans forward, watching me closely. "What were the circumstances of her death? Do you know them?"

"I am quite certain that my friend was not killed by an African."

"Quite certain? How can you be certain?"

For a moment I don't know what to say. Jenkins detects why that is.

"I take it you have a theory of the murder."

"I assume a lover killed her."

"She never had an African lover?"

"I guess what I meant was that she was not killed by an African driver or waiter or lodge boy. Someone she met in Tsavo."

"She took some care in choosing lovers?"

I feel myself squirming under these questions. "As one of her former lovers, of course, I think she

chose them carefully." I try to smile but cannot manage it.

"If an African did not kill her, does that mean there's no story in it for you?"

"What I'm trying to say is: I don't believe she was dispatched by the GSU." The Government Services Unit is a band of thugs that takes care of government dirty work. Jenkins smiles tightly, understanding now that I really have worked as a reporter in Nairobi. I feel we are back on equal footing. I take advantage of that. "Nor do I think she was killed in the way Josiah Mwangi Kariuki was killed." Kariuki, a Kikuyu politician and former secretary to Jomo Kenyatta, the country's first president, was assassinated by GSU thugs for threatening Kenyatta's political primacy. "Nor do I think she was the girlfriend of a government minister who became inconvenient."

"Good," says Jenkins. "We don't want a love-nest scandal that taints officials." Then suddenly he asks, "Did you kill her?" He carefully watches my reaction to this question.

It's so preposterous, so surprising, that I feel like laughing. "No. Would I be here if I had?" We measure each other. "I haven't been in Kenya for over a year. That's a matter of record." I offer him my passport to examine.

"Our borders are very porous. The passport proves nothing." After a moment he asks, "Are you the father of this child?"

"She's never told me so, but I assume that I am."

"Who do you think killed her?"

"Someone who's well out of your jurisdiction."

"Are you acting on his behalf?"

"No. I just have to know what happened. I loved her."

"Who told you that she might be dead?"

"Her husband. He's South African. An Afrikaner from Bloemfontein in the Orange Free State." I give him the name and description of Sarie's father for I can hardly implicate Hazen without causing myself problems. It's a difficult lead to follow and, if pursued, will only result in denials. "She's a very independent woman," I explain. "Her husband told me that she'd been gone for some months. He hadn't heard from her."

"Why isn't he the one looking for her?"

"He can't come into black Africa. Not with a South African passport. She had American passports and could travel wherever she wanted."

"Passports? More than one?"

"Two. One for entering South Africa. One for black Africa."

Jenkins watches me. He knows that some of what I've told him is untrue, but he doesn't know how much.

"It's an unhappy marriage," I say. "He's much older. That's why I was her lover."

Jenkins studies me for a long moment. Then he instructs me to return at two o'clock. Kamau will show me some pictures.

—⁂—

The movie footage I watch that afternoon is definitely that of a tourist. It begins with random shots of animals—elephants and rhinos, zebras and wildebeest, impalas and little Tommy gazelles—poorly composed, many of them poorly focused, some shot at such a distance that they lack a center of interest. Next there is footage of Asian tourists standing before a fleet of Volkswagen mini-buses painted with zebra stripes.

I'm sitting in a small conference room. The images dance on the wall. Inspector Kamau, who stands behind me at the projector, says, "We know nothing about this woman. So if you could help us, we'd appreciate it."

Now the footage shows a sign: "Welcome to Tsavo National Park."

Kamau says, "A Korean took this. Tourist visits from Korea have been down ever since."

The footage cuts to two distant forms rising above roadside vegetation. The vehicle starts toward them. The ride is bumpy, the focus uncertain. As the vehicle nears the forms, they become clearer. They're lions. I can imagine the excitement of the tourists at coming upon these beasts.

The vehicle stops. The movie's quality improves. The lions munch on a kill. The camera zooms in on the object of the lions' appetite. The focus moves in and out, then clicks in. It becomes clear that the lions are eating a woman's body. The vehicle's horn begins to sound. It blasts urgently.

"Once the driver realized what it was, he tried to stop the lions feeding."

"The body is naked," I say. "Were clothes found nearby?"

"No clothes."

"Was she dead before—"

"Yes. By asphyxiation."

The lions do their best to ignore the van and its blaring horn and the screaming camera enthusiasts hitting the windows, banging on the side of the van. I would find it very difficult to watch lions feeding on any human body that only hours—or moments—before was alive. But this is a body I've held in my arms, that I've cherished and caressed. I hold a hand up to block the sight of it.

Kamau explains, "The only way to get the lions off the body was to drive almost upon it."

I watch the screen through the protective lattice of my fingers. The lions move off a few yards and the body becomes clearly visible. The shot zooms in on it, moving from the skull, its dark hair torn, down the back past flesh chewed off at the shoulders, down to ankles cut by sandal straps. The shot lingers on the right buttock and zooms closer. On it is a tattoo.

"What's that?" I ask. But I know what it is.

"A tattoo of Africa. Who'd expect to find that on a white woman's bum?"

I rise from my chair and turn my back to the images on the wall. "I guess I've seen enough," I say.

Inspector Kamau turns off the movie. He excuses himself and leaves me alone. What I've just witnessed is not entirely a surprise. But still I'm shaken.

Kamau returns with Commander Jenkins. They appraise me, weighing the effect of the evidence on me.

Kamau asks, "Who is she?"

I say, "It's hard to make a positive I.D. from that." Because I am reluctant to articulate what I know.

"How about from that?" Kamau hands me some photos. They are morgue shots. One is a close-up of Joss's face. Oh, Joss! How could they?

Jenkins says, "She died of suffocation. There was semen in her body. We've kept samples. But there was no sign of rape." So he made love to her before he—or they—killed her. That way her defenses were down and she was already naked.

"There was no I.D.?"

"No I.D.," says Kamau. "Just the tattoo. We've asked about her in every hotel and tourist lodge in the country."

"Is she the Bennett woman?" Jenkins asks. "Did she have a tattoo?"

I nod that she did. "We traveled together for a month eight or nine years ago."

"You said her name was Valerie, I believe," says Jenkins. But he knows very well that I did not tell him that.

"Jocelyn. I called her Joss."

"A Valerie Bennett was registered for two nights at Hunter's Lodge. On the dates we think this woman was killed."

Kamau adds, "Hunter's Lodge is less than fifty miles from where the body was found."

"You think the victim was called Valerie Bennett?" I ask.

Jenkins will not be drawn. "What do you think?"

"I knew the woman as Joss," I say. "I never heard her called Valerie."

"Valerie Bennett answers the description of this woman," Jenkins says. "The manager of Hunter's Lodge saw her put her luggage into a car driven by a white man and go off with him. We think your Jocelyn and our Valerie are the same woman."

I agree that seems probable. I ask for copies of the morgue photo and the one of the tattoo on the right buttock.

"If you're not here as a journalist," Jenkins asks, "why would you need photos?"

"I thought I might show them to her husband."

"You can't be his friend," comments Jenkins, "if you do that."

—m—

While Kamau goes to get me copies of the photos, Jenkins watches me intently. I say nothing, thinking of poor Joss. How could she have gotten herself into this fix?

Stray remarks suddenly click into focus, comments she might have made on a walk or while we held each other in the night. As I put them together, Hazen must have arrived in St. Louis on home leave from an overseas assignment, determined not to leave for another foreign post without a wife. He met Valerie, swept her off her feet, talked marriage to her. Then he met the vivid, beautiful, and exciting Joss. She swept him off his feet. They ran off together. Somewhere along the line to the next post they married.

Valerie never forgot Hazen. And she never forgave Joss for stealing him. She married, probably on the rebound, and the marriage did not last. At some point she reconnected with Hazen, at a time he was ready for someone less exciting, less beautiful, less vivid, a woman who would make a good ambassador's wife. They began to meet for secret trysts just as Joss and I had done in Paris. And at some point they began to plan.

Joss thought Hazen brought her to Kenya to see animals while enroute to Malawi. In fact, he brought her to Kenya to kill her. With the excitement of a new post and an ambassadorship, they were getting along again. Once more they were making love. In my mind I see Joss lying asleep and naked in bed, sated with lovemaking and curled against Hazen's body. Hazen slowly slides away from her. He's careful not to disturb her sleep. Rising from the bed, he tiptoes across the room. He takes a pillow. He moves back to the bed, straddles her unsuspecting body, and pushes the pillow onto her face. He holds it down on her until the writhings and struggles cease. Then he dresses, drives up the Nairobi-Mombasa highway to Hunter's Lodge. Valerie is waiting for him. The light plastic surgery, not to reconstruct her face, but only to make it look a bit more like Joss, has already been done. They return to Hazen's room at Kilaguni Lodge, wrap Joss's body in a sheet and load it into the car. They dump the body, return to Hunter's Lodge, and spend the rest of the night there. In the morning the manager of the lodge sees Valerie leaving with a white man.

When Kamau returns with the photos, I ask, "Does a case like this go into the unsolved bin?"

"Oh no, we'll solve it," Jenkins says. "Maybe you'll help," suggests Kamau.

"Don't I wish I could," I reply, but I have no intention of helping. It's Pepper who needs my help, not Jenkins and Kamau.

"Journalists interested in a case?" Jenkins says. "That makes a murderer nervous. A nervous murderer makes mistakes." We shake hands all around. "I don't trust journalists," Jenkins remarks. "But I'm happy to have information when I need it." Then he asks, "What's she to you now? A good story?"

I say, "The murder of a woman you loved? That never makes a good story."

Returning to the New Stanley, I do not walk with a spring in my step. I do not congratulate myself for investigative tenacity. Or for amazing luck. Or for turning the tables on Hazen and his dreadful consort. I hardly think. I am so overcome with sadness that I merely shuffle along. When I reach the New Stanley, I have coffee at the coffee shop named for the thorn tree that stands before the hotel.

Jealousy has prevented me from liking Maxwell Hazen. Now I loathe him. Still, if he were with me I would embrace him. I feel certain that some part of him loved her. Admired her beauty. Wanted to be charmed, rather than assailed, by her perversity. Vowed that her obstinacy would never break his patience. Resolved that he and she would make good parents for their child, who would be his child regardless of the biological father. How tragic to be driven to kill your wife! I cannot help but think she drove him to it. I am sure she must— even now—still be playing with his head as she has so long played with mine.

But she is playing with mine no longer. For Hazen, I think, she may never die. Even though he killed her, she will continue to haunt his thoughts, to roam around in his dreams, to appear to him on sidewalks and in crowds.

This is not the case for me. When I saw the photos of her body in the morgue, I felt unspeakably lonely. Sitting in the Thorn Tree now, sipping my coffee, watching the pedestrians and the tourists and the traffic on Kenyatta Avenue, I feel an enormous emptiness inside me. But I know she's dead. She will not haunt me. I'm alone again. For years I've been a man who had a woman. Not a woman I lived with, but one who was always with me. Not a woman who expected fidelity—which I did not give her—because she knew her hold on me was too strong for other women to break. I did not even realize that she was with me in this way until I saw the photos of her dead. Now I'm alone. She's not with me anymore.

By the time I reach the transit lounge at Embakasi, where I wait for the flight back to Dar, the hollowness inside me has filled itself with sadness. I find myself thinking about my life. With Joss dead it's no longer rooted to anything, certainly not to the fantasy of our somehow making a life together. I would not have thought that Joss put meaning into my life. And, no, she didn't. But I understand now that she put aspiration into it. Without her it seems there's nothing. I love my work, but how long can a man be content supplying exotica for his readers' morning coffee? Why is it suddenly that I feel old? That I feel the years slipping by, out of my grasp? Should I go back to the States? But if I did, what would I expect to find there? Is it different work

I need in my life? Or different people? Are there any people in my life now who are truly meaningful to me?

—⁂—

On the plane back to Dar I think about lying beside Joss in the Paris hotel, staring into the darkness above us as I held her. About begging her to leave Hazen and come live with me in Johannesburg. About her saying she did not have it in her to be faithful to one man. She would not want to hurt me the way she had hurt Hazen. But, most of all, it would not be good for Pepper. Pepper needed the stability of parents who stayed together even if they made life hell for one another. "We don't make life hell for her," she assured me. "We both love her. She's the one thing we did right together."

It never occurred to me then to ask if Hazen were truly her father. When Joss said that Pepper was something she and Hazen had done together, what could that mean except that she was Hazen's natural child? I now knew that she meant that raising her was what they had done—and would continue to do—together.

Ever since we had first been together in East Africa, I supposed that, even though Joss was promiscuous, I was special to her, the man she would choose to spend her life with if that choice were possible. Now I saw that as an illusion. I realized that I was merely one of a whole team of men who gave interest to her life. Probably I did not make the first string. She had had lovers who could boast of noteworthy achievements. When she knew me, I had accomplished nothing. I was eking out a living writing journalism on spec. When we were together, I was young, vigorous, American, and not bad looking. It was a good bet that my sperm count was high. So if she were looking for a man to make her pregnant, I was a good choice. The math suggested that I had fathered her child. I realized that if she had had any special regard for me, she would have told me in Paris that I was Pepper's father. Because she had not, I had to assume that she was truly committed to Pepper's other father, the man who killed her.

And why had Hazen done that? To have the last word? Had he killed her knowing it was the only way to finally end the war between them? What would happen to Pepper now? The child must have strong suspicions of what happened to her mother. That was why she was sick. That was the real poison that kept causing her to relapse. Kay Kittredge's dream no longer seemed far-fetched. Since Hazen and his consort had killed once, I assumed that it would not be difficult for them to kill again. And so the question presented itself: if I didn't rescue Pepper, who would?

—⚋—

Back in Dar es Salaam I return to the hotel. A little uncertain of the reception I'll find, I knock on the door of Maggie's room with trepidation. When she opens it, she gives me a smile. I'm relieved. "Look who's turned up," she says. "Come in."

I enter with an envelope of photos in my hand. Maggie's suitcase is open on her bed. On a pillow lies one of the weird Makonde carvings that tourists often buy in Dar. "Been shopping?"

"I tried to call you in Nairobi about an hour ago," Maggie says. "The New Stanley said you'd checked out. I wanted you to know—" She shrugs. "It's time I fly away home."

I watch her, saying nothing, uncertain whether "home" means our place in Joburg or Colorado Springs. She returns to the bed and goes about her packing.

"You like?" she asks, holding up the Makonde.

It's a sculpture of a wizened old man hunched over like a beetle. He seems to have six legs and, as is characteristic of Makonde, alternate light and dark layers of wood give interest to the piece.

"That's what I'll look like," I say, "if you're going back to the States." She smiles at that, but makes no reply. "Are you?"

"Not immediately. For a while I've got to fly doctors and tourists and whoever around southern Africa. But after a month or six weeks..." She shrugs again. "I can stay with Clive and Liz."

"No need for that," I say.

"It's been great fun, you know," she says.

"Let's not end this with clichés." She looks at me as if I've hit her. "There's been too much honest feeling for that."

"The words we use would be important to you."

"Professional preoccupation. Sorry." I suggest we have dinner. She claims she's already eaten, but I know she's done no more than nibble on crackers open on the desk below the window. On my good behavior I ask permission to help myself to crackers. She grants the permission. At the desk I lay out the photos of Joss and Not-Joss that she's already seen, as well as the morgue shots that Kamau gave me. Once I've arranged them, I say, "You might look at these."

She glances toward them. "Haven't I seen them already?"

"Not all of them."

We both feel a tension between us. In order not to exacerbate it, Maggie comes over to the desk and scans the photos. I watch her. When she gets to Kamau's photos, she stops. She gazes at them, holding her breath. There's a new tension in the room now and the tension between us has dissipated. Finally she turns and looks at me. There are tears in her eyes.

"Oh, Tommy! How awful!" She comes to me and we embrace.

Suddenly there are tears in my eyes, too. I wipe them away and she pulls back to look at me. She gives me the comforting kiss of a friend.

"She really was beautiful, wasn't she?"

I nod. "And intelligent. And often funny. And devious. Willful. Manipulative. Selfish. Intriguing. And married."

"I'm so sorry," Maggie says. She embraces me again.

"A bitch. But what a bitch!" I try to laugh, but I cannot.

"Maybe we should have some dinner, after all," Maggie says.

—◆—

At dinner Maggie tells me about an affair of hers. On her first flying job she and a fellow pilot fell in love. She lived with him secretly, not telling her parents.

They got engaged, then a week before the wedding he disappeared for three days. When he re-emerged, he broke the engagement. His rejection deeply humiliated her. "You were probably lucky," I tell her. She nods.

But to cancel the church, the reception, the band, the caterer. Telephoning the guests, some of whom had already arrived from out of town. Returning the presents. She acknowledges that she lost confidence in herself. She did not date men for more than a year.

"You will get over it," she assures me. "I wasn't sure I could. But I did."

"It's not anything I have to get over," I say. She does not believe me. And, of course, the circumstances of Joss's death will always haunt me. I explain that, in fact, I was only one in a string of lovers. "The man she hated was the man she really loved."

"Be glad she wouldn't leave him for you."

I remind her that it's likely I'm Pepper's father. That leads to a discussion of how to rescue her, how to expose Hazen and Not-Joss. All the ideas we explore are impractical and, by the time we've finished a bottle of wine, our notions are so ludicrous that we're laughing. We end up back in her room lying side by side on her bed, holding each other, fully clothed once again, and staring at the ceiling.

Finally I say, "I think we should get married." Maggie pulls away from me and shakes her head. "I'm not seeking a mother for Pepper," I assure her. "I want to anchor my life— Somehow." I stop. Why is it so hard to say what I feel?

"Being Pepper's mother doesn't scare me," Maggie says at last.

"I'm really not—"

Maggie raises a hand to quiet me. "Let me tell you something," she says. She explains that shortly before the wedding that never happened she discovered she was pregnant. A lovely surprise, she thought. She wanted a family and was ready to start one. On learning the news, the fiancé was quiet at first, then laughed ironically. "Many fine families start this way," he said. But he did not embrace or kiss her. Two days later he disappeared.

"I was frantic with worry," Maggie says. "Then he came back and called off the wedding. I got terribly sick." I pull her to me and kiss her forehead. Finally, answering my unasked question, she says, "I miscarried." Tears form in her eyes.

I embrace her and kiss her. "Don't cry," I tell her. "I'm here and I love you." As I hold her, staring at the ceiling of the room, my journalist's skepticism tiptoes across my mind. I banish it. I am not going there. Maggie moves out of our embrace. She sits up and wipes away her tears.

Gently I pull her down beside me again. "We're going to be okay," I say. I tell her I did a lot of thinking in Nairobi. I tried to come to terms with my recklessness, a trait I've cherished in myself. Now maybe it's time to bring it under control. I knew that recklessness was why I'd gotten involved with Joss. It had led me to enter Hazen's residence like a common thief. To enter the Colonial Club's ladies lounge.

Because of it I had flouted Banda's interview rules; I wondered if my doing that had truly set back Hazen's quest to get Banda to trust democracy. I wondered in Nairobi if my story about the leopard-man murders might really play a part in determining whether Malawi received a US aid package for the Lilongwe development project. I do not want my coverage to impact the lives of Africans negatively. I wish my coverage could give my American readers a sense of compassion for Africans. Writing exotica stories to titillate readers makes them feel superior to less fortunate people. That is not the career I want. I say that my life needs to get anchored. Maggie admits she has thought the same about hers.

"Then knowing Joss was dead," I say. "That seemed to open up a whole new period in my life. I think I want to be anchored by a family."

Maggie rises again and sits on the end of the bed. She gazes at the photos still lined up on the desk across the room.

"What I feel for you," I say, "is good, strong. Not the destructive passion I felt for Joss." She does not reply. I ask, "Is this just a fling for you?"

She lies down quietly beside me and whispers, "No." After a moment she adds, "And if Pepper needs a mother, I'm up for that."

At the end of the next week we fly back to Johannesburg. Before we have a chance to change our minds, we have a magistrate marry us.

When we arrive back at the house from seeing the judge, the telephone is ringing. When I answer, the voice says, "Thank God, I've gotten you at last." It's Kay Kittredge calling from Blantyre. "The ambassador and his wife are taking the kid to South Africa next week. There's a clinic they've heard about in Durban. Remember my dream? I thought you'd want to know."

Chapter Fifteen

I n a Cessna for which Clive has no scheduled charters, Maggie flies us 950 miles north of Johannesburg and brings us down low over Lake Malawi, sparkling in the morning sun. We land at Salima, a lakeside town. Bakili waits for us in his VW bug. As we scramble out of the plane, he announces, "We must get to Blantyre, my friend. Kamuzu's called some kind of demonstration. That's unheard of!" We jump into the bug and race to Blantyre.

As we pass villages set among the small mountains that rise like cones out of the green land, Bakili—quite unexpectedly—sings the praises of Maxwell Hazen. "At night he turns into a sorcerer, I think," Bakili laughs. "Maybe even a lion." Bakili holds down the car horn. Children scurry to the roadsides. Women walking with bundles on their heads stop to watch us pass. "I'll take you to the demonstration. You'll see what he's done."

We leave Maggie with Beryl at Bakili's house and hurry to the center of town. When we arrive there, Bakili parks the car on a side street and hands me a broad-brimmed safari hat. "Wear this," he commands. "Pull it down over your face. Remember: You're persona non grata in this country." I pull the hat low over my eyes. "My friend," Bakili groans, "you will never make a white hunter."

Outside the Central Police Station a huge rally is in progress. People mill in the street. Drums sound. Hawkers sell food. Marchers form a makeshift parade and shuffle along, the more energetic dancing, their bodies shiny with sweat. They circle drummers who pound out mesmerizing rhythms. Some members of the crowd wear the colors of Banda's party and carry posters with his picture. Others, dressed in Musopole's colors, tote posters with the portrait of him; I saw at his office one in which he sought to look both like a statesman and a paramount chief. Others posters say, "Find the leopard!" "Give Us Jobs!" "All Malawians Hail Kamuzu!" "Arrest the murderer!" They are in English due to a possibility of international TV. A contingent of school children marches with a banner that says, "We love Kamuzu!"

Bakili moves along the edge of the crowd. I follow him. We take places against a bank building across from the police station. Bakili nudges me and cocks his head. In a second-story window of the police station I see the diminutive President acknowledging the adoration of the masses. A couple of paces behind him stand Hazen, Foresta, and Sykes, all in sunglasses. Off to one side, careful not to upstage the President, is Charles Makanga Musopole. I ask Bakili, "Why's Muso up there with Banda and the US embassy?"

"He's joining the government," Bakili tells me. "The crisis is over."

"Over?"

"Your friend Hazen who got you deported, he palavered those two into a settlement. I told you: he must be a sorcerer."

"What about the leopard-man?"

"The murders will stop."

"Does the crowd know that?"

"Just wait."

Members of the crowd continue to dance. Some clap their hands to the basic drumbeat; others twirl about, raising and lowering their signs. School children begin to shout, "Kamuzu! Kamuzu!" Banda moves to the rhythm of this shouting. Others in the crowd take it up.

Far away a siren screeches. Bakili nudges me and nods. The paraders continue to move. The drummers play on. As the siren approaches, the crowd falls silent. A police van arrives at the edge of the crowd. Slowly it moves among the people. They have now fallen silent. They push against one another to let the van approach. It arrives at the police station, its siren blaring. The siren cuts off. An ominous silence fills the street. Policemen leave the van.

I glance up at the window across the road.

Musopole now stands beside Banda. Hazen, Sykes, and Foresta have moved forward to watch a drama that has clearly been staged. I glance at Bakili. He's too caught up to look at me.

Policemen open the van's rear doors. They reach inside and pull from the van what at first seems a pile of rags. In fact, it's a man. He has been so brutally beaten that he's half dead. He cannot stand. The crowd cranes its neck to see him. Its silence deepens. A policeman pulls from the van a leopard mask with a cloth hood attached. The silence intensifies. Then a murmur starts. It moves through the crowd. Someone spits at the beaten man. Men burst from the crowd to kick him.

Police push them back with truncheons. Crowd leaders shout, "Kamuzu! Kamuzu!" The crowd quickly takes up the chant. It is mesmerizing, deafening. Policemen drag the broken man inside the station.

Once again Bakili nudges me. "Let's go. I've got to write this up."

We push through chanting bystanders, duck around the edge of a building, and start for the car. "That's not the leopard-man," I shout at Bakili. He ignores me, hurrying along. He moves into an alley. I follow him. We walk fast. When I get up beside him, I say again, "That's not the leopard-man."

Bakili shrugs. "Of course not." I stop walking.

Bakili asks, "That surprises you?" He looks at me, baffled. "The President would have insisted on someone to show off as the killer." He starts moving again. I catch up with him.

"So who is he?"

"A village misfit. Musopole got him."

"Got him from whom?"

"A chief somewhere owed him a favor." Again I stop walking. Bakili pauses for a moment; gestures me to follow and starts moving again. He says, "The man is a symbol that order's been restored."

"And that's okay with people? That they haven't got the actual killer?"

Bakili stops walking. He regards me with astonishment. "How long are you in Africa, my friend? The killings were a way for the President and Musopole to talk to one another. They will stop now. That's what people want."

"But the police beat him. They almost killed him."

Bakili looks surprised at this remark. "He must be beaten," he says. "As an example."

"And that's it? Justice done."

"That's it. The killings stop."

Bakili resumes hurrying along. I follow behind. "And Hazen negotiated all that?"

"What a service to our country. The man's a lion."

As we hurry along, a huge cheer rises from the crowd.

After nightfall Maggie and I drive out to the Hazen residence. When I near the house, I turn off the headlights and proceed slowly up the murram road where I left the Land Cruiser the day I snuck into the house. I park it so that we can leave, if we must, at top speed. Maggie and I are dressed entirely in black.

Maggie wears a black skullcap with her hair tucked up inside it. We have also blackened our faces. The only thing that shows in them is our teeth and the whites of our eyes. Under one arm Maggie carries a thick blanket bought in a store in the heart of Johannesburg where people go to outfit their night watchmen. Grasped under the other arm is the garment she has sewn me out of African mammy cloth bought in Bazaar Street in Nairobi. I carry a hammer, a flashlight and a wooden crate sturdy enough to support our weight.

The house sits on a rise of land. As we approach it, we see the night watchman sitting under the tree before his small fire. Behind him a Chevrolet station wagon is parked. The Hazens have guests.

We skirt the stucco wall that surrounds the house until we are behind it. At a likely spot well away from the watchman's post I set the wooden crate beside the wall, stand on the box and hammer down as best I can the glass shards stuck along the top of the wall. I take the blanket from Maggie. I fold it several thicknesses and place it over what remains of the shards meant to discourage people like us. I hoist myself up and jump down on the other side. Maggie tosses the garment to me and follows me over the wall. I pull the blanket off and tuck it under my arm. Now that we are safely on the residence grounds, we move stealthily toward the private living quarters wing. We are careful to move soundlessly, keeping away from the watchman. In the darkness we are all but invisible. Even so, the tension we feel puts a tension into the atmosphere. The watchman senses it and rises. Still well away from the house, we watch him move cautiously out of the warmth of the fire. We fall to the ground. The watchman turns on his flashlight and shines it about ostentatiously enough for Hazen and his guests to know that he's doing his job. I wonder what the watchman will do when the time comes. He has a panga, no gun. Every watchman I've known would run. Is this one different? He goes back to the fire and sits down.

Maggie and I rise and hurry noiselessly to the far end of the house where Pepper's room is located. We move to the door with glass panes that opens into her room. Maggie holds the blanket over the glass panes and I strike a single blow on a pane near the door handle. The glass cracks, the sound largely muffled by the blanket. We pause to listen. I crawl far enough out into the yard to check on the watchman. Either he has not heard the window breaking or has decided not to investigate. In a crouch I scurry back to Pepper's door. I push against the broken glass with the handle of the hammer and work enough of it out so that I can put my hand on the door handle inside. I unlock and open the door. We enter soundlessly and tiptoe toward the bed.

"Pepper?" I whisper.

I run the flashlight over the bed and pull open the mosquito net. I direct the light above the child's head so as not to blind her. She gazes at me—whom she can barely see—with a strange equanimity. It's as if she has seen so many curious goings-on since arriving in Malawi that my appearance does not push her deeper into confusion.

"I promised that I'd come back," I tell her. "Remember?"

She continues to gaze at me, saying nothing.

I turn the flashlight on myself and explain that I have blackened my face for a masquerade. "Do you remember me now?" She says nothing. "When I came before, I said I had lunch once at your house in Rabat. You showed me the kittens that had just been born."

She whispers the word "kittens" as if it were magic and smiles.

"Do you still have your mother's picture?"

She nods. I introduce Maggie and tell Pepper that we have come to take her to a place where she'll be safe. "Will I see my Mommy?" she asks.

"We'll tell you about your mother just as soon as you're safe." Then I ask, "Do you want to see my masquerade costume?" Maggie opens the cloak and pants she has sewn me. They're of mammy cloth with a leopard skin pattern. I put on the pants and belt them tight so that the leopard tail curls up behind me. I have Maggie bathe me in the flashlight's beam. I sashay around, showing off the tail. Pepper giggles. With Maggie's help I slide my arms into the sleeves of the cloak and my hands into the leather work gloves fitted with razor blade claws. Maggie pulls the cloak over my head, adjusts it about my body and around the tail. She fits the hood over my head and the mask over my face. The mask has large eyeholes rimmed in a frightening red. Its pointed teeth drip blood of the same color. Once the cloak is on, Maggie again splashes light onto me. I move beside the bed and whisper, "Have you heard of the leopard-man,

Pepper?" She watches me with wide eyes. "Tonight I am the leopard-man!" I emit a couple of comical meows. Pepper giggles. I move about the room in a crouch, meowing. Maggie holds the beam of the flashlight on me. Pepper's laughter encourages me. I tell her I am off to the masquerade and, being careful of the razor claws, give Maggie's hand a squeeze. I move into the hallway and close the door behind me.

The plan's very craziness is what makes me confident it will work. All it needs to do is create a diversion. The surprise should do that. If the men were military, the plan might fail. But diplomats don't put their bodies in jeopardy. Two minutes of confusion is all we need.

I wait for some moments in the darkness, allowing my eyes to grow accustomed to the surroundings. I move along the hallway in a crouch. It's a movement I've practiced for several days, awkward and ungainly, but I'll need it for no more than thirty feet.

Once I'm ready, I make my way out of the hall. My heart is pounding so loudly that I'm sure it can be heard. I drop down to the floor. I enter the large living room, crawling on my knees. As I crouch behind a chair, my back flushes cold with a sudden fear that something will go terribly wrong. I take control of myself the way Hazen himself might. Peeking around a chair arm I see the Hazens seated at a card table with Roy and Dina Foresta. Behind the ambassador is a door leading outside. Between them and me lies an arrangement of sofas facing an immense fireplace.

Crawling close to the floor I move behind a sofa. From it to the card players will require a short run. As I settle behind the sofa, I hear the two couples discussing the leopard man's capture.

"Musopole told me what needed to happen to make the killings stop," Hazen says. "I passed that along to Kamuzu. I encouraged him to consider the palavers of the old days when every elder had his say under the big tree."

"Your facility with Africans is simply amazing," says Foresta.

"Well, I've kicked around a bit. Kamuzu bringing Musopole into the government was a case of letting him under the big tree."

"What's amazing," corrects Not-Joss, "is Max himself."

"When I got back to Musopole," says Hazen, "he promised me the murders would stop." An astonished exclamation from Hazen. "Musopole even provided the leopard-man! One of his chiefs had a troublemaker to get rid of."

Dina Foresta deals the table another hand of bridge. As the bidding starts, I hear the watchman come to the door. Again the cold wash of fear along my back. The watchman begs the ambassador's attention.

"Bwana! Bwana!" he calls, then chatters away in words I can't make out. Has he discovered the broken glass on Pepper's door?

I hear Hazen ask, "What are you saying? A leopard?" I glance around the end of the sofa. Hazen stands at the door. Foresta comes beside him. He leans toward the man. He speaks with excessive slowness and very loudly as if anyone who does not speak English must be mentally retarded.

"In the yard?" bellows Foresta. "You mean: In. This. Yard?"

"It's some kind of joke," says Not-Joss from her wheelchair. "Tell him you got the leopard-man business all resolved."

"I'll go check," says Foresta. He disappears outside.

"You should have Marine guards out here," says Dina.

Hazen opens his wallet and withdraws some bills.

"Not too much, Max," advises Not-Joss. "He'll be drinking. He probably has been."

I observe Hazen hand the watchman the bills. The man is baffled. He is trying to warn of danger and Hazen pays no attention. Hazen presses the bills on the watchman and tries some Swahili. "Hakuna chui."

Hazen shows the man the door. "No leopard tonight," he tells him. "Leopard all finished now." The watchman disappears. Hazen returns to the table and touches the shoulder of Not-Joss with an ambassadorial smile of confidence. Dina is mollified as well. She freshens ice and drinks from bottles on a drinks tray.

Foresta returns. "Nothing out there," he says. "Everyone has a grievance against America,"

Not-Joss contends. "So why not the leopard-man, too?"

They laugh at this. The men return to their seats. I watch the card players pick up their hands. "Africans have the oddest way of working things out!" Not-Joss exclaims.

"But they do work them out," says Hazen. "That's the important thing. Where were we?" The card players return to bidding their hands. I crawl closer, only half-hidden now by furniture.

Watching the quartet, I sense the alertness of Not-Joss.

She listens, shushes the others. They all listen to the silence. Not-Joss puts down her hand. The others watch her, surprised. "Something's in the room," she says.

Again my back goes cold. Am I caught? I lie very still. Not-Joss looks behind her. She points at me. "There! See it."

They all look toward me. I rise in a crouch. I race forward, screaming a guttural cry. Foresta pushes back. He offers me a straight path to Hazen. I dive onto the table, my leopard pelt and mask there to terrify them. I slide into Hazen. He tries to escape. I grab the lapels of his jacket with my claws. He cries out. I rake my claws down his front. My claws slice his clothes. He screams, terrified.

I turn to the others, hissing, pawing the air with my claws. I circle toward them. I overturn the table onto Hazen. "Do something!" screams Not-Joss, stuck in her wheelchair. I move toward her, pawing the air before her, hissing so vehemently that my saliva flies into her face. "Do something!" she cries again. Dina holds Foresta back. He stands before her, shielding her.

I turn back toward Hazen. He scrambles to his feet. He's terrified. He rushes outside. I reach for the drinks tray. There's a plate of fruit on it. I grab the fruit knife. I topple the tray and brandish the fruit knife under the nose of Not-Joss. "Do something!" she screams. I hiss and paw and dance before her. Suddenly she jumps out of her wheelchair. What? I retreat. She rushes at me.

I flee, thinking: She can walk! The bitch walks! She was faking! Outside I stalk Hazen. He's circling about the yard in a panic. Not-Joss charges outside. I corner Hazen, seize him. Not-Joss screams, "Watchman! Watchman!" But he's run off.

I lift Hazen off his feet. I rush him against a tree. Hitting it, he grunts and crumples. He groans. Not-Joss scurries toward us. She shrieks, "Get him! Get him!" But the Forestas are immobile at the doorway. Hazen whimpers.

I rush away. Not-Joss crouches beside Hazen. I throw off the leopard cloak and mask. Fleeing in the darkness, I hear Hazen squeak weakly, "You walked!" Not-Joss shrills, "Oh, my god!" She realizes what the Forestas will suspect. "I walked!" she exclaims. "I walked! It's a miracle!"

I circle behind the house. At Pepper's door Maggie awaits me. Pepper is in her arms. She transfers the child to me. "Let's go," I say. We hurry across the yard. The front gate is open. The watchman must have fled through it. We hurry that way.

We rush through the open gate. We make our way to the car. Maggie slides into the passenger seat. I put Pepper onto her lap. I drive slowly away from the residence, without headlights. I try to control my trembling. "You okay?" Maggie asks. I say nothing.

Before we encounter traffic, I turn the headlights on. Now Maggie can see. She realizes that I'm shaky. She stares at me, astonished. She holds Pepper against her. "You told me there was nothing to worry about," she says. "Why're you shaking?"

"I may piss my pants."

She laughs and corks my shoulder. I pull to the side of the road, grip the steering wheel tightly, and let the trembles rip. The steering wheel shakes. Maggie sings a lullaby to Pepper who watches me with wide eyes. I jump out of the car, pull off my leopard trousers and leave them by the roadside.

We get back to Salima after midnight. Pepper has been asleep on Maggie's lap and we put her to bed without waking her. I lay my palm across her forehead. She's not feverish. Maggie and I wash the blackening from our faces and our bodies. She grabs sleep while I keep watch over Pepper.

At first light we are back at the plane. With only a banana for breakfast, Pepper's chipper as I strap her into her window seat. I make sure the door is firmly locked. Pepper watches Maggie at the controls. As the plane moves us into position for takeoff, Pepper presses her forehead against the window. We hurtle down the runway. Pepper wraps her arms around mine and grins at me. I say, "We're off!" Pepper repeats the words. Maggie lifts the plane into the dawn. Pepper peers below us at the deep blue of the lake as Malawi recedes behind us.

Chapter Sixteen

As I drive us home from the airport, Pepper sits with Maggie on the rear seat. She moves from one side of the car to the other, watching the city move past. She is all energy. I wonder: Is this normal for a child? Or a manifestation of illness? I realize I know nothing about children. I haven't been around them in years.

When we arrive at the house after stopping to buy clothes for Pepper from the skin out, she is yawning. She explores the house, like a wind-up toy that needs rewinding. She ends up in the room we've prepared for her. Maggie opens the bed. Pepper crawls in. I cover her with a blanket. Soon she's peacefully asleep. I look down at this bundle of flesh and bone, intelligence and imagination, feeling strangely paternal. For a moment her eyes open only enough for us to see the bottom half-circles of her pupils. Then they close. Her lips draw back in—is it a smile? Or the beginning of a whimper? I'm not sure which.

A loveseat stands across the room below a window that overlooks the garden. I take Maggie's hand and lead her to it. "Let's sit with her a while," I say. I sit and pull her down beside me. For a time we say nothing, listening to the muted rise and fall of an eight-year-old girl's breathing. My daughter. Our daughter. Hardly more than two weeks ago I assured Clive that Maggie and I were just two Americans in somebody else's country, too young for serious. Amazing.

Maggie and I talk in whispers about Pepper's future. First, we must get a doctor in here to help us put her on the path to recovery. Next, we'll need to get her more clothes and items for kids that we know nothing about: books, toys, goodies. Down the line we'll have to find other children for her to play with. And a school.

What do we tell her about who we are? And about her parents? We agree never to bad-mouth either Hazen or Joss. We decide to tell friends that Pepper is my sister's child; she's come to live with us for a while. Eventually we will say we've adopted her. Obviously it's best to keep the true story to ourselves. As for what we tell Pepper, that's something we'll have to take a day at a time. We sit together, whispering, sometimes just holding one another.

Eventually I go to my office to check the mail. I return to her room with reading to catch up on. By dinner she has not wakened. Maggie and I decide to let her sleep. After a quick supper I return to the loveseat to keep watch. Pepper sleeps on, lightly snoring. I watch till almost midnight, then join Maggie.

When she and I tiptoe into Pepper's room the next morning, she is kneeling on the loveseat watching Zakes, the gardener, mow the back lawn. We greet her, pleased that she's up. She glances at us, then returns to looking out the window as if to avoid dealing with strangers. Maggie carries a breakfast tray. I have a stand on which she can set it so that Pepper can eat in bed.

We invite her to return to bed. She does this obediently, but without looking at us. Maggie and I wonder. Is this going to be more complicated than we hoped?

"Can you eat this?" Maggie asks. She offers Pepper a bowl of what my mother always served me when I was sick: bread chunks in warm milk. She eats—dutifully at first, then with some appetite—and things seem better.

I explain to her once again that she is in Johannesburg in South Africa. Maggie assures her that she will get well here, staying with us.

"Is my Mommy here?" Pepper asks, risking a look at us. "I want to see my Mom." Maggie and I exchange another look. Pepper reads us immediately. "She's not here, is she?" Pepper looks back at her food. She acknowledges sadly, "She goes away a lot."

"Would you like something more to eat?" Maggie asks when she finishes. "You did a very good job on the bread and milk."

"Do you have toast?" Pepper asks. "And grape jelly? Grape jelly is my favorite."

"Comin' right up!" announces Maggie. She grins at me because grape jelly is also a favorite of mine. It must be in the genes.

"You have to tell us all your favorite foods," I say. I kneel beside the bed so that I'm at her level.

She glances over at me. "That lady in Malawi, who wanted people to think she was my Mom . . . Who is she?"

"We don't know. What we know is that you're here and you're safe. And you're going to get well."

"I would get better," the girl says. "Then I'd get sick again."

"You're going to stay well here."

At that news Pepper risks a smile. Her eyes soften and for just a moment I see Joss in them. "Is my father here?" I shake my head. "Sometimes he is good to me," she says. "And sometimes he's mean. When he's angry, he says I'm not his little girl. Who's little girl am I then?"

"How about being my little girl? Our little girl? Maggie and I have no children and we would love to have you stay with us." The child nods, but she's uncertain. "One of these days, Pep, we'll talk about your father. It's a complicated story." We look at one another. I smile at her. "It's so good to have you here!" I say. She smiles as if my enthusiasm were a little silly. "Just get well now, okay?"

Maggie appears with buttered toast, thickly spread with grape jelly. She's pleased to see us talking, me on the floor. When I take the bread and milk bowl from her tray, Pepper reaches up and hugs me.

The day of our return to Joburg I check both the English-language and the Afrikaans-language press to see how they're covering the kidnapping of the American ambassador's daughter in Blantyre. It's a big story, strong on human interest, since the nightmare that haunts all white parents in apartheid South Africa is a revolt of Africans that might include their children being kidnapped or murdered. But it's a big story only if someone tells it. So far no reporter has unearthed it. There is not a word about the matter in the papers.

There can be only one explanation for that: the embassy in Malawi is sitting on the story. Hazen's overriding desire will be to discourage scrutiny of his family and personal life. And so he will have justified this embargo as a way to facilitate contact with the kidnappers. Out of a reluctance to give American enemies any ideas, the State Department must have approved this strategy. But State must dramatize its commitment to the safety of its officers and their families overseas. So it will certainly have begun an investigation by CIA, security, and possibly even law enforcement agencies. The fact that Malawi is a never-heard-of-it, end-of-the-world place means that few media people are likely to stumble on the story.

After a week without a scrap of coverage, I telephone Bill Sykes in Blantyre, ostensibly to check on a report in the Johannesburg Star that the leopard-man killer has been arrested. I explain that, if the report is factual, I'll do a follow-up piece for the Big Guy. It will detail the upbeat ending of a downbeat story. "Hazen thinks my paper and I are interested only in publishing negative pieces about Africa," I tell Sykes. "That's just not the case. Malawi deserves to have the upbeat ending published." Sykes gives me the Malawi government line, never mentioning that Makanga Musopole has joined the Banda government and the connection with the so-called leopard-man's arrest. He suggests that I check his information with the flack van der Merwe.

As we conclude our conversation, I note that I've heard a crazy rumor that Ambassador Hazen's daughter has been kidnapped. "Can you confirm or deny it for me, Bill?"

Sykes says that he never deals with rumors.

When you're the spokesman for an American embassy, he tells me, there are so many rumors flying around— about CIA shenanigans, illegal payments, and even sexual peccadillos—that he has learned never to offer comment on rumors.

"Speaking of sexual peccadillos," Sykes says, "whatever happened between you and Mrs. Hazen at the Colonial Club? She contends you tried to rape her." Sykes assures me that he does not find the accusation credible. Mrs. Hazen is, after all, a cripple and he met my girlfriend at the Mount Soche. "What actually happened there, Craig?"

"I don't dignify rumors either," I reply. "People will go to great lengths to discredit a journalist, but that charge takes the cake. And furthermore," I say, "that 'girlfriend' is my wife."

Sykes says he's heard—from his pal Kay Kittredge, I assume—that Mrs. Hazen lived quite a wild life at other posts. Would I know anything about that? I don't dignify rumors, I repeat, especially ones I know nothing about.

Once I get off the line with Sykes, I phone Kay. She knows immediately why I've called. She says she needs to get to a secure line—which undoubtedly means someplace outside the embassy—where she can talk off the record. "It's got to be off the record," she stresses.

—⋘—

"I've got retirement to consider." She returns the call half an hour later, telling me that she's at a pay phone at the Mount Soche Hotel. She gives me the number and I call her right back. "That poor child," she says, confirming the kidnapping. "What a miserable life she led! She's dead by now. We all know it. Those savages who took her have probably cut her body into little pieces to use as magic charms. Sometimes Africa can be so cruel!"

I ask if there are any leads in the case. Has any group claimed responsibility? Has anyone demanded ransom? Kay says she has no information about any of it. Hazen and the security people, she says, "don't tell nobody nuthin'." When I ask how Mrs. Hazen reacted to the kidnapping, Kay says, "That Lady MacBeth!"

She's gone into seclusion. 'Unable to face the anguish,' they say. I'm sure Hazen insisted. The talk is: she's always sedated these days. That means she doesn't have to answer any questions. They're a very tricky pair, those two!"

I've got enough leads from sources to pursue the story. Or at least to tip off the Big Guy's man at the State Department about it. But I have as much reason as Hazen to keep it hidden and hope no one stumbles on it. I do nothing about it.

—⅏—

Pepper begins to settle in. She explores the house and garden. She putters with me in the flower beds. She gets to know Zakes, the gardener who comes three days a week, and Matilda, who has done cooking and housework for us in the mornings, but now begins to come all day every weekday. Maggie and I make sure Pepper is never alone in the house. I start to write stories there; previously I have done them in a small office I maintain in town. Maggie and I cut down on trips away from Johannesburg. We make certain we are never gone at the same time. Pepper's health improves. She begins to trust us, to smile, for example, when we come upon her unexpectedly. She hugs us after we say prayers at bedtime and seems happy to have us kiss her goodnight.

We school her in the story we've concocted about her being my sister's child who's on an extended visit. Of course, she recognizes the story as a fabrication, a lie. We do not discuss the necessity for it. Pepper seems to understand that if we have done right in rescuing her—and I'm sure this is what she believes—we have also done wrong in the eyes of the law. We do not talk about her parents. That's a subject we will have to talk about at some point, but we will let her bring it up. She doesn't. I come to feel certain that she senses that her mother will always be absent—that "she goes away a lot"—and that the absence results from something done by her father and the woman pretending to be her mother. Now and then I catch her looking off into space with eyes of unspeakable loneliness and sorrow that I want more than anything to see sparkling with happiness. There is nothing Maggie and I can do to make those eyes brighten other than to love Pepper and win her trust for that love. Occasionally she calls us Mom and Dad and I tell myself that we are making progress.

—⚏—

One afternoon hurrying along in a section of fashionable stores I glance ahead of me on the sidewalk and stop dead in my tracks. Walking toward me on well-shaped legs, her hips rolling, her feet in high-heeled shoes, is a woman I'm accustomed to seeing in a wheelchair. Valerie Bennett. She's been in the stores, totes a shopping bag, and has her arms full of parcels.

She strides along in a gait that reflects the ready-for-life vitality in her face. Clearly she enjoys the glances of men whose necks turn as she passes by. I step out of the flow of pedestrians and watch her. I'm amazed and amused at her audacity.

She catches sight of me. She hesitates, then hurries to the curb and into the street to avoid me. As she darts across it, dodging through traffic, she drops a package. I hurry into the street and retrieve it. When I catch up with her on the opposite sidewalk, her expression is apprehensive.

"Mrs. Hazen!" I say.

"Don't come near me! Not after what you did to me!" She reaches out for her package and I withhold it.

"What I did was unpardonable," I say. Looking at her, I can't help being affected by the transformation. A woman I'd seen as mousy and damaged is now beautiful, sensual, sexual. I can understand Hazen's fascination. "I apologize."

Now that she sees me responding to her as a man does to a woman, she's confident that she'll retrieve her package. She becomes almost flirtatious. "You didn't expect to find that tattoo, did you?"

"I had to be sure."

"You thought of all my lovers, I'd remember you." She smiles disdainfully. "Didn't you?" I shrug. "And if I didn't remember you, I must be an impostor. That's what you thought, isn't it?"

"I plead guilty."

She beholds me, wondering what kind of a lover I'd be. "Were we so good together?" she asks.

"You're the best I've ever had."

Now she wonders if Joss was really so accomplished. And reminds herself that flirtations with skeptics like me are ill-advised. "That's all a thing of the past. I must fly."

I do not relinquish the package. "You've regained the use of your legs. How fantastic! How astonishing!"

"I did something I never thought I'd do, not in a million years," she confesses. She will keep talking in order to get the package. "But I wanted to walk again." She pauses, anticipating the astonishment she will see in my face. "I consulted a native healer."

I do not disappoint her. "You what?"

"Yes. Out in Soweto. He had a shop in a shed, full of the most stomach-wrenching items: dead snakes, monkey skins, dried leaves, pulverized seeds."

"What happened?"

"He concocted a potion for me." She enjoys lying to me; I enjoy watching her do it. "I didn't dare inquire what was in it. I just forced it down my throat."

"Really? I can't believe this."

"On the way back into town I thought I'd die. But the next morning I could walk. That was yesterday." She smiles charmingly. "I really must fly!"

"I ought to do a story on that," I say, fishing my notebook out of my pocket. "What's the man's name?"

She laughs. "Can't spell his name. It's Zulu, I think. Can't even pronounce it. And I'm not sure he'd want publicity. I must run." She takes the package from my hands and starts away.

"How's Pepper?" I ask.

"Gone to the States," she says, turning back for a moment. "To live with Max's mother."

"Good," I say. "I'm sure that's where she belongs."

Watching her regain the seductive, hip-rolling gait, so full of undamaged freedom, I recall what Musopole said of her. The guy has an eye. I'm certain now there never was an accident. That was all pretense designed to secure the sympathy of the embassy staff. I follow her. She makes me think of Joss: her boldness and audacity, her sexiness and readiness to flirt. Trailing behind her, I think how useful it would be to know more about her: where she stays in South Africa, the name she uses when she's here. But I'm not adept at tailing people and she manages to lose me.

Back at home I'm determined to call every decent hotel for whites in the city. This is to satisfy my own curiosity for there's no action I can take against her. At the city's finest luxury hotel, the President, a guest is registered under the name of Valerie Bennett.

—◆◆◆—

By the time Pepper has been with us for six months, we have got her in school. She goes off every morning on her bike in her school uniform and comes home using the latest South African slang, some of it in Afrikaans, the nuances of which neither we nor she really understand. Maggie and I are beginning to feel like a real married couple. I am putting on a little of the weight that signals settledness and contentment, and our regard for each other is deepening to the extent that we can foresee a time when we will feel that we have always been married to one another. We think with ever less frequency of former lovers.

I learn that the Deputy Secretary of State for Africa will host a meeting in Lusaka, the Zambian capital, for all American ambassadors serving in southern Africa. There's no story in this meeting for me and I have always found Lusaka a difficult place to work. But I need to get up to neighboring Rhodesia.

White settlers there have unilaterally declared their independence from Britain and trade sanctions are hampering the economy. If I can find the right contacts, I can turn the settlers' efforts to smuggle basics into the country in defiance of sanctions into interesting Sunday morning reading.

But the real reason to go to Lusaka is to have a chat with Maxwell Hazen.

Since this is the reason for the trip, Maggie and I agree on the wisdom of getting Pepper away from our house in Joburg. Hazen may realize that we have the girl. We must hide her someplace where police cannot easily find her. The three of us fly down to Cape Town and take a cottage overlooking the beach at nearby Camps Bay. We plan excursions—to the Cape of Good Hope, to the top of Table Mountain, to Franschhoek and Stellenbosch and the nearby vineyards. Once the women of the family launch these excursions, I slip off to Lusaka.

The American ambassadors are lodged at the Lusaka Inter-Continental. I stay at the less prestigious Ridgway. On the first night of the meeting I strike up a conversation in the Inter-Continental bar with a couple of Americans from the embassy. One is a security specialist in from Washington on hand to keep the Deputy Secretary and the ambassadors safe. The other is a young political officer, a woman in her second overseas assignment. The security guy is trying hard to charm her. Since she's not interested, she's happy to chat with a staffer from a do-gooder non-governmental organization who's taking a look at anti-apartheid guerrilla groups.

"Have you been to Rhodesia?" she asks me.

"I go there next."

"Lucky you," she says. "I'd love to see Victoria Falls from the Rhodesian side. But since UDI, it's strictly a no-no for American diplomats to enter Rhodesia." She lowers her voice. "Unless you've made ambassador."

"What's that mean?" asks the security guy. "They going over?"

"Four of them," the young woman says. "Friday night. Once the meetings are over. I made reservations at the Victoria Falls Hotel this afternoon."

"Our detail's not going," says the security guy. "All we need is to get picked up down there carrying."

"It's a boys-will-be-boys deal," says the woman. "That's no fun with guards."

I cross over into Rhodesia the next morning. In Vic Falls I take a room at the Ilala Lodge, but hang around that grand monument to colonialism, the Victoria Falls Hotel. It does not seem to be suffering from sanctions. On Friday evening sitting in the hotel bar, I catch sight of Maxwell Hazen. He's in the sedate hotel drawing room relaxing below larger-than-life-size portraits of King George V and Queen Mary, drinking post-dinner liqueurs with his three boys-will-be-boys colleagues. Sitting at the bar, watching him, I'm able to telephone him. A waiter delivers a telephone to Hazen, attached to a long cord. Hazen reacts with surprise. No one is supposed to know he's here.

"Hello?" He speaks softly into the receiver.

"Mr. Ambassador," I say. "Tom Craig here."

Hazen glances about in confusion. How do I know he's here? He does a quick survey of the room, wondering if someone is watching him as indeed I am. "Welcome to Victoria Falls," I say. "Have your meetings gone well?"

Hazen mutters excuses to his colleagues and rises. He takes the phone from the waiter and moves out of earshot of his associates.

"I wonder if we could have a chat?" I say.

"I'm afraid not, Craig. The Deputy Secretary is running us ragged."

"The Secretary's in Lusaka. What about right now?"

"Are you in Victoria Falls?"

"I'm in the hotel. I'm looking at you." Hazen glances about the drawing room, but he sees no one who resembles me. "You're standing in the drawing room," I say. "George V could give you a kick if he were alive."

This assertion unnerves Hazen. He makes a full circle, hunting for me. His colleagues watch his befuddlement. Hazen realizes finally that I'm in the bar. He peers in its direction. I wave. He stands erect and turns his back on his associates.

"I'd like to talk to you about your wife," I say. "About her condition."

"After what you did to my wife, I should have sent hit men after you."

"Your late wife, sir. She and I were lovers. I'm not sure you knew that." Hazen turns to look at me, his expression furious at first, then a little frightened. "I have a deal to propose."

Hazen turns his back again on his colleagues. "No deals. I could have you arrested."

I whisper into the receiver. "You can talk to me. Or I can talk to the Deputy Secretary." Hazen says nothing. "Meet me in half an hour at the Victoria Falls overlook."

"I won't be there. Craig. I don't play these games."

"I've written an article about you, Mr. Ambassador, that will destroy your career. Meet me at the overlook in half an hour. Don't bring anyone with you."

I hang up. Hazen stands for a moment, his back to me and his colleagues, taking possession of himself. He turns and hands the phone back to the waiter. He looks at me, uncertain what to do. I leave the bar and walk through the drawing room.

—⁓—

At Victoria Falls the Zambesi River, flowing out of Zambia, plunges into a deep, but narrow gorge. In this trough it swirls about, sending mist high into the air, until it finds its course out of the gorge and rushes eastward toward the Indian Ocean. On the Rhodesian side of the falls an asphalted walkway stretches the full length of the gorge. It offers a remarkable view of the force of nature at work.

I drive out to the overlook and park well off the road opposite the entrance. Crossing the road, moving toward the rushing sound of the water, I carry a large flashlight, stuck in my belt, and an envelope of photographs. There is a full moon. The path is well lit by moonlight. I reach the entrance pavilion and take refuge in the darkness of its roof's overhang. I want to see Hazen before he sees me. I want to be certain he comes alone.

Finally a taxi pulls up. Hazen leaves the vehicle, telling it to wait, and walks nervously toward the pavilion. His senses are alert, but the moonlit darkness reduces what his eyes can see. The humidity caused by the mist interferes with his sense of feel, and it's hard to hear anything but the pounding of the water. Hazen approaches the entrance pavilion and hesitates before the darkness in which I stand. "Craig?" he calls. "Is that you?"

"Ever seen the falls at night?" I ask, stepping out of the darkness.

We examine one another, each wondering if the other has brought a weapon. But that does not seem Hazen's style.

"They're beautiful in the moonlight," I say. "Let's have a look." I gesture Hazen toward the overlook path. He hesitates, reluctant to allow me to follow behind him. Finally he starts forward.

I say, "I ran into your wife on a street in Joburg."

"So she said."

"She was walking. I didn't know African medicine could work such wonders."

"It was all mesmerism. She relapsed when she got back to Malawi."

We follow the path to a point where we can see the falls. At any time they are splendid, even when the water is low and you feel cheated, even when it is high and the mist pelts down on the overlook path as if it were rain. Tonight, in the moonlight the view is magnificent. Water cascades over the rocks, bright in the moon shimmer. I stand beside Hazen. For a moment we are not adversaries, but two mortals astonished by nature.

Hazen comes out of the spell of the falls. He asks, loudly enough for me to hear above the roar of the falls, "Why am I here?"

"When I met Joss Bennett nine years ago in Nairobi," I say, "I fell under her spell. I was young enough then not to argue with good luck. She didn't want to talk about herself. She lived with me. That's all I wanted."

Hazen makes no reply. I take him by the elbow and gesture him along the overlook path.

"It turned out she was married," I tell him. "That stunned me. Because we had great rapport." Hazen does not reply. "She and her husband had an open marriage," I continue. "Infidelities on both sides. Loved each other, hated each other, but wanted it to work. Thought a child might help."

After a moment Hazen says, "I've never met any Joss Bennett that I know of, Craig. Jocelyn is not a common name, but if that's the only connective—"

"Trouble was," I interrupt, "her husband couldn't produce offspring. Low sperm count." I put my hand on Hazen's shoulder as if in commiseration. He shakes it off. When I glance at him, he looks away, ashamed of his male inadequacy. "I learned that years later when I met Joss again in Morocco. I met the child, too. A sweet, bright, intelligent girl of maybe six. It was my impression that, like a lot of Foreign Service children, she got fobbed off on servants. The parents were busy angling for professional advantage."

Hazen stops walking and stares straight ahead of him, trying to reconstruct in his memory my meeting Joss and Pepper in his living room in Rabat. He cannot do it and breathes very slowly, uncertain where this talk is leading. "The past is past, Craig," he says. "Jocelyn and I are trying to move ahead in the present."

"I made love to Joss that afternoon in Rabat. I returned to the house after you left for the embassy. Joss told me the child was mine."

"Have you any idea," Hazen asks, "how many men she told they had fathered her child?" It's Hazen's turn to put his hand on my shoulder. I pull away. He pats me in commiseration. "We tested her," he says. "Pepper's my child." Then he adds, "Pepper was kidnapped six months ago. Can you imagine the nightmare I live wondering what's happened to her?"

I say nothing. Hazen stops walking and turns to me. He stares at me for a long moment. "You have Pepper, don't you?" We look at each other across the darkness. I do not answer his question. "How is she? I love her, you know."

We come to a place where the path splits. In one direction it continues along the gorge. In the other it goes to a ledge overlooking the falls. I start along the ledge path. Hazen hesitates. Finally he says, "Have you any idea the number of men Joss had in the afternoons? How many she met in Paris? Not just you. Can you imagine how that behavior impacted my career?" I watch the mist rise up from the falls. Hazen laughs without mirth. "You can bet I knew who Tom Craig was when I heard the name. Philandering bastard."

"You had your share of affairs."

"Only enough to maintain my self-respect."

"Why not divorce her?"

"She refused a divorce. She liked me providing a home for her in exotic places, moving to new posts every few years where she could find new adventures." After a moment he adds, "But that's over now. You've seen her: broken by an accident, a shell of what she was. We're managing somehow."

I leave him and move to the edge of the precipice.

In the African way there are no railings here, just the falls in their splendor. "You can see the whole length of the falls from out here." In the roar of the cascade I have to call to him. Finally he joins me, but keeps well away from the edge. I do not go near it either. In the spectral illumination of the moonlight, we stare at the water hurling itself into the gorge. It coats us with mist.

He asks, "You going to throw me into the gorge?"

"You're the murderer."

"I'm no murderer," he yells. "I'm sorry she got her hooks into you. You and all the others."

When I pull the flashlight off my belt, Hazen crouches. I take photographs from the envelope I carry. Hazen rises, still on guard. I direct the beam of the flashlight onto the morgue photo of Joss. "That's how she looked when the lions of Tsavo got finished with her."

We stare at the photo a long moment. Suddenly Hazen snatches it from me and flings it into the gorge. It catches an updraft and rises with the mist, finally floating slowly toward the Zambesi. "There are others," I say.

Hazen asks, "What do you want?"

"An American passport for Pepper. Her last name Craig. Here are a couple of photos." I offer Hazen a small envelope with Pepper's passport photos. He puts his arms behind his back.

"You think I've got blank passports lying around my embassy to pass out to extortioners like you?"

"I think you can probably find one."

"Passports are scrupulously controlled, my friend. My consular officer keeps the blank ones in his safe. He alone issues them because he knows that if one goes missing his career is finished."

"I think we know whose career may be finished."

Hazen is careful not to seem rattled. "During an inspection of a post where I was serving," he says, "a blank passport came up missing. No officer left that embassy building until it was found."

"Fascinating anecdote."

Hazen folds his arms across his chest. "It was retrieved from a vice-consul's desk. He was sent home the next week."

"Maybe you'll get sent home, Mr. Ambassador." We measure one another through the moonlit darkness. "Given your capabilities, I'm sure you can swing a passport." Again I offer the envelope with Pepper's photos. Again he refuses to take it.

"And what do I get from you?"

"The story I'll send my paper if you don't come up with the passport. The complete—dossier, I believe you'd call it."

"Your paper will never publish that story," Hazen informs me. "There's a libel suit in it." He smiles. "Do you think your paper's going to make me rich?"

"Let's find out." We stare at each other. Across the gorge the falls continue their thunder. "I give you the dossier and my promise never to touch the story again." Hazen says nothing, considering his options. "We make the exchange one week from today. In Nairobi."

"Not Nairobi. "

"I was with her in Nairobi, that's why. On the Norfolk Hotel terrace. At 9:00 a.m. A week from today. I'll be having breakfast."

Again, I offer the envelope of photos. Hazen takes it, sticks it in a pocket. He turns to leave. He takes two steps up the path. Then suddenly he rushes me. He wraps his arms about my chest, pinioning my arms. He lifts me off my feet. He pushes me toward the edge of the precipice. I kick his legs out from under him. We fall to the ground. We roll toward the edge. We start sliding. Hazen releases me. He grabs at vegetation. We keep rolling. The falls thunder across the gorge. The mist moistens our hands. It makes everything slippery. I manage to grab the base of a bush. Hazen rolls past me. I seize his belt and hang on. He dangles over the gorge. I hear his cry above the roaring of the water. "Help me,

Craig!" he shouts. He looks down into the boiling cauldron below. He blubbers for help.

Somehow my feet lodge securely on rock. I hang on to Hazen. Slowly he manages to work his way back from the ledge. He lies flat on the ground, panting with fear and exertion. I scramble to my feet. I take Hazen's hands and pull him to safety. We both sit, away from each other, sweat pouring off us. Finally Hazen asks, "Why did you save me?"

"I need that passport."

Chapter Seventeen

A s I sit down at a table on the Norfolk terrace, I nod to the waiter sweeping the steps Joss climbed that night she appeared out of the darkness. The sunlight is bright. It will be warm by noon. Right now the air is cool, fragrant with freshness and possessed of a clarity that makes vibrant the blue of the sky and the reds of the bougainvillea. "Jambo," I call to the waiter in Swahili. "Habare ako." He replies, "Mzuri sana," and gets me a cup of coffee.

In order to feel myself in control of this morning's agenda, I am staying this trip at the Norfolk. I am in one of the quaint, unheated cottages at the rear of the property beyond a garden where peacocks and superb starlings are kept in an aviary. I've come out onto the terrace well before the appointed hour, picking up both a Daily Nation and an East African Standard at the reception. Breakfasting at other tables are men I recognize. We nod to one another, but do not speak. I sit looking toward the center of town, past the buildings across the road of the still aborning University of Nairobi. I see African students shambling along, but not Hazen. Since he is not registered at the Norfolk—I checked with reception last evening—I assume he will come down this road. If he comes at all.

I order eggs, bacon, and toast, and look through the Nation. The layout has improved since the days that Bakili and I worked there, but the quality of the writing has fallen. The tone of the paper is as lively and assertive as ever—it's the truly African sheet—whereas the East African Standard with its gray front page, seems as English colonial as ever. I keep glancing up at the road, but Hazen does not appear. Since I do not really want to breakfast with Hazen, I begin to eat when my eggs arrive. As I am scanning "Dear Susannah," the Nation's lovelorn column, I feel a tension sweep across the terrace, almost like an electric charge.

I look up and Hazen, briefcase in hand, is pulling a chair away from my table. He's come onto the terrace from the reception and gotten the drop on me.

"May I join you?" he asks. I sense that his instinct is to offer his hand. But he suspects I might not take it. He simply sits. When the waiter approaches, he orders coffee, no breakfast. "What sort of story brings you here?" he asks, trying conversation.

"You bring the passport?" Why pretend that I approve of him sufficiently to make conversation? I continue eating.

Rebuffed, he inquires, "And you have the dossier?"

I lay before him a large mailing envelope containing the dossier. I keep my hand on the envelope, preventing his opening it, until he has shown me the passport. I remove my hand and take the passport. Hazen quickly opens the envelope and pulls out its contents. I glance over at the others having breakfast on the terrace. Then I open the passport. It appears to be in order. Pepper's name is listed as Pamela Bennett Craig. Birthplace: St. Louis, Missouri, USA. The appropriate date. Place of issue: Pretoria, South Africa. All that needs to be done is for her to sign it in accordance with her new name. Pep smiles at me out of her passport photo and the smile warms me.

Hazen says, "I brought these along. There's one for each of us. I hope you don't mind." He places before me a letter, addressed To Whom It May Concern, in which we acknowledge the transfer of documents on both sides. It means that if I go after him for murder, he can come after me for kidnapping. "One can't be too careful," Hazen observes. He has already signed and dated both copies. I do the same, take one, and hand the other back to him.

Hazen studies the piece I have written about him for the paper. It begins by noting that Ambassador Maxwell Hazen and his wife Jocelyn seem to be an exemplary diplomatic couple. It describes their extraordinary dedication, their perseverance in the face of Joss's accident, her confinement to a wheelchair, their daughter's mental health problems, and her disappearance at the hands of a "leopard-man" terrorizing Malawi for months. Then it reveals that, in fact, Hazen and his impostor-wife murdered his actual wife by suffocating her in Kenya. While Hazen reads it, I signal the waiter for my check.

"Quite an interesting article," Hazen comments. "You're a fascinating guy."

"More suited to gossip rags than to a serious newspaper," he opines. "But very readable." I do not reply. Hazen withdraws the photos I've included and examines them. He glances around the terrace, measuring the others breakfasting with us. He gazes at the photos and shakes his head. "I did love her, you know. If she'd run away with you, she'd have driven you to do the same thing." I say nothing. He returns the photos to the envelope and puts them into his briefcase. He looks at me. "How did you get Pepper? May I ask?"

"Trade secret," I say.

"Were you in that ridiculous costume?" I turn back to The Daily Nation.

"Pepper's a lovely child," Hazen says. "Joss and I never wanted her hurt." He leans toward me, ready to push up from his chair. "I'll take care of my own coffee," he says. He takes a twenty shilling note from his wallet and sets his coffee cup on the edge of it. I notice that Kamau's men rise from their tables and take their positions. "I assume we agree," he says, "that if there's publicity about this matter, Pepper's the one who's damaged."

"We do agree on that."

We look at each other. Again Hazen's instinct is to offer his hand, but he suppresses it. I glance at the check. Hazen rises, takes his briefcase and starts away from the table. I sign the check and leave a tip on the table and I do not look up. But I'm conscious of Kamau moving toward Hazen as he goes down the terrace steps. I hear him say, "Mr. Hazen? I'm Inspector Kamau. Could you come with me please?"

I get up from the table and move toward the entrance of the hotel. I'm aware that Hazen has hesitated. He understands now why I insisted on Nairobi. Probably he is looking around at me, feeling betrayed. But I never promised not to contact the police. As I enter the hotel, I hear Hazen run down the street. I hear Kamau call, "Stop! Stop!" Kamau's men start after him and I know that Hazen will never outrun them.

I continue into the hotel and pass through the garden down to my cottage. There I place a call to the American expatriate history professor who acts as the Nairobi stringer for the Big Guy. I alerted him the night before to stand by this morning. Now I suggest he hurry to the Norfolk where, it seems, the Kenya police have apprehended the American Ambassador to Malawi in connection with the murder of his wife. I tell him that since I am in Nairobi on personal business I would prefer that he handle the story. He need not notify the Big Guy that I'm here. He agrees, realizing that the story will be ongoing and his wallet fatter.

I check out of the Norfolk, take a cab to Embakasi, and catch the noon flight to Johannesburg and Cape Town. I reach Camps Bay in time to tuck Pepper into bed. Because I've had a successful trip, Maggie and I relax the rules a bit. For a while we sit together on the bed, our arms about each other, Pepper between us. Holding each other, we talk late into the night, a family.

The End

Cune Press

Cune Press was founded in 1994 to publish thoughtful writing of public importance. Our name is derived from "cuneiform." (In Latin *cuni* means "wedge.")

In the ancient Near East the development of cuneiform script—simpler and more adaptable than hieroglyphics—enabled a large class of merchants and landowners to become literate. Clay tablets inscribed with wedge-shaped stylus marks made possible a broad inter-meshing of individual efforts in trade and commerce.

Cuneiform enabled scholarship to exist and art to flower, and created what historians define as the world's first civilization. When the Phoenicians developed their sound-based alphabet, they expressed it in cuneiform.

The idea of Cune Press is the democratization of learning, the faith that rarefied ideas, pulled from dusty pedestals and displayed in the streets, can transform the lives of ordinary people. And it is the conviction that ordinary people, trusted with the most precious gifts of civilization, will give our culture elasticity and depth—a necessity if we are to survive in a time of rapid change.

Books from Cune Press

 Aswat: Voices from a Small Planet (a series from Cune Press)

Looking Both Ways	Pauline Kaldas
Stage Warriors	Sarah Imes Borden
Stories My Father Told Me	Helen Zughaib & Elia Zughaib
Girl Fighters	Carolyn Han

 Syria Crossroads (a series from Cune Press)

Leaving Syria	Bill Dienst & Madi Williamson
Visit the Old City of Aleppo	Khaldoun Fansa
Stories My Father Told Me	Helen Zughaib, Elia Zughai
Steel & Silk	Sami Moubayed
The Road from Damascus	Scott C. Davis
A Pen of Damascus Steel	Ali Ferzat
White Carnations	Musa Rahum Abbas
The Dusk Visitor	Musa al-Halool
Jinwar and Other Stories	Alex Poppe

 Bridge Between the Cultures (a series from Cune Press)

Empower a Refugee	Patricia Martin Holt
Muslims, Arabs & Arab Americans	Nawar Shora
Afghanistan and Beyond	Linda Sartor
Music Has No Boundaries	Rafique Gangat
Apartheid Is a Crime	Mats Svensson
Curse of the Achille Lauro	Reem al-Nimer
Arab Boy Delivered	Paul A. Zarou
Escape to Aswan	Amal Sedky-Winter
Confessions of a Knight Errant	Gretchen McCullough

WCW West Coast Writers

Fluid	Lisa Teasley
The Other Side of the Wall	Richard Hardigan
Kivu	Frederic Hunter
Finding Melody Sullivan	Alice Rothchild
Afghanistan & Beyond	Linda Sartor

Cune Press: www.cunepress.com

Frederic Hunter served as a Foreign Service Officer in the United States Information Service in Brussels, Belgium, and, shortly after its independence, at three posts in the Republic of the Congo: Bukavu, Coquilhatville, and Léopoldville. He later became the Africa Correspondent of the *Christian Science Monitor*, based in Nairobi.

A playwright / screenwriter, Hunter's award-winning stage work, *The Hemingway Play*, was given a reading at the Eugene O'Neill Playwrights Conference, presented at Harvard University's Loeb Drama Center and produced by PBS's Hollywood Television Theater series. Other plays have been performed at the Dallas Theatre Center, ACT in San Francisco, and the Ensemble Theater in Santa Barbara.

Movies Hunter has written have been produced by PBS, ABC, and CBS. Research for his PBS drama *Lincoln and the War Within* led him to write the historical novel *Abe and Molly: The Lincoln Courtship*. He's taught screenwriting at the Santa Barbara Writers Conference, at UCSB, and at Principia College where he also taught Modern African Literature. Hunter's Africa experience is the basis for several current novels from Cune Press.